PROVENANCE

PROVENANCE

A Novel

Carol Smilgin

CAROL SMILGIN

iUniverse, Inc.
Bloomington

Provenance

iUniverse books may be ordered through booksellers or by contacting:

iUniverse
1663 Liberty Drive
Bloomington, IN 47403
www.iuniverse.com
1-800-Authors (1-800-288-4677)

ISBN: 978-1-4620-1469-9 (sc)
ISBN: 978-1-4620-1472-9 (dj)
ISBN: 978-1-4620-1470-5 (ebk)

Printed in the United States of America

iUniverse rev. date: 06/21/2011

In memory of my friend Felice whose true story—as told to me, supplies the background for Georges Lartigue's family's flight from Belgium in PROVENANCE

ACKNOWLEDGMENTS

I will always be indebted to my critique partner, Deborah Szwarce for her corrections, helpful ideas, and endless support; Lynne Heitman for her encouragement; Nina del Rio for her help and Lucian Symmons—both of Sotheby's, NY, for his discussion of provenance issues; Wally Exman, for his editorial advice; Gordon Jensen, for his help on security systems; Ron Weiss, for his help with construction management terms; Brewster Miner for his knowledge of automobiles; my readers-Sheila Whitehouse, Nancy and John Weller; Mary Littleford and Arlene Kay for their helpful comments; Julia Paterson for calendars; Dave Parker for music titles; Barbara Minikakis for Greek words; Nina Griggs for references in France and Spain; Dr.Tom Hagamen and Dr. Mary Beth Hagamen for their advice on psychiatric disorders and hospitals; and Natalie DeVoe of the Metropolitan Museum, who, several years ago, took me to my first German Expressionist exhibit, and recently supplied details on, *Mada,* Gustav Klimt's painting of a young girl.

Special thanks go to: Victoria Reed—formerly head of provenance research for the Princeton University Art Museum—who granted me an interview and introduced me to the two books that helped launch *Provenance;* to Carol Hughes, whose online course and special advice, enabled me to further develop the plot; and to Melissa Grella, my proof reader/copyeditor, whose amazing attention to detail helped with several last minute additions.

Lastly, I'd like to thank my sons, John and Caleb, for their interest and John for specific details on events leading up to WW II. To my friends—far too many to mention here—who, during the past several years listened to me talk about the novel, thank you. I will always be grateful for your attention, patience and encouragement.

AUTHOR'S NOTE

Provenance is a work of fiction. The names, characters incidents, and places are the product of the author's imagination with the following exceptions: Victor's Bar in Santorini, Greece, did exist in the 1980's and my son John and I spent an evening there. We also climbed the volcano as depicted in the story.

There is no Gallerie Des Artists on Rue du Bac in Paris, no Galleria de Marcho in Lisbon, nor is there a Mendes Galleria art gallery near the Castellana in Madrid. The Paris auction house Hotel Drouot, however, is well known, as is the restaurant, Café Runtz.

The restaurant, Le Poquelin, at 17 rue Moliere in Paris' 1st Arrondissement, does exist; the décor is as attractive, the atmosphere as hushed, and food as superb as I've described.

The "Million Dollar Stair" in the St. Regis Hotel on East 55th Street, in Manhattan got its name from the fact it cost one million dollars ($1,000,000.00) to carve it out of a single block of marble.

The painting, *Emma,* was never confiscated, because it never existed, though Gustav Klimt is a famous Austrian painter renowned for his portraits of women.

The Nazi ERR condemned the work of both Wassili Kandinsky and Ernst Ludwig Kirchner, and details about them in *Provenance* are accurate as are those of the other Expressionists.

References to Hitler, his art, and the backgrounds of other Nazis—including (thanks to recently declassified material) those who escaped with the help of the Vatican Ratlines—are factual and as up to date as recently published material and the Internet allow.

Art is the unconditional grace of the imagination.

Patrick Overton

PROLOGUE

Madrid, Spain
October 2007

Jeffrey Lawler adjusted his neck scarf, and, turning up the collar of his raincoat, stepped out of the metro at Banco de España just as a blast of wind and rain assaulted him. He paused to struggle with an umbrella. Then, using it as a shield, he struck out toward the Paseo de Recoletos.

For the past week and a half, Jeffrey and his wife, Rebecca, had been visiting his grandmother, and today was the day they were scheduled to return home to Portugal. But instead of packing, he was on his way to meet one Deitrich Radtke at the ever-popular Café de Gijon.

In the late 1940s, Radtke had been one of the art consultants working for Gustav Mendes, owner of the Mendes Galleria near the Castellana, from whom Jeffrey's grandfather frequently bought paintings. When Ernst Lawler died in 2006, Jeffrey inherited a number of them. However, one—a Wassily Kandinsky—had gaps in its provenance. And while the other—an Ernst Ludwig Kirschner—had the remains of an ownership stamp on its back, there was no written record accompanying it.

With the gaps on the Kandinsky falling between 1933 to 1947—the time of raids by the Nazi Degenerate Art police—that and the lack of documentation on the Kirschner, made both suspicious, virtually rendering them unmarketable. This led Jeffrey to believe that because they fell into the classifications of Modern and Expressionist Art, they'd been confiscated and set aside with other works waiting to be destroyed. Instead, they'd been sent to Madrid and 'exploited' or sold illegally to his grandfather. As to why his grandfather bought them, Jeffrey could only guess. As a result, he'd been probing the backgrounds of Radtke, Gustav Mendes, and the gallery since.

His research had paid off. More and more evidence pointed to the fact that Gustav Mendes had been involved with Nazi-looted art during the War, regularly receiving crates of paintings shipped from Holland and Belgium, through France and across the Bay of Biscay to the port of Balboa. Despite Mendes' death in 2005, the gallery remained open. His daughter, Señora Gallina, was the new owner, and Deitrich Radtke, though now in his eighties, came in several times a week.

Hoping to schedule an appointment with Radtke, Jeffrey had flown to Madrid the previous month, visiting the gallery on the pretext that he wished to expand his collection of German Expressionist Art. But Radtke hadn't been there. And so, he'd left his engraved business card with a note stating that his grandfather had been a regular customer and that he was curious about two pieces that had discrepancies in their provenance. He ended by saying he looked forward to Radtke's help in solving the mystery. He'd all but given up on hearing from him when, yesterday, Radtke telephoned.

Perhaps he might also know why Grandfather wrote Bruno Lohse's name across a blank sales receipt from the gallery. What the devil had made him think of Lohse in the first place? Could he have met him at the Entartete Kunst exhibit in 1937? He'd met Goering. During the War, Lohse worked for Goering. Had Radtke also been at the exhibit? Had he done business with them as a result?

Huddling deeper into his raincoat, Jeffrey circled the Plaza de Cibeles, pausing in front of the Palacio de Communicaciones to wait for the signal to cross at the corner where the Plaza met the Paseo de Recoletos. Adjusting his hold on the umbrella, he glanced at his watch. Café de Gigon was on the far side of the Paseo at number 28, and, despite the foul weather, it looked like he was going to be on time. Just then, the signal changed and he stepped into the street.

Still holding fast to the umbrella, Jeffrey didn't see the dark grey Mercedes with smoked-out windows come around the corner from Calle de Acalá and head straight for him, until it was too late. Frozen where he stood, he was powerless to react.

The heavy sedan struck, tossing him into the air and directly into the flooded path of the car behind the Mercedes.

As shock and pain consumed him, he managed one final thought, "Rebecca."

CHAPTER ONE

Las Vegas, Nevada
Summer, 2010

Rebecca Lawler gazed out the window at her swimming pool shimmering in the afternoon sun. It was hot and she was anxious to return to her vacation home in Portugal where a constant breeze wafted up from the sea.

Rebecca, her sister, Adelaide, and Adelaide's attorney Tom Hutchins had been meeting in her living room with two detectives from the sheriff's office to hear the final results of their investigation into the January death of Adelaide's husband, Jim Broker. In March, once the police had given them permission to leave, Rebecca insisted that Adelaide return to Portugal with her for some much needed R&R. They'd remained there since, returning two days ago for this meeting.

Resettling herself on a green wicker couch with flowered chintz pillows, Rebecca rescued a wayward lock of dark auburn hair and fastened it to the rest arranged on the top of her head with a tortoise-shell pin. Just then, Adelaide returned from seeing the detectives to the front door.

"At last that's over with," she said, collapsing into a matching, green wicker chair. Rebecca glanced at her watch "They were here for over an hour." She laughed at her sister's grimace. "Something tells me you could use a drink."

"I'd kill for a glass of red wine."

"One red wine on the way. Tom? A drink?"

"Are you planning on joining Adelaide and me?"

"Yes. I'm going to have some wine."

"In that case," Tom said, "I'll have a scotch on the rocks with a splash of soda."

Adelaide started to rise but Rebecca waved her back.

"I'll get it, Addie. You stay and relax. Back in a minute," she added, on her way out of the room.

Adelaide rested her head against the back of the chair and closed her eyes.

"When are you and Rebecca returning to Portugal?" Tom asked.

"The day after tomorrow."

"Why so soon?"

"Because I have an appointment in Lisbon on Saturday and want to get back several days beforehand," Rebecca said, returning with their drinks.

"And from there she goes to Kiffisia, Greece to visit Jeffrey's parents before making an overnight stop in Santorini," Adelaide added.

"Busy lady, "Tom said, nursing his scotch. He glanced at Rebecca. "What's taking you to Lisbon?"

"I've an appointment to take two paintings to a dealer in hopes of selling them. Jeffrey and I were in the process of selecting those we wished to sell when . . . Jeffrey had his fatal accident."

Tom looked up. "Your husband was killed?"

The question was not unexpected, but it took a minute for Rebecca to collect her thoughts. "We'd been visiting Jeffrey's grandmother in Madrid. On the day we were to leave, Jeffrey got a call from someone he'd been trying to reach for over a month. On his way to meet him he was struck and killed by a car."

Tom stared at her. 'I'm so sorry. I had no idea. Please accept my belated condolences."

"Thank you, Tom. That's most kind." She took a sip of wine, hoping to dislodge the lump in her throat.

"Was there an inquiry?"

"Yes. But just as a formality. The worst part came later when I had to decide where he should be buried." Tears threatened, but Rebecca blinked them away. "The idea of cremation always horrified me. In the end, Abuelita—Jeffrey's grandmother—persuaded me to agree to it. But the arrangements seemed to take forever." She shook her head remembering. "There were so many forms. Despite her age, Abuelita is very sharp." She looked at Tom. "She's in her nineties. She hired attorneys and constantly kept on top of things. Still, it took forever."

"Did the authorities ever find the car or the driver?"

"No, not even after two witness detailed the information on the license plates."

"Sounds like the plates were either stolen or counterfeit."

"That's what I've come to think."

"Do you happen to know who Jeffrey was meeting?"

"Yes, a man by the name of Deitrich Radtke."

"Do you know why he wanted to see him?"

Rebecca did, but in light of what had happened, the knowledge of it made her uneasy. Though only a hunch, she couldn't dismiss the feeling that Jeffrey's death and the reason he was meeting Radtke were somehow connected. "Not really," she lied. "Why?"

"Only curious. My apologies for the third degree."

"That's all right, Tom. I know it's well intentioned."

"It is indeed." He smiled, studying her, "At any rate, take care of yourself." He raised his glass in her direction. "And the very best of luck."

"Thanks. I have a feeling I'm going to need it."

CHAPTER TWO

Galleria de Marcho
Lisbon, Portugal

Georges Lartigue stared at the two paintings before him. He was fairly certain that one, an early Ernst Ludwig Kirchner nude circa 1909, had been confiscated by the Nazis. But instead of being destroyed, it had been stolen with the intention of either trading or selling it illegally. The other, a Wassili Kandinsky abstract oil-on-cardboard, while rare, could have been acquired legally. It would, of course, depend on the provenance.

Georges been working in the office of his gallery, Des Artistes, on Paris's Rue de Bac, when the call came through from his colleague and friend, Senhor Carlos De Marcho, requesting he come to Lisbon. He'd arrived at his friend's gallery just before noon and had been enjoying a coffee and biscotti. He approached the Kirchner.

"As you said on the phone, Carlos, these two paintings are exceptional. The fact either of them exists is remarkable given the Nazi's purge of what they considered degenerate art. As you know, Kirchner and Kandinsky topped the list. Today, along with Klimt and Klee, the sale of their works continue to set record heights. When one is available, the auction houses, Christie's and Sotheby's, go on a crusade to alert their big buyers."

"Yes, that and the recent surge of interest in German art make the Kirchner especially valuable."

"Indeed," Georges said. "I think we agree that both will sell well."

Georges circled them, examining the backs for telltale marks or stickers of ownership—a "J" for Jew, a swastika or a number indicating its inclusion in a Nazi inventory—anything that would indicate where these pieces might have been, but none could be seen. As a provenance researcher, he was especially intrigued. "You say the lady who brought them in was attractive?"

Senhor De Marcho's face lit up. "Ah, *sim*, yes. A very beautiful woman by the name of Rebecca Lawler came in with them." He shrugged. "At first I thought she wished an appraisal. Instead, she asked if I could arrange to sell them for her."

"And you, of course, said yes. But I'm curious, I trust you have the documentation?"

"Not as yet. She said she first wanted to see if I was interested in helping her. She mentioned there were others."

Georges looked up. "Others?"

"Yes. Apparently, Mrs. Lawler's late husband inherited over a dozen works of art from his paternal grandfather. As the Lawlers had a sizeable art collection of their own, they wanted to sell the pieces that either didn't suit their tastes or fit in with what they already had in either of their two homes. The primary residence is outside of Las Vegas, Nevada. The one in Portugal is a vacation home."

"And so, my friend," Georges said, refreshing his coffee from the urn on the counter and adding sugar and a dollop of milk, "what did you tell this beautiful Mrs. Lawler?"

"That I'd be happy to help her and, whenever convenient, I'd like to see the rest. If they're anything close to these, they have to be worth a small fortune."

"Mrs. Lawler's vacation home is here in Lisbon?"

"No, in Santa Barbara de Nexe, near Faro. Recently, however, she's been spending most of her time in Las Vegas. If I can make an appointment to view the others, would you be able to do so?"

"Depending on when," Georges answered, putting his coffee cup on a nearby table. Moving to the paintings, he lifted each off its stand and reversed it, hoping to get a better view of the back. But as before, it was difficult to get a good look due to the elaborate frames. "My friend Sally Livingston arrives next week and a wedding of a close friend is on the twenty-sixth."

"I have Mrs. Lawler's address and phone number," Senhor De Marcho said, returning to his desk and retrieving a business card. "Suppose I telephone her now?"

"By all means," Georges said, pocketing his professional eyeglass and retrieving his coffee cup. "How long a trip is it to . . . what's the name of the place again?"

"Santa Barbara de Nexe, only a fifteen-minute drive from Faro. We can fly to Faro from Lisbon. To drive would be impossible, although we Portuguese are fast drivers, or, as you French are prone to say, *'sont fous'* . . . crazy, yes?" He reached for the telephone.

"Oui," Georges agreed. "Believe me, your reputation precedes you." Minutes later, he heard Senhor De Marcho replace the receiver. "I am so sorry, my friend. It seems the lovely Mrs. Lawler is in Greece."

"Who was that on the phone?"

"Her sister, a Mrs. Adelaide Broker. Mrs. Lawler will be returning Monday. But that is no help to you or to me."

"You say Faro has an airport?"

"But of course. Are you thinking you'll return to Paris tonight as planned, but if I can get an appointment early in the week, you'll accompany me to Faro?"

"Oui."

"Mrs. Broker said she expects to hear from Mrs. Lawler later today. She'll tell her we phoned, and one of them will get back to us. In the meantime," Senhor De Marcho said, endowing Georges with a broad smile, "let us take a stroll to where we can have some good food that can only be enhanced by an exceptional wine."

Georges drained his coffee cup, leaving it on the counter next to the urn. "You know of such a place?" he asked, struggling to be serious.

"Ah, you French think you're the only ones with a flair for haute cuisine. Come."

With Senhor De Marcho leading the way, he and Georges left the gallery.

"Senhor de Marcho called today," Adelaide Broker told Rebecca over the phone later that afternoon, Portugal time.

"Really? What did he have to say?"

Adelaide relayed the conversation. "He was hoping to schedule a time when it would be convenient to meet with you. I told him you'd be back on Monday; he said he'd telephone again once you returned."

Wonderful. Perhaps that means he'll help me. "Would you mind calling him back and asking if we could meet Tuesday?"

"No, of course not. I'll call as soon as we hang up. How's Greece?"

"Beautiful."

"And Jeffrey's parents?"

"Very well. I'm calling you from their home in Kiffisia."

"Is it as beautiful as you remember?"

"Yes. But you know I love stone houses with dark wood interiors and leaded glass windows." Her eyes misted at the sudden thought of Jeffrey. She quickly changed the subject.

"Oh, and Addie? Don't forget—I'm flying to Santorini tomorrow and will be staying at the Atlantidas Villas in Oia."

"I know how fond you are of that island," Adelaide chided. "So, if you don't appear Monday, I'll just have to come get you."

"As tempting as that might seem," Rebecca said, "have no fear. You'll see me Monday."

* * *

That Saturday night, her petite form clothed in a white T-shirt, blue batik wraparound skirt and sandals, Rebecca sat in a small restaurant in Oia watching a waiter bring her a half carafe of retsina and a plate of assorted Greek appetizers.

"*Efharasto poli,*" she said, once he'd finished placing the items on the table.

"*Parakalo,*" he replied, with a smile revealing a row of beautiful white teeth.

He poured the wine for her, and with a nod and another smile, he left.

For the most part, Rebecca found Greek men attractive and enjoyed observing them . . . from a distance, so as not to appear bold.

She sampled the appetizers, sipped the resin-infused wine, and gazed across the majestic caldera. In the center, the dark mass of *Vulcanes*, the dormant but still active volcano, penetrated the surface of the sea, its curved peaks and valleys just visible in the fading light. It was dusk, the wind had come up, and stars had begun to peek through the darkening sky.

Fantasy, pure fantasy.

She looked toward Fira, the town perched atop the neighboring volcanic rim, its strings of lights dancing in the evening breeze one thousand feet above the sea. *I wonder if Victor's Bar is still there.*

It has to be. Perhaps I'll stop in tomorrow for a visit. A tingling sensation ran through her. *Then again, perhaps not. Too many memories. Yet . . .*

A waiter at the hotel where she and her friends had stayed on their trip following college graduation had mentioned it the evening they arrived. Once she'd heard it described, she had made her decision.

"You see," he told them, "the bistro is carved out of the volcanic ash of Fira. To get there, you must walk down a dozen steps. Then you relax on this beautiful terrace overlooking the caldera, sip an aperitif or two, and listen to opera. Believe me, if you go, you will never forget it."

Rebecca did go and it had been the most memorable evening of her young life. But there was a reason. She drifted . . .

CHAPTER THREE

Victor's Bar, Fira
Santorini, Greece

It was mid June, the night was warm, and a full moon shone from a star-studded sky, bathing the volcano in a ghostly white light.

He arrived shortly after she'd been served her drink, and she couldn't take her eyes off him. Given the atmosphere, it was as if Apollo himself had descended the stairs and stepped into the small bistro. Blond, with thick unruly hair, chiseled features, a full mouth, and long-lashed, brown eyes, he was wearing tan chinos, sandals and a pale pink, open-collared oxford shirt with the sleeves rolled, exposing a tan forearm lightly covered with golden hair. Her stomach fluttered.

Lean and tall—perhaps six-foot one—and obviously American, he reminded her of the way Phidias, the Classical Greek Sculptor, had perfected the human form. She knew she was staring, but couldn't help herself, and the smile he gave her as he passed to sit two seats away in the only vacant chair, left her weak.

He appeared to be by himself as was she, her friends having opted for a livelier evening.

Soon, the couple on her left got up to leave, and before she could gather her thoughts, the blond god lowered himself into the chair next to her.

"Hello," he said, the rich tones of his voice as mellow as the evening.

"Hello," Rebecca replied, daring to look at him.

"Beautiful spot, isn't it?" he said, gazing upward into the moonlight beyond. Strains from Wagner's "Liebestod" drifted from within.

"I can think of none as beautiful," she answered, following his gaze.

"Ever been here before?"

She turned to look at him. "You mean to Victor's or Santorini?"

Their eyes met and he grinned, "I guess I mean both."

"Neither," she said, studying him. "This is my first trip to Greece."

"And you came alone?"

She laughed at his shocked expression. "To Victor's, yes, but not to Greece. I'm here with three friends, but they decided they wanted more action tonight."

He shook his head. "Well, whatever they opted for, it can't match this."

"What about you?" Rebecca asked.

He looked at her, eyes sparkling. "Yes. What about me?"

The waiter arrived as she was about to reply.

"What are you drinking?" her new companion asked.

"Campari and soda, and I'd like a glass of water, too, please."

He repeated it to the waiter, adding, "and a seven-star Metaxa for me, parakalo."

"What? No Ouzo?" he asked once the waiter had gone.

Rebecca gave him another steady look and answered, but felt he hadn't heard for, not only did he remain mute, he was now the one who was staring.

She was about to repeat herself when a slow blush crept up his neck and he said, "Excuse me?"

She smiled. "I said I like Sambucca, but not Ouzo. The licorice flavor is too sharp and it's neither syrupy nor smooth. What I meant by my previous question was, what about you? Is this your first time to Victor's or to Santorini?

"No. I was here two years ago. Never forgot it."

He looked across at the volcano and pointed. "Are you planning to take the boat out and climb Vulcanes?"

She looked. "Can you?"

He nodded. "Yeah. Interested?"

"I might be. Where would I meet you?"

"Are you staying here in Fira?"

"No, on the other side of the island in Kamari."

"Okay," he grinned, "I'll come get you."

"You have a car?"

He dazzled her with another smile. "No, the local bus."

"You mean you'd come all that way?"

"It's only a twenty-minute ride. Besides, then I can grab a morning swim there before we go, that is, if I can bum a shower afterward. The black volcanic sand on the beach there is very fine and adheres like glue."

She sent him a sidelong glance. "All right. That seems like a fair trade off. You can either use the shower of our male companions next door, as I'm sure they'd be happy to oblige you, or the one in the room I share with another girl. The choice, of course, is yours." She laughed at the gleam in his eyes.

He laughed too. "There's a choice?" Then, growing more serious, he added, "Perhaps your friends would like to come with us."

"I can ask. That's very nice of you."

The waiter returned with the drinks and they were quiet for a time, lost in the moment.

Several minutes later, he leaned toward her. Instinctively, she pulled back. But then he extended a hand. "By the way, I'm David."

She gave him hers. "I'm Rebecca." She was about to say, "Thomas," but like him, she omitted her surname.

At one-thirty a.m., he put her on the last bus to Kamari, then took a taxi to his hotel in Oia.

The next morning, Rebecca and her roommate, Gina, were having breakfast on the terrace when David appeared, arms extended, with a wet beach towel in one and a backpack in the other. Rebecca thought he looked wonderful and felt heat rising to her cheeks. "How was your swim?" she asked.

"Great."

She introduced Gina, then added, "You'd probably like to take that shower."

He looked down at his dripping form, feet and ankles covered in dark sand. "How'd you guess?"

She steadied him with a look, but couldn't resist the urge to tease. "I'm sorry to report that our two friends have yet to put in an appearance. So, like it or not, I guess you'll have to use our shower." She knew from his grin it was what he'd had in mind all along.

"Be back in a minute," she told Gina, and led David up the stairs to their room on the second floor. "The shower's only a curtain over a raised section in the floor with a drain. Don't worry if water gets on the floor. It's unavoidable." She handed him the keys. "Enjoy."

He looked down at her and for a moment she thought he might kiss her—not too unpleasant a thought—but the moment passed.

"Thanks, Rebecca. I really appreciate it."

By the time David rejoined them, Rebecca and Gina's friends, Robert Boyd and James Hill, had arrived and had just ordered breakfast. Rebecca introduced David, who sat down and ordered as well. The five of them chatted and compared experiences for the next half-hour.

The bus arrived just as they finished eating. They grabbed their backpacks and water bottles and boarded.

Once arriving in Fira, they walked through the small town with its whitewashed buildings and blue-domed church, past the stairway that led to Victor's, and made their way to the wide six-hundred-step staircase that dizzily wound down the 1,100 feet of the caldera to the water below. A hushed sense of expectancy hung in the air.

Bob was the first to comment, "Wow."

James laughed. "My sentiments exactly."

Gina and Rebecca shared a look.

With a glance at David, James said, "Well, I guess there's no time like the present."

David laughed. "Okay, then. Let's go!"

Starting out, Gina and Rebecca held hands. But they soon developed confidence, and proceeded on their own.

On the way down, they passed donkeys who were carrying visitors going up while the animals' owners cracked whips over their heads and shouted obscenities such as, "Malaccas," at them, which basically meant their miserable state as a donkey was the result of their laziness as humans.

On reaching the bottom, they climbed into a small boat manned by "Dimitri"; once on board, they began the journey to Nea Kameni, the larger of the two volcanic islands.

To Rebecca, it seemed the closer they got, the more ominous Vulcanes appeared. Black boulders of miscellaneous shapes and sizes lay piled at the waterline, while varying shades of grey and black volcanic ash in some places 40 to 50 feet high formed the sides of the volcano itself. Rebecca fully expected to see a door slide open and two long green arms reach out to claim them.

She looked across the expanse of water at Fira perched atop the cliff of multiple layers of colorful pumice reaching over1,000 feet into the sky. "I feel so insignificant."

"You're right," James, the taller of their male friends, said. "The view's awesome."

Dimitri pulled the boat in closely, but they still had to wade ashore. "Volcano," he said, pointing to the water. "Zesto," he repeated several times. "Hot. Good," he added, rubbing his arms and legs.

"He's right," Rebecca said. "It is hot. It's also yellow and has an unpleasant odor."

"The odor and the color comes from sulfur," Gina said. "It's in the water. Just like it is in Hot Springs, Virginia."

"Good for rheumatism and such," David added. "But we'd better get a move on so we can finish before the sun gets higher and it becomes unbearably hot."

They followed him past a crater that lay on the side of the volcanic mass to the top where they gaped in disbelief at two enormous cones, each sunken on either side of a long central ridge that bisected them.

"Anyone want to take a walk down?" David asked.

No one said a word.

"Come on, Rebecca. How about it? Nothing will happen. Honestly. I've done it."

Not to be viewed as a quitter, Rebecca nodded mutely.

"Aww, what the hell," James said.

"I'll stay and keep Gina company," Bob, said. "Someone has to, right Gina?"

And so, heart in her throat, Rebecca, with James behind her bringing up the rear, followed David down the sand-like ridge bordering the cavernous depths of the volcano. When they reached the lowest point, they stopped.

"Here," David said to her, "give me your hand and look up."

The feel of her hand wrapped in his large one strengthened her resolve. But when James moved closer, she didn't hesitate to reach back and take hold of his arm. Then she looked up and sucked in her breath.

"How's that for scale?" David asked.

"Jesus . . .," James said.

Rebecca only stared. This is what it must look like outside the gates to hell.

"How tall would you say Gina and Bob look, David?" James asked.

"Half inch, give or take," David replied.

Rebecca's grip suddenly tightened. "I think I just felt something."

"Yeah, so did I," James said.

"Just a small tremor. Earthquakes are a frequent occurrence. Not to worry. The last big one was back in 1955. That time the volcanic eruption sent flaming boulders—some half the size of a house—showering down on Oia. One of them still rests near the pool at the Atlantis Villas. It's taller than I am,

and I'm six foot one. Several buildings on the edge of the caldera in Fira slid down into the sea. But Oia suffered the most. You can still see several partially crumbled buildings when you walk through the town. Today when they build houses, the roof is rounded to better withstand earthquakes." He laughed at their horrified expressions. "Okay. Had enough?"

"I think so," James said. Rebecca could only nod.

"Then let's start the climb back."

They took one last look into the cone-shaped pit of the volcano, and despite slipping and sliding in the pumice under foot, they made it to the top in less than five minutes.

"You guys were so small!" Gina said, once they returned to where she and Bob were waiting.

"So were you," Rebecca replied, relaxed now that they were all together again.

James reached for David's hand. "Thanks, David. That's something I'll never forget."

"Yeah, it does tend to stick in one's memory."

The next day was their last in Greece, so David took them to the archaeological excavation at Akrotiri.

There, under the expanse of a protective tin roof, they saw the partially reconstructed remains of what once had been a lush Minoan metropolis.

"The guide book said the entire core of the island exploded back in 1500 B.C.," Bob said, "'which caused the sea to rush in and send ash into the atmosphere that blanketed areas as far as Egypt. Skies worldwide were darkened for months which is evidenced today by the stunted growth rings of the California Redwoods.' I know it's considered to be five times the size of Krakatoa that erupted in Indonesia back in the 1800s. Back then over 36,000 people were killed." He smiled at David. "As you can see, the subject fascinates me."

"Amen to that," David said. "Some believe Santorini is the fabled Atlantis."

Bob grinned. "I believe it."

"Yeah. So do I."

"I remember from a class discussion in college," James said, "that it's not only mentioned in Egyptian papyri, but Plato discussed it too."

Rebecca decided to research it once she'd returned home to California.

Hunger pains persisted, bringing Rebecca back to the present and reminding her that she hadn't eaten since lunch . . . she checked her watch . . . five hours ago.

She sampled the dolmades, taking several sips of wine in between. Then, after spreading a spoonful of yogurt and garlic mixture on several pieces of pita bread, she had another sip of wine. As anticipated, everything was delicious.

She noticed the light wind continued to stir the paper lanterns above Fira. From across the way, snatches of opera music reached her ears as the light breeze gently blew over her. The effect was so sensuous and the view so beautiful, it wasn't long before she retreated into her reverie.

David had asked her to have dinner with him that final evening. And so, at the end of the day, they bid good-bye to the others and hopped on the bus for Oia.

The moon had crested on the horizon and fragrances of freesia and thyme were in the air, as they sat sipping retsina on the terrace of a family-owned restaurant.

They dined on assorted mezethes that included eggplant salad, hummus, taramosalata, dolmades and miniature calamari, and then shared a main course of moussaka.

Stuffed, they took a stroll along the walkway, stopping in many of the shops. Nearing the end of town, they doubled back, when David, on the spur of the moment, decided to grab a blanket from his room, buy another bottle of wine and two pieces of baklava, and take the dirt path down to a small beach below.

Once there, they spread the blanket on the sand. David stretched out, propping himself up on an elbow, and they sipped sweet wine, nibbled the baklava, and watched the moon climb into the sky.

David made a remark Rebecca couldn't hear and when she leaned forward to ask what he'd said, he reached up and unclipped the comb in her hair, running his fingers through the glossy strands as they fell onto her shoulders.

She started to straighten, but he was quicker, and placing his hand on the nape of her neck, he pulled her down, rolling her onto her back. For Rebecca, this was a first. She was always popular, but until now, she'd never shown interest in any particular male.

David's mouth caressed hers while his fingers fumbled with the buttons on her blouse. Then, after a moment's hesitation, he pulled the garment free from her slacks. Slipping a hand beneath, he cupped a breast, teasing the nipple through the brassiere's thin fabric and sending chills down Rebecca's spine.

Moments later, he removed his shirt and helped Rebecca slip out of hers.

Lying back on the blanket, David reached up and unhooked her bra. With her hair spilling over him, Rebecca brought her mouth to his, moaning as he massaged her breasts.

Aching for more, she rolled on her side and pushed off her slacks. But before she could settle, David took her hand and placed it against the rigidity threatening to burst through the front of his trousers.

It took a minute for her to understand. With her breath quickening, she unfastened his belt, grasped the tab on his zipper and lowered it, freeing him.

She'd never encountered a fully, aroused male before. Though it excited her, she hesitated, unsure of what she was expected to do.

"Touch me," David said, his voice a hoarse whisper. But when she continued to do nothing, he reached over and caressed her arm. "Rebecca, touch me."

And she did.

Some time later, he removed the last of his clothing, and pulling her to him, rolled her onto her back. He pushed her hair away from her face, kissing her languidly and thoroughly, before trailing his lips along her jaw line and then down to her breasts, where he took his time.

When she sunk her fingers in his hair and began to writhe beneath him, he moved his hand down her abdomen, pulled off her bikini panties and slipped between her legs.

She moaned, twisting her head from side to side as he fingered her. But when he probed deeper, he came up against her barrier . . . and stopped, lifting his head.

"Rebecca . . ."

"No, David, no. Don't stop!"

He rested his head alongside hers, breathing heavily.

"David, please," she panted against his ear. "Please. I want it to be you."

In another minute, David raised his head and moved over her propping himself on his elbows. Spreading her legs with his, he advanced until he made contact. He hesitated, but Rebecca now took the lead; with a sudden thrust of her hips, she forced the breakthrough.

She knew he heard her sharp intake of breath, for he remained still before he again began to move. Eyes wide, Rebecca gazed back at him and adjusted to his rhythm.

Her release came first. She gave herself up to the wave of sensations engulfing her which peaked when she felt him explode inside her.

Rolled together in the blanket, they fell asleep until just before dawn when they awoke and made love again.

The sun's rays had just begun to pierce the horizon when they decided to take a swim before anyone in the houses above took notice.

To Rebecca, the inky blue water felt like silk against her skin as she sliced through its surface, laughing and swimming circles around David in an attempt to prevent him from catching her.

Sometime later, they climbed out to lie on the blanket and invite the sun to dry them.

At eight, still damp, they reluctantly packed their things, and going over to the dirt road, climbed it back to the town. There they enjoyed a delicious Mediterranean breakfast of melon, olives, yogurt, feta cheese, and freshly baked bread, all accompanied by syrupy Greek coffee.

In silence, David escorted her to the bus stop in Oia. As the bus approached, he turned, and with his fingers anchored in her hair, took her head in his hands and kissed her.

The screech of brakes broke the spell. In another minute, the bus came to a halt where they stood surrounded by others waiting to make the trip to Kamari.

"Goodbye, Rebecca," David said, tracing a finger down the side of her face and across her lips.

"Goodbye, David," she answered, her gaze locked with his.

He stepped back and waited while she boarded and then waved as the bus pulled away.

Rebecca returned his wave, and watched while he looked in her direction, until the bus rounded a curve, and he was lost from sight.

She hadn't asked his last name, whether he had a job, or his plans for the future. The only information she had was that he lived in Connecticut and had gone to college for two years before taking a break.

It wasn't important, because once he'd stepped through the doorway of Victor's, Rebecca knew he'd be the one. It was never a matter of choice, and it was the reason she felt neither sadness nor remorse at their parting.

Fanciful? Unreal? Perhaps. But she'd always have the memory.

She sighed and turned to the person on the bus who'd just spoken to her . . .

Except no one was there but the waiter—and she was not on a bus . . .

"Kiria?"

Startled, she looked up in confusion and saw that although her wine glass was empty, she'd eaten only half the appetizers. "*Parakalo Kyrios.*"

"*Parakalo, Kyria*, not to worry," he replied, humor dancing in his eyes.

She reached for the menu, scanned it, and quickly gave him her order. He filled her wine glass and with another smile, retreated.

She spread more eggplant mixture on a piece of pita bread and realized she was still hungry.

The waiter soon returned with more food, and before long, she finished most of what was on her plate. Sitting back, wine glass in hand, she looked across the caldera, where *Vulcanes* lay quietly, and tried to shake the feeling threatening to overtake her. If she were not a rational person, she would have sworn . . .

But that's ridiculous.

Or was it?

She raised her head, closed her eyes and inhaled. The moon was up, and the scent of thyme and freesia were in the air. Then, as if by magic, softly from out of nowhere, distant strains from Wagner's "Liebestod" reached her ears.

CHAPTER FOUR

Gallerie des Artistes
Rue du Bac, Paris

Jacket slung over a chair, Georges Lartigue sat behind closed doors in his office, his muscular, five-foot eleven-inch frame hunched over the desk. He'd returned late from Lisbon, and had been working since, hoping to catch up on a research project he'd promised the Louvre in two days.

Someone closed the front door. *Mais j'ai fermé a clef la porte.* He started to rise but froze as the door to his office opened slowly.

A female figure dressed entirely in black stared back, one hand on the doorknob. He gasped.

Miranda? Non. Impossible! Details of what had been a three-year living nightmare played through his brain.

She gave the door a shove, her body now a silhouette in the vacant space framed by the halo of the doorjamb.

"Hello Georges."

Silence.

She moved into the room. "Surprised?" she asked, her smiling lips a red streak. "Though I guess I can't blame you. I mean, it has been a long time, hasn't it?"

Georges swallowed hard, then found his voice, "Seven years since you went missing."

She lowered her gaze. Fluttered her eyelashes. "Really? That long?"

"Yes, Miranda, that long." Resigned, he gathered the scattered papers, slid them into a folder and placed it in a drawer. His heart was thudding with such force, he was certain she could hear it.

Leaning back, Georges managed the kind of restrained smile one might give a trying child. He was done agonizing over unanswered questions left in the wake of the car accident that had ended with a vehicle nose down in a river at the bottom of an embankment, claiming the life of her male companion. The windshield was shattered, and the passenger side door was damaged and partially open. A Citibank credit card bearing Miranda's name, a lipstick, and a set of keys to their apartment, were found on the floor beneath the seat.

Labeled as missing, an all-out search for her body ended several months later without results. But six and half years passed before a Manhattan circuit court judge finally signed the declaration establishing Miranda's death.

Georges didn't care where she'd been, or how she'd found him. He didn't want to know. He only wanted her gone. "Why are you here?"

She fingered the paperweight on top of his desk. "What, not even a little pleased to see me?" When he didn't reply, she continued, "I need money, *darling."*

He dropped the smile. "Miranda . . ."

She held up both hands, her eyes shiny with tears. "Just until I get a job."

Or find another gigolo. He refused to be moved. He knew all her ploys—the tantrums, threats, hysterical panic attacks . . ."And just where do you plan on doing that?"

"Why here, of course, in Paris. I do speak some French, you know. Besides I've applied for a work visa." She reached into her handbag, produced a handkerchief and gently blew her nose.

"I presume you mean *la carte de séjour?"*

He smiled at her blank look. "No matter, but why Paris and not New York? I should think it'd be easier for you to find work closer to home, despite your linguistic abilities."

She leaned over the desk, neckline gaping, eyes soulful. "But you Georges, are here."

Enough! He stood and retrieved his briefcase from the closet. "Miranda, surely you must know that I no longer care." His thoughts were racing. Somehow he had to get both of them out of there.

With a defiant gesture, she backed against the desk and hoisted herself onto the highly polished surface, exposing more of her lengthy, well-shaped legs, clad in sheer black fishnet stockings, which she then proceeded to cross. A toss of her head sent long dark tresses spilling down her back. Bracing herself, she pumped one mule-covered, high-heeled foot in the air and ogled the man in front of her. "You might not, but what about your friend, Miss Livingston?"

He gaped at her, having forgotten the lengths to which she'd go.

Georges put his briefcase on the desk, opened it and removed his checkbook. Reaching for a pen, he wrote out a check for four thousand U.S. dollars, cash. There was a ripping sound as he detached it and held it out to her.

Miranda took it, scrutinized the amount and shot him a triumphant look. No tears now. He replaced the checkbook, clicked the briefcase shut and removed it from the desk. Grasping her firmly by the arm, he eased her off.

Still clutching her arm, he ushered her through the gallery and out the front door. Once outside, he paused to lock up, activating the alarm system which caused metal panels to slide across the walls, concealing the art beneath. Again taking hold of her arm, Georges escorted her to the nearest taxi stand.

But before she could get in, he pivoted her to face him. "*Attention*, Miranda. That check represents *all* the money you're going to get; if you make any attempt to further harass me or anyone associated with me, I will seek legal assistance to restrain you. Is that clear?"

There was a momentary flicker of fear in her eyes, but in the next instant, it was gone.

She twisted herself free from his grip and with fire in her eyes spat, "*Perfectly.*"

As Georges watched the taxi pull away, he wondered where on earth it would take her, but he knew it would never be far enough. For the woman he'd just sent off, had once been his wife.

CHAPTER FIVE

"Bonsoir, mon ami. I'm glad you could meet me on such short notice," Georges said to Brian Neville, as Brian strolled into Le Poquelin at 17 rue Moliere in Paris' First Arrondissement.

After a warm, backslapping embrace, Georges studied his handsome friend's trim, six-foot, two-inch frame, and nodded his approval. "*Bon.* You are well, yes?"

Brian's blue gray eyes lit up as he grinned, "Couldn't be better."

The owner, Monsieur Lassé, approached, and Georges introduced Brian.

"*Bienvenue.* Welcome, Monsieur Neville." He turned to Georges. "As requested, Monsieur Lartigue, I saved you the table in the corner."

"Trés bien. Merci beaucoup."

Monsieur Lassé seated them and signaled a waiter. "Philippe will assist you this evening, Monsieur Lartigue but if there is anything I can do for you personally, please let me know."

"D'accord. Merci encore," Georges said, accepting the unfolded napkin from Philippe.

Though small, Georges had chosen the restaurant for its hushed, elegant atmosphere and personal service. Linen-covered tables, lush carpets, and large bouquets of flowers—accompanied by a superb menu and excellent wine list—assured a relaxed, memorable evening.

"*An aperitif, mon ami?"* Georges asked. "Some wine *peut-être?* or would you prefer to start with a drink?"

"Perhaps a drink. Scotch and soda *pour commencer, s'il vous plait,*" Brian told Philippe.

Georges ordered a Campari and soda.

"You were obviously upset on the phone when you mentioned that you had a particular problem you wished to discuss," Brian said, toying with his dinner knife.

Georges hesitated only a moment before his reserve disintegrated and the words burst forth. "It seems I have a wife, one who has appeared from the dead, and I need your help."

He knew the news came as a shock, but true to form, Brian maintained his ever-suave demeanor. "That's quite a challenge."

Their drinks arrived.

"*Salut*," Brian said, raising his glass. He sipped the scotch and studied the ice. "Okay, fire away."

"*Salut,*" Georges repeated; taking a pull on his drink, he folded and unfolded the corners of his cocktail napkin while he told Brian about Miranda's visit. When he finished, both were silent.

Brian was the first to speak. "We've known each other a while, my friend, but in all that time, I never had a clue you'd been married."

Georges shifted in his seat, uncomfortable at the mere mention of it. "At the time, I was living in New York and working at Sotheby's.

"We were young, Miranda and I," Georges continued, "too young. And one weekend on the spur of the moment, we decided to get married. Of course, my parents, oh my parents . . ." He helped himself to a breadstick.

"I admit I was attracted to her. She was stunning," he hesitated, "and very, very sexy." Snapping the breadstick in half, he hurriedly buttered an end and popped it into his mouth.

"In addition," he continued several seconds later, "I felt sympathy for her because she was Jewish and had lost most of her relatives during the war.

"Miranda's mother was only a child when she was orphaned in 1940. Her parents had left her in the care of an aunt while they returned to Poland planning to rescue *their* parents. Instead, all were rounded up and sent to Treblinka. Her mother never got over the loss. Several years after Miranda was born, she suffered a nervous breakdown, was institutionalized and ultimately committed suicide.

"To make matters worse, Miranda's father disappeared shortly afterward, leaving Miranda in the care of his less-than-enthusiastic sister."

Georges took a sip of his drink. "I identified with Miranda, you see, because my mother and her side of the family are Jews."

He knew that this, too, came as a surprise to Brian, but was certain it didn't matter. However, it did make him realize how little they both really knew about each other. While close, their association had always been professional—until Brian introduced him to Sally Livingston.

He noticed Philippe in the distance. "Are you hungry?" he asked Brian.

"We can order if you like, but don't let it interfere with your story."

"Suppose I go on, then, and start by giving you some background on my own history?"

"Even better."

Georges took a sip of Campari. "Once the invasion of Poland had taken place and the Germans were advancing west each night, my grandmother, mother, and uncle would take refuge in the basement while my grandfather and the cook stood on the porch at the back of the house watching enemy shells explode in the distance.

"By mid-May, however, Grandfather decided they'd gotten too close and moved everyone to their house on the coast. Several days later, he learned that King Leopold had fled the country and Belgium had fallen to the Nazis.

"And so, it was from the coast that they, with nothing but what the car could accommodate, left everything—including many magnificent paintings from Grandmother's family—in the house in Brussels, and began their journey southwest along the coast into France. There were five of them packed into that car: Grandfather, who was driving, Grandmother, her father—my great grandfather, Mother, and Uncle.

"Progress was all but impossible because the roads were thick with refugees carrying anything they could in carts, on their backs, or strapped to animals. Stopping for petrol was a nightmare. Added to that, Great Grandfather suffered from urinary frequency, requiring them to make additional stops.

"Due to Hitler's order to seal the port at Dunkirk, allied soldiers and armaments were everywhere—trapped in a pocket between the advancing German army and the sea. To add to the mayhem, German Stuka planes regularly swooped out of the sky and strafed the area, causing everyone along the road to drop to the ground . . . everyone, that is, except Grandfather. He used it as an opportunity to make time and, gunning the motor, would zigzag along the road in an attempt to gain whatever mileage he could. Needless to say, they moved at a snail's pace.

"They ate whatever they could—raw eggs found in chicken houses, and vegetables from gardens and fields. They slept in barns and ditches, or under houses and storage sheds, stopping at every port along the way in hopes of booking passage on anything scheduled to leave.

"Several weeks later, they at last arrived in Marseilles. Within days, Grandfather surrendered his passport to someone offering to help them leave France but was then thrown in jail for not carrying it.

"Somehow, Grandmother managed to engage an attorney for him. Then she, with Mother and Uncle in tow, made three trips to Madrid, determined to persuade the Fascist government there to give her the necessary visas that would allow them, to travel through Spain into Portugal. It was in Portugal that they had found passage on a ship going to the United States.

"Several weeks later, Grandmother succeeded. A judge freed Grandfather and urged them to leave the country, which, of course, they did. But halfway across the Atlantic, their visas ran out. Had they not been on an American ship, *mon ami*, I would not be sitting across from you today."

Several seconds passed before Brian spoke, "What an incredible story! Where did they settle once they arrived in the U.S.?"

"Virginia. Mother has always said that the streets of Washington were washed with her mother's tears. She was a difficult person, but because of her persistent pleas to the government on their behalf, many friends and relatives, most of them Jews, were able to leave Europe and come to the United States.

Brian took a sip of scotch and studied Georges. "You're fortunate, you know."

Georges looked up. "How so?"

"You said your grandmother was difficult, but from what you've just told me, she was also a strong, dedicated woman. From what little I know, I'd say you've inherited that strength."

"*Ah, mon ami. Merci beaucoup.*" He watched the ice as he swirled it in his glass. "If only it were true."

They were silent for several minutes until Brian asked, "Whatever happened to the house in Brussels?"

"It made it through the War intact. My parents visited it in 1962, and Mother was astounded to find that, despite people living in the house, the piano remained in its original position."

"And the art?"

Georges opened and closed his fingers. "Poof. Gone. Confiscated by the Nazis."

"Is that what prompted you to become involved with provenance research?"

Georges nodded. "Who knows? Perhaps one day it will lead me to something. There was one painting in particular . . . a portrait of my great grandmother, painted by Gustav Klimt when she was sixteen. At the time, Klimt was a friend of the family." He sighed.

Brian finished the last of his drink. "There's so much we take for granted today, isn't there?"

"Ah, *oui.* But now," he said, straightening, "perhaps we should order. Would you like to choose the wine?"

"No thanks," Brian said, raising his hands in protest. "I prefer to leave that in the hands of an expert."

Georges picked a vintage Pomerol and accepted the cork while Philippe poured some into a glass for him. Lifting the goblet, Georges studied the wine's deep, burgundy color before taking a sip. He smiled. "*Bon. Trés bien.*"

Philippe partially filled their glasses. Brian sampled it and the gleam in his eyes indicated his approval. "I knew you'd choose something exceptional."

"Getting back to my marriage," Georges said, after another swallow of wine. "I knew within the first six months that it had been a terrible mistake, realizing, too late, that sympathy should never be a *raison d'être.*" He helped himself to a piece of bread and spread it with butter.

"It wasn't long before it became apparent that my new wife suffered from delusions. At first the hysterical eruptions, or 'panic attacks' as the doctor called them, occurred infrequently. However, they increased with time, as did a tendency for violence. She'd throw things and smash things, all while screeching threats.

"I wanted to end it, resign my position at Sotheby's, leave the United States and go live in France. But, whenever Miranda suspected I'd leave, she'd threaten suicide."

The waiter returned with their first course. Georges took a bite of his country paté while Brian sampled his soup. "The langoustine bisque is good?" Georges asked.

"Excellent."

They ate in silence until Georges finished the last of his country pâté, and continued.

"Eventually, Miranda began seeing other men." He noticed Brian's quizzical look and shrugged. "How did I know? How does any husband know—disconnects when I answered the phone, the smell of liquor on her breath when she arrived home late? There were times she didn't come home at all. Then came the car accident." He filled Brian in on the details.

Philippe brought the main course

"And now, Miranda's here in Paris?" Brian asked.

"Oui, and apparently knows about Sally." Georges attacked his entrée.

"Or, at any rate, *thinks* she does," Brian added. He took a bite. "You were right. The duck is delicious. I don't suppose Miranda mentioned where'd she'd been all this time?"

Georges' silent stare gave him the answer.

"Sorry. Forget I asked."

"What I need," George said, the urgency in his voice clear, "is to have an attorney in the United States check into whether, in view of Miranda's reappearance, I'm still married."

"Ouch," Brian murmured, more to himself than to Georges.

"Exactement."

"But if a judge issued a declaration of death, wouldn't that bring an end to the marriage?"

"That is what I need to know for sure," Georges said, slicing off another piece of meat, "and I'll pay whatever it takes to find out. Again, my apologies for springing this on you so close to the wedding."

"Believe me," Brian said, laying his fork aside and reaching for his wine, "I'm more than happy to help. I'll get in touch with my brother Larry. He's a New York attorney and it shouldn't be difficult to find the information. What a time you've had."

"Yes, my coming to France helped put distance to it and ease the memory, but now that she's come back to life . . ." Georges raised his glass and took a hefty swallow. Philippe immediately appeared to top off their glasses.

"It might be in your best interests to take a few precautions," Brian said once Philippe had gone.

"Such as?" Georges asked.

"Increased security—at the gallery and your home. It's too bad you don't know where Miranda's staying."

"I did not wish to know, nor could I bring myself to ask. I went into shock when I saw her there in the doorway. You cannot imagine . . ." he closed his eyes and shook his head.

"Have you mentioned any of this to Sally?"

"Ah, and therein lies the problem. No, I have not." His eyes met Brian's. "I always suspected something like this might happen, and, if you'll pardon the candor, it has been the reason for my reluctance to deepen the relationship."

"Oh, I thought you had. But then it's really none of my business."

"The problem is," Georges continued, "I was looking forward to a time when Sally and I would become closer. Miranda, after all, was supposed to be dead." He sighed and shook his head.

After another minute, he said, "There are other things to consider too. My mother's family was very well off, monetarily as well as socially. Thanks to my grandmother, the family money is still intact.

"Alarmed at the rise of National Socialism, she took it upon herself to read *Mein Kampf.* Recognizing what the future held for Jews if Hitler came to power, she began transferring all her assets into my grandfather's name. It was safe, you see, for he wasn't Jewish and had already established a Swiss bank account. That's where the money remained until after the war when, bit-by-bit, Grandfather removed the funds and deposited them in his bank in the United States.

"The fact that Miranda and I were married in New York with its community property laws, could pose a significant threat to my financial future if it turns out we're still married. It was the main reason my parents were so upset."

"It was your grandmother's family who amassed the art collection?"

"Oui. They lived in Vienna. They were not only collectors, but like many other Jews, were philanthropists and supported the arts. Then came the war, and everyone knows what happened to Austria's Jews with the

Anchluss in1938. Fortunately, they had money and were able to buy their way to freedom."

"Thank God for that," Brian said, finishing the last of his entrée. "I'll call my brother tonight. Given the time difference, it'll be six in the evening when it's midnight here. At some point, though, you might wish to reconsider your decision and tell Sally. By not doing so, she might become vulnerable," he hesitated, "if for any reason Miranda decided to . . ."

Georges stared at his friend. "You think?" But then he recalled the many emotional displays designed to intimidate and, in the end, get Miranda whatever she wanted.

"If you're still hesitant and don't wish to mention anything to her," Brian continued, "you might think about erring on the side of caution by posting security in the vicinity of your apartment as well as the apartment Sally's renting while she's here for the wedding."

"You're right as usual," Georges said. He straightened suddenly. "*Mon Dieu!*"

Brian looked up. "Something wrong?"

"I just agreed to help a colleague with a project he that he said involves a beautiful woman. If Miranda were to find out about her, she might also . . ." He looked at Brian. "Believe me, you have no idea what she's capable of."

"I'll take your word for it, but for now, let's just deal with the immediate problem. As soon as I get back to the hotel, I'll give Larry a call and I'm serious about your making arrangements for the extra security."

"I promise to look into it when I get back to the office." Georges gave Brian his first smile of the evening. "Once again, I'm in your debt."

"I can't say I know anything about that. As I recall, I was always handsomely paid for my professional services. Anyway, this time it's different. I'm at your complete disposal as a friend."

Grateful, Georges nodded acknowledgement. "*Merci beaucoup. Et maintenant,*" he said with a wave, "*enfin, je suis terminer,* at last I'm through."

Choking back a laugh, Brian shook his head. "You've certainly had my full attention this evening."

Georges continued, his mood obviously improved, "Now, let's order dessert and you can tell me everything about you, Carrie, and the wedding."

CHAPTER SIX

The following Tuesday, Georges was on another flight to Lisbon. There, during a brief stopover, Senhor De Marcho planned to join him for the continued flight to Faro.

Seated by the window next to Georges was David Neville, an art dealer and partner of a gallery in New York who'd come to Paris to be the best man in his brother Brian's wedding. At Georges' coaxing, however, he'd agreed to arrive several days early and accompany Georges to Faro.

"Thank you again for coming," Georges said, once they were airborne out of Charles de Gaulle airport. "I appreciate your taking the time."

David looked at him. "You made it sound so tempting, I couldn't afford not to. Now tell me again how you came to be involved?"

Georges told him of his visit with Senhor De Marcho.

"You said the two paintings you saw were exceptional?"

"*Oui*, especially one. Mrs. Lawler's husband inherited them from his paternal grandfather who'd been a big collector before and after the Second World War.

"Mrs. Lawler and her husband want to sell them?"

"Mrs. Lawler is a widow."

"Then, the paintings are part of her husband's estate?"

"I would imagine so. At the time, Senhor De Marcho wasn't aware of the particulars."

Georges reached into his briefcase, extracted several sheets of paper, and passed them to David. "These are the notes I made on them. Believe me, you won't be sorry you've come.

"Mrs. Lawler also has a home in Las Vegas. She and her husband were substantial collectors, but between their two houses and what Mr. Lawler inherited, they had more art than they had room for.

"She told Senhor De Marcho that the pieces she'd taken to him were two of several neither she nor her husband cared for and had set aside until arrangements could be made to sell them. Unfortunately, his death intervened before they could do it together."

David read through Georges' notes. "So, the lady's full name is Rebecca Lawler?"

"*Oui,* and her husband's name was Jeffrey."

David grinned. "Senhor De Marcho told you she was beautiful?"

"*Oui.* 'A woman, a very beautiful one, came into the gallery' is what he said."

David set the sheets on his lap, and for a minute, gazed out the window. "I met a Rebecca once. And she *was* beautiful. But it was a long time ago."

"Yes, and . . ." Georges said.

"And nothing!"

"Ah, you Americans."

David spun to look at him. "*You're* American."

"Only half, born with the heart and mind of a Frenchman."

David snorted a laugh. "Well, if you must know, this Rebecca and I only spent three days together. It was during the time when I was taking a break from academia. I had *no* college degree, *no* job, *no* money and *no* prospects. I was going in whatever direction my instincts took me, hardly a position in which to initiate any kind of a relationship."

"But those three days . . . they were good ones, yes?"

David looked at the papers in his lap and nodded. "Yeah, they were good ones."

"And now you are a successful businessman."

"That's true."

"But are living with someone."

"Also true." David was beginning to squirm.

"And?" Georges persisted.

"Ha! You're a fine one to talk, you old bachelor."

Georges shrugged. "What is it about us, eh, my friend?"

"I've often wondered."

"Do you love this lady with whom you share your home?"

"Her name is Elise," David said. "Elise Crawford. And yes, I love her."

"What of marriage?"

For a minute, David remained silent. He'd taken no offense at Georges' questioning. Georges, after all, had known him as long as he'd known Brian, and like Brian, David knew that Georges thought of him as a brother. But along with the conflicts he already had over his live-in situation, it caused ambivalent emotions to surface. "Frankly, I don't know," he said at last.

"At least you're honest. *Peut-être,* the love you share is not that kind of love."

"I've thought of that."

"How does your Elise feel do you know?"

David heaved a sigh. "She'd like to get married."

Fortunately, at that point their conversation was interrupted with the announcement that they'd soon be landing in Lisbon.

David returned Georges' notes and unfastened his seat belt, glad for a chance to escape. "Since we won't be changing planes, if you'll excuse me, I'm going to make a quick trip to the bathroom.

* * *

The taxi with Senhor De Marcho, Georges Lartigue, and David Neville drove up a pebble-stone driveway and stopped before an impressive, white iron gate attached to two heavy stone pillars, each topped with the latest model of security camera. Fastened to the pillar on the left was a white ceramic plaque on which was written, *La Casa des Palomas*, in dark blue letters. "The house of doves," Senhor De Marcho translated.

Anchored to each pillar was a tall, white iron fence that fanned out, presumably surrounding the property.

"Está âlo?" asked a bodiless voice emanating from somewhere within the left pillar.

Senhor De Marcho gave his name; almost immediately, the gates began to open. Once through, they continued further up the driveway toward a white stucco, two-storied house that stood, its red tiled roof shimmering in the sun, overlooking a distant sapphire colored sea. Bougainvillea climbed over one corner, the bright blossoms in stark contrast to the whiteness of the house. The driver stopped in front.

David whistled softly. "Nice place."

Georges and Senhor de Marcho agreed.

They paid the driver and approaching the entrance, rang the bell.

Hearing footsteps, they looked up to see a beautiful, raven-haired woman coming towards them. Stunned, David stared at her for the resemblance to what he remembered about Rebecca was startling.

"Senhora Lawler?" Senhor De Marcho asked hesitantly.

She opened the screen door. "No, but please come in. Mrs. Lawler's on a long distance call in the other room. I'm her sister, Adelaide Broker. As they entered, she extended her hand.

"Georges Lartigue," Georges said, briefly bowing over it.

Senhor De Marcho followed suit. "Pleasure, Senhora."

Adelaide turned to David. "David Neville," he said, shaking her hand.

"Mrs. Lawler should be along any minute. In the meantime, come in and make yourselves comfortable."

They followed her into the living room, where, on the opposite wall beyond open French doors, lay a broad, partially protected terrace.

David joined Adelaide on the couch. Georges and Senhor De Marcho took chairs opposite them.

Adelaide studied David. "Is Neville a very common a name?"

"To be honest," David said, "I've never thought about it."

"I only mention it because earlier this year a rather tragic event put me in contact with an exceptional man by the name of Neville . . . Brian Neville to be exact."

"Really? Well, if it's the Brian Neville I'm thinking of, he's more than likely my brother."

"But the resemblance . . ."

"I know. I take after my mother's side of the family. They're all blondes."

"Then I hope you'll forgive my inquisitiveness, but if this Brian is your brother, isn't he about to be married?"

"Yes. In fact, the wedding's this weekend."

"David is to be best man," Georges interjected.

"May I ask how you know Brian?" David asked.

Adelaide dropped her eyes and was silent for several seconds making David wonder what he'd engendered.

She glanced up. "I'm sorry. I was trying to choose my words. Brian and I met in Las Vegas during a very difficult time for me. My husband Jim had been assassinated several days after he and the other members of the Board at Broker Industries had been approved for large increases in their life insurance. Brian was in charge of the reinvestigation on behalf of the insurance company." She paused. "It was in my home that Brian was burned from the incendiary device someone threw into the house."

Georges and David shared a look. Georges knew all about Brian's injuries and the long period of treatment he'd undergone in the burn unit of a Las Vegas hospital.

"Brian is a wonderful man, Mr. Neville," Adelaide continued. "He couldn't have been kinder or more helpful to Rebecca and me. We'd left the house an hour or so before it happened and felt terribly about not being there to help."

"Brian told us how much it had meant to him when you and Rebecca visited him in the hospital. And, please call me David."

This time when she smiled, Adelaide's face lit up, and David noticed how it enhanced her loveliness. "Then you, David, must call me Adelaide. Visiting Brian was the least we could do. I trust he's fully recovered?"

"Indeed he has, with little or no residual scarring."

"I'm very relieved to hear that. Please give him my warmest regards the next time you see him. And now, I think I hear Rebecca coming."

The three men stood and turned toward the sound in anticipation. But nothing could have prepared David for the jolt he sustained as his breath left him. Speechless, he stared at the auburn-haired beauty coming toward them.

Skin the color of golden honey and dressed in slim white slacks and a tee shirt over which was an open, blousy, yellow flowered shirt tied in a knot at her waist, she radiated sunshine. Manicured toes poked from her sandals and her hair—the hair that David had never forgotten—was wrapped in a large twist and secured on the top of her head with tortoise-shell pins.

Before David or anyone else could say a word, Rebecca came to an abrupt halt, and, staring at the handsome, brown-eyed blonde before her, slithered to the floor in a dead faint.

CHAPTER SEVEN

Georges was the closest and the first to move. He quickly closed the gap between himself and the slight form lying crumpled on the floor.

Concern galvanized David into action, and he followed to hover beside her. Adelaide was right behind him.

Senhor De Marcho stood aside but was ready to offer help if needed.

Adelaide knelt beside her sister. "Becca?"

"Perhaps a cloth and some cold water," Georges suggested.

"Yes, of course," Adelaide said. She got up and hurried toward the kitchen.

"I'll come along in case you need help," said David, following.

* * *

Rebecca's head hurt—so did her body. *Why is this bed so hard?* She shifted position. It didn't help.

Something cold and wet was put on her forehead. She tried removing it, and collided with a hand. Someone said her name.

"Becca? Can you hear me?"

"Addie?" The cold wet cloth was removed. Another took its place.

"She doesn't seem to have hurt herself," she heard a man's voice say. She opened her eyes and tried to focus, but what she saw made her close them again. *It can't be . . . it isn't possible . . . it makes no sense. What would he be doing here?*

"Can you sit up if we help you?"

She wasn't sure of anything, but decided to try, and again opened her eyes . . . this time more slowly.

Her sister knelt beside her on the left and a pleasant-looking man was standing next to her. But it was the handsome face belonging to the lean physique squatting beside her on the right that caught her attention.

And, she knew. It belonged to David . . . *the* David . . . *her* David. *My David?* Where'd she come up with that? *My brain must be muddled.* She laughed softly.

"I think she's coming around," she heard him say and realized she had never forgotten the mellow tone of his voice.

She tried pushing herself into a sitting position; two pairs of hands reached out to assist her.

"Easy does it, Rebecca," the same voice said.

"Thanks, I will," she answered. Her efforts had made her lightheaded and a bit dizzy.

"Perhaps we should call the doctor," Adelaide said.

"No, no," Rebecca protested. "Really. It was just the excitement."

Adelaide looked from David to Rebecca. "You sure?"

Rebecca nodded.

"In that case, sit there another minute, and I'll get you something to drink."

"I'd love a Coke," Rebecca told her.

With that, the Lawler housekeeper, Maria, appeared with another clean cloth and bowl of ice water. "How is the Senhora now?"

Adelaide switched bowls with her. "Better, I think. Would you be good enough to bring Mrs. Lawler a Coca-Cola?"

"*Sim,*" Maria replied, "but of course," and she returned to the kitchen.

A man in work clothes briefly appeared in the doorway but disappeared under a barrage of Portuguese from Maria.

Rebecca was now upright sitting tailor fashion. "Poor Ricardo," she said, looking at the faces around her. "He's my gardener and a very sweet man, but he's just been told that Maria's in charge and he's to mind his own business."

"How about a lift to the couch?" David asked.

Rebecca gave him her full attention. Then, putting her head in her hands, she started to laugh. Seconds later, David joined in. At last, they stopped and she looked up at him. "David, what in the world are you doing here?"

Just then, Maria arrived with the Coke.

"*Obrigada,* Maria. Thanks. I'll take it over on the couch." Rebecca started to get up.

But even with extra hands helping, she was still wobbly and she stumbled. With one big swoop, David caught her up in his arms.

"I still can't believe it," he said, chuckling as he carried her.

She gave him one of her stares. "I've never fainted before."

"Then I guess the difference between us is that I tend to pass out *after* the shock's worn off."

"Oh, great! Let's hope it's not before we get to the couch."

That started them laughing again. As a result, David's movements became awkward, and his lips grazed her cheek as he bent to set her down. Rebecca's skin began to tingle where his lips had touched it "Thanks," she murmured, rubbing the spot. "Glad we made it."

"Believe me, not as much as I am," he said, still chuckling.

Maria handed Rebecca the Coke. "Thanks, Maria." She took a sip and looked at the others. "My apologies, gentlemen. I guess by now you realize I'm Rebecca Lawler. You must also realize that David and I've met before. It was in Santorini twelve years ago, but we haven't seen or heard from each other since." She took another sip of Coke.

"Right," David said. "Other than our first names, the only things we knew about each other were that Rebecca was from San Francisco and had just graduated from college, while I was from Connecticut and taking a break from academia."

"I visited Santorini just last week," Rebecca continued. "To come home and find David standing in my living room was such a shock, I guess I fainted."

"Thanks for the explanation," Adelaide said, obviously relieved. "Needless to say we were all in the dark."

"Would anyone else like a drink . . . coffee, tea, something cold?" Rebecca asked.

"I bring a tray," Maria said. With a nod to Rebecca, she hustled out of the room.

"I'll go along to see if she needs help," Adelaide said. Carrying the unused bowl of ice water, she followed Maria into the kitchen.

Rebecca took one last sip of Coke, then put the glass on the coffee table. "Please. Everyone sit. Hello, again, Senhor De Marcho."

"Senhora," he said, smiling and inclining his head in her direction.

"Georges Lartigue," Georges said, advancing to greet her. "Senhor De Marcho's friend from Paris. And with me," he added, nodding toward David, "is David Neville, friend and art dealer *exceptionnel* from New York, with whose gallantry you are fortunate enough to be familiar."

Rebecca laughed. "What a marvelous sense of humor." She glanced at David. "So the name's David *Neville?*"

"And the brother of *Brian Neville*," Adelaide said, coming back in the room carrying a tray with an ice bucket and glasses. After putting the tray on the coffee table, she returned to the kitchen.

Rebecca looked at David. "Is what Adelaide said true? You're Brian Neville's brother?"

David grinned. "Yes. Don't let the hair fool you."

Rebecca recalled a conversation she and Adelaide had had soon after they'd arrived in Portugal. "Didn't Brian just get married?"

"He's about to be," David corrected. "How did you and Adelaide know?"

Rebecca hesitated, shifting to curl her legs beneath her. "The day of the fire before Brian was burned, Adelaide and I met with him and his associate, Paul Smith. As a hobby, my brother-in-law made films and DVDs of people enjoying themselves at parties and special events held at his home. The problem was, they'd been taken without the knowledge or consent of the participants. As a result, Jim kept them at home under lock and key in the library. Upon learning about them, the insurance company recognized the potential for blackmail and sent Brian and Paul to review them. Their professional manner so impressed Adelaide that she took them into her confidence, disclosing suspicions she had about Jim's murder that, up to then, she'd withheld. She also gave them privileged information about Broker Industries' business practices that she'd previously been hesitant to reveal. Please, try to understand. At the time, she had no idea who was responsible for either Jim's death or the fire and was concerned that, whoever it was, might also wish to harm her.

"It was Brian and Paul who insisted she have additional security posted in and outside of the house. Later, thanks to the recommendation of Bill Height, the attorney heading up the reinvestigation for the insurance company, Adelaide found an attorney." She looked at David. "His name is Tom Hutchins. Perhaps you know him?"

David shook his head. "No, I can't say that I do. But I know Bill Height."

Rebecca's stomach cramped. "It . . . it was Bill Height who, over a month ago, told Adelaide about Brian's forthcoming marriage to . . . to Carrie Norman, correct?"

David nodded. "Correct. You know Carrie as well?

"Not really," she said, uncomfortable. "Her husband, John, was one of the attorneys handling the original investigation. John and I happened to spend an evening together when he and his partner came to a lavish dinner party at Adelaide and Jim's home."

It had been more than a month since she'd thought about that evening's affair with John Norman. Just as in the past, the memory of it caused guilty feelings to nag at her conscience. Rebecca was already a widow, but John was married to Carrie. During the evening, John mentioned Bill Height, saying they were close. *I wonder how much Bill Height knows.*

To steady her nerves, she took a deep breath. "Addie and I were shocked, and much saddened by the news of . . . of John's death," she continued. She couldn't bring herself to say "suicide."

Refreshments arrived. Adelaide and Maria did the honors.

Once everyone had been served, Rebecca regained her composure and turned to Georges. "Tell me, how did you and David became involved in this project of mine."

David looked at Georges, and Georges at Senhor De Marcho.

"Ah, Senhora," Senhor De Marcho began, "the paintings you left with me happen to be most unusual—especially one, that, I suspect, has a very interesting history."

Rebecca retrieved her Coke from the coffee table and took a sip. *If I only knew what it was.*

"I, therefore, summoned Monsieur Lartigue, who is not only a good friend, but is considered to be an authority on research involving the backgrounds of various works of art. That is, looking into their past, or what's better known as their provenance." He paused.

"Yes," Rebecca said. "I'm familiar with the term."

"Then perhaps you're aware of the increased attention now paid to the provenance of a piece when it comes up for auction or is bequeathed to a museum or other public institution. This is especially true when it comes to the type of European paintings Hitler prized, which the Nazis stole and traded for thousands of what they called 'exploitable' works."

Rebecca nodded but made no comment.

"Next," Senhor De Marcho continued, "we come to the art of the nineteenth century and modern, or contemporary, art. This includes works by French Impressionists and German Expressionists . . . one, by Ernst Ludwig Kirchner, you left at my gallery." He looked at Rebecca.

"Again, I have to check the exact date as to when Jeffrey's grandfather acquired it," she said, uncurling her legs and straightening, "But I know he traveled to Munich in 1937 to attend Hitler's 'degenerate' art exhibit, *Entartete Kunst*, where so much of the Expressionists' work was on display."

"That is," Senhor De Marcho went on, "of course, what makes that piece so unusual."

"Not to mention valuable," Georges broke in.

"Because following that exhibit in March," Senhor De Marcho continued, "the Nazi Degenerate Art Police, or ERR, raided 20,000 works of art from the *Kronprinzenpalais*, Germany's first museum of contemporary art, and other museums where 'degenerate' or unacceptable art was on display. The purge included over 400 pieces by Ernst Kirchner, Max Beckman, Emil Nolde, and Franz Marc, to mention only a few. All were sent to the 'degenerate art warehouse.' From there, they would be destroyed, sold, or, as I previously mentioned, 'exploited' abroad."

"As late as 1939," Georges added, "nearly 5,000 paintings, sculptures, and works on paper, all labeled 'unexploitable', were burned in the courtyard of the main fire station in Berlin. We're amazed, therefore, that the pieces you left exist at all."

Rebecca finished her Coke giving the ice a swirl. "Because of our interest, Jeffrey and I spent a great deal of time researching the background of the pieces he'd inherited. Since there were several by German Expressionists, we became quite familiar with the history surrounding their work. Like you, we were amazed any of them had survived."

"To get back to what your husband inherited," Senhor De Marcho said, "I believe you told me his grandfather started his collection in the late 1930s and continued to buy up until the time he died in 2006. Is that correct?"

"Yes, that's correct."

"And since you are now the benefactor of what he left your husband, I presume you have all the necessary papers and proof of ownership, perhaps even a *catalogue raisonné?*"

"It's all in the safe."

"And you, of course, have access?"

"I do."

"Please, forgive me Senhora. I don't mean to offend but only wish to emphasize how important this is, especially if you wish to place the paintings at auction. Auction houses can be very finicky about this sort of thing. If any questions were to arise, the paintings could be rejected outright, or the house could insist on having an independent firm check to make sure they were acquired legally. That process could take months, during which the paintings would be held."

Rebecca's heart sank. *Which will probably be the case once it's discovered that one has an incomplete provenance while records on the other—except for the remains of an unreadable ownership stamp and Ernst Lawler's receipts of purchase—are missing completely.* She was hoping, somehow, they could work around it.

"You see, Mrs. Lawler," Senhor De Marcho continued, "both Monsieur Lartigue and I think you should place them at auction. Only then, will you the get the price those pieces deserve."

"In other words," Rebecca asked, "you recommend auction over a private sale?"

"In this case, yes," Georges said. "Kandinskys have soared in value over the last few years. In addition, Christie's has been selling German art as an entity unto itself. As recently as last year, the resulting sales sent it to the top spot at Christie's, Europe. It's experiencing a turnover higher than that of any other category, including twentieth century art. Does the idea of auction bother you?"

She thought of Jeffrey's planned meeting with Deitrich Radtke and, again, had the hunch that something about it wasn't quite right. "Only that it draws so much attention."

"We can certainly arrange to have someone attend the auction as your representative," Georges suggested.

"Yes. I'd like to take time and consider that." She looked at David.

"And you, David, what do you think?"

"Unfortunately, I've not had the pleasure of studying the two pieces in Lisbon. However, Georges was so impressed that he asked me to come to Paris several days earlier than planned so that I could accompany him today to see the others."

"Don't let David off too easily," Georges said. "He, too, is an art historian well versed in this type of thing. I asked him to come because I felt another pair of expert eyes would be valuable."

"Though just how expert has yet to be determined, I fear," David said. He grinned and spread his hands. "But for what it's worth, here I am."

And your appearance all but giving me heart failure. "Doing what you do though, David," Rebecca, asked, "don't you find it amazing that there can be so much history wrapped up in one piece of art, or that owning it can be so involved and problematic?"

They looked at each other. "Like you say," he replied with a smile, "it's pretty amazing."

And Rebecca understood that what he just said had little to do with paintings.

CHAPTER EIGHT

"If you'd like, I can show you the others," Rebecca said, now fully recovered. She glanced at her watch. "There's just enough time before lunch, that is, if a one-thirty lunch meets with your approval?"

Everyone agreed it did.

She stood. Upon seeing their concerned expressions, she added, "No. Really. I'm fine. Just getting my balance."

They followed her onto the terrace up an outside stairway made of the same stucco as the house, across a small balcony with sweeping views of an azure sea in the distance, and into a room that was obviously a bedroom/study.

Rebecca gestured toward two daybeds and several scattered chairs. "Please, make yourselves comfortable."

She went to a floor-to-ceiling closet, removed two frames and positioned them against the opposite wall. "I'm sorry not to have stands."

"Not important," Georges said.

Before him, were a Cézanne landscape and an apocalyptic drawing of Potsdmer Platz by Ludwig Meidner. "*Trés Bien!* Your husband's grandfather knew *de l'art.*"

"Jeffrey told me he'd been a passionate art devotee for as long as he could remember."

"Ah, but in addition, he had a superb eye. One can love art, but it is a gift to *know* art."

"True. Now, if someone will get the Max Beckman street scene in the other frame, another can help me bring over the two lying between the acid-free paper in the third drawer of that storage chest," Rebecca said, pointing.

Eager to help, David and Georges jumped up, and while Georges made room to prop the Beckman between those already against the wall,

David helped Rebecca secure the other two on the corkboard above. There was a Dégas sketch of a nude and a rare watercolor-and-India-ink painting on paper by Kandinsky.

Rebecca watched in anticipation as they examined them.

"You've quite a treasure trove of modern art here, Rebecca," David complimented

"Thank you," she said, beaming. "While Jeffrey and I recognized their value, they did not mix with or complement what we already have. There's even more in the house in Las Vegas, so perhaps you can understand why we wanted to sell these."

"If what you have in Las Vegas is anything similar to what you have here," David continued, "I'd have to say I agree with you."

"Is it your intention to have us take the two unframed pieces today?" Georges asked.

"It's up to you. They're heavily insured. I only need to sign the releases."

"And we, of course, will furnish you with the proper receipts," Georges said.

"Will you be taking them to Lisbon?" Rebecca asked Senhor De Marcho.

He and Georges exchanged glances. "No, Senhora. As much as I'd like to have them, I feel you'd be better served if they were to go to Paris with Monsieur Lartigue."

"And what of the two I brought you?"

"For the moment, it would be my pleasure to keep them. But soon, they, too, should go to Paris."

"In the meantime," Rebecca said, "I think you should be the one to keep their data."

Senhor De Marcho thought a minute, and with obvious pleasure, said, "Perhaps the Senhora is right."

Going to the desk, Rebecca reached underneath and depressed a button. At the same time, she removed a hand-held keypad from a drawer and punched in a series of numbers. A panel in the rear wall slid open, revealing a safe with its door ajar. Retrieving two large files and a stack of release forms, she returned to her seat, placing them on the table in front of her.

She opened the first file and removed five medium-sized envelopes, each stamped with a name corresponding to the pieces before them.

Reaching inside the envelope labeled Wassily Kandinsky, she withdrew a photograph showing the artist in his Paris studio with the painting in the background. There was also an insurance certificate, copies of pages from the Paris Kandinsky Society's *catalogue raisonné* listing the piece, a receipt of purchase, and copy of a check with Jeffrey's grandfather's signature, dated April 10, 1940, four years before the artist died.

"As you can see," she said, "everything you'll ever need is here."

"Bravo!" Georges cheered, obviously impressed. "For auction purposes it's essential the Kandinsky Society list each piece in their *catalogue raisonné*. Today, the market is flooded with excellent forgeries. You also have an important photograph. *Trés, trés bien*."

"All thanks to Jeffrey's strict adherence to detail." She removed the second file. "And these," she said holding up two smaller envelopes, hoping they wouldn't ask her to open them, "have whatever information there is on the two paintings in Lisbon."

"Are the certificates, receipts, *catalogues raisonné* and proofs of purchase your only copies?" David asked.

She glanced at him. "No. Although Jeffrey was meticulous about such things, I was the one who had the second sets made and authenticated."

"Smart gal."

"Not at all. I was just doing my job. It would have upset me to think I'd spent the better part of my career as an art consultant without learning *something*."

Color highlighted his cheeks as David choked out a laugh. "No. I guess you're right."

"Lunch is about to be served," Adelaide announced from the doorway.

"Be right with you as soon as I make out these releases," Rebecca said.

Georges withdrew a pen from an inside pocket and prepared the receipts.

"Done!" Rebecca said a few minutes later, inserting the forms into their corresponding envelopes. She stood. "Is everyone as hungry as I am?"

"If what we smell has anything to do with what's on the menu, I think the answer's unanimous," David said as he and Georges put the two unframed pieces in their protective coverings and inserted them into cardboard tubes.

Rebecca laughed. "Sounds like a 'yes' to me, Addie."

Carrying the artwork, the three men followed Rebecca and Adelaide down the inside stairs to the marble-tiled foyer of the main entrance.

They ate indoors since the area on the terrace was too small for the five of them.

After a first course of mixed cold appetizers—including a Portuguese specialty, freshly grilled sardines—Maria deposited a large, multicolored, ceramic tureen of bouillabaisse in the center of the table, accompanied by crusty bread and mixed salad.

Thanks to two bottles of well-chilled Vinho Verdi, everyone was on a first name basis. Toward the end of the main course, the conversation drifted back to the paintings.

"Since we've agreed to leave the three framed pieces here," Rebecca said, "I can have them packed, insured, and shipped to you tomorrow, Georges."

"Are you sure you to want run the risk of having them sent?" David asked.

"It just seems the fastest way to get them there," Rebecca replied.

"Why not bring them to Paris?" David suggested.

It didn't take long for Georges to catch the drift. "Excellent idea."

"And if you bring them this week, you could go to the wedding," David continued.

At Rebecca's blank stare, he added, "No obligation, you understand, only if you'd like to. But it's going to be in one of the most beautiful churches in Paris, and you'd be able to see Brian and meet Carrie."

"And meet my friend Sally Livingston," Georges added.

Rebecca was having a difficult time making sense of what had happened to her life. One minute it was all as it had been; in the next, it was completely turned upside down. To add to that, she'd just been invited to the wedding of the century.

She leveled a look at David. "That's very kind of you, but I think it would be better if I . . ."

"If you what?" David said, challenging her stare. He looked at Adelaide. "In fact, why don't the two of you come?"

Always anxious to assist a friend, Georges withdrew a small case from an inside jacket pocket and turned to Adelaide. "Rebecca already has my card, but, just in case, here's another. It has the address and telephone number of my gallery. If you let me know the day and time of your arrival, I will have a car meet you."

"Talk about salesmanship," Rebecca said, looking at Georges. "I don't know what to say."

"'Yes', is good," David said.

"Addie?" Rebecca said, appealing to her sister. "Help!"

But Adelaide seemed to be lost in thought.

"Addie?" Rebecca repeated.

"Yes?" Adelaide replied, coming to.

"What do you think about going to Paris?"

"And coming to Brian's wedding," David added.

"It's one thing to take the paintings to Paris, but quite another to crash a wedding," Rebecca said, sitting back and looking hard at David.

He endowed her with a bright smile. "How could it be viewed as crashing when I've just invited you personally?"

Rebecca rolled her eyes. "You're incorrigible."

"How about it, Adelaide?" David asked.

Rebecca looked at her sister and knew right away that Adelaide loved the idea.

"Why not, Becca? Heaven knows. Paris is always a treat. Besides, I'd love to go to the wedding."

"Done," David said, with an emphasizing smack on the table.

"Addie, what have you gotten us into?" Rebecca asked. She found the thought of meeting Carrie disquieting and wondered how much Carrie knew about the evening she'd spent with her husband at the Brokers' party over a year ago. The last thing she wanted was to upset a bride on her wedding day. Her stomach lurched. Perhaps there was a way of meeting them before.

"When is the wedding?" she asked.

"Saturday at six," David said, beaming. He flashed her a smile, "P.M., that is." His elation was obvious. He fiddled with his wine glass.

Reaching for the bottle, Georges got up and topped it off, then did the same for the others.

Still apprehensive, Rebecca looked at David. "Is there some way we could see Brian and meet Carrie *before* Saturday?" She smiled. How could she not? David's enthusiasm was contagious.

"Perhaps we could all have dinner the day you arrive," Georges suggested as he continued to pour wine.

"What day do you think you'll come?" David asked Rebecca. Not getting an immediate response, he turned to Adelaide.

"Friday?" Adelaide said.

"Thursday," David said, "in the morning, so you'll have the day to unpack and relax before dinner."

Rebecca was incredulous. "Are you *always* this decisive?"

He threw her a look. "When it comes to my best interests, yes."

"Oh? And this is?" She couldn't help baiting him.

David rose to the occasion. Cocking an eyebrow, he said, "Wouldn't you say that remains to be seen?"

Laughing, she threw up her hands. "I give up. Fine. We'll be there Thursday. Won't we, Addie?"

"Thursday it is," Adelaide answered, excitement visable in her eyes.

Rebecca looked at Senhor De Marcho, who, after two glasses of wine, asked that he be called Senhor Carlos. "*Perdåo,* sorry, Senhor Carlos. By now you must think we're all a little crazy."

He laughed, a deep resonant sound, startling everyone. "No, Senhora. Not at all. I am enjoying myself too much."

Suddenly, David looked at his watch. "What time is our flight?"

"Five-thirty," Georges said, checking his. "*Mon Dieu.*" It was a quarter past four.

"Exactly," David said, pushing back his chair.

"I'll drive you to the airport," Rebecca offered. "I'll get my bag." She stood and left on the run.

As they made their way to the door, everyone started talking at once, resulting in much laughter. Rebecca reappeared, and with David and Georges each carrying a tube with precious artwork, led them out toward her dark blue Volvo station wagon.

After many "thank yous" and "good-byes" to Adelaide, the men got in the car.

"See you Thursday," David said, giving Adelaide's hand an extra squeeze before sliding in next to Rebecca.

"Looking forward to it," she laughed and waved until the car passed through the gate and disappeared.

Adelaide found it most interesting that David and Rebecca had met in Santorini twelve years ago. It had to be why the island was such a favorite of Rebecca's. *In my mind, it makes today's coincidence most significant.*

She sighed and, with a little smile, walked toward the house. There was lightness in her step that had not been there before.

A wedding in Paris. How perfectly marvelous.

CHAPTER NINE

Large blue eyes stared back as Sally Livingston ran a comb through her wavy blond hair and gave her reflection a nod of approval.

Exiting the cramped lavatory of the Air France jumbo jet, she made her way back to her seat minutes before the "Fasten Seatbelt" sign went on, prior to their landing at Paris' Charles de Gaulle Airport. Since she was staying in Paris a while, she'd brought more than her usual amount of luggage and was pleased Georges had insisted on meeting her. Thinking of him made her smile.

An attractive man with thick wavy hair, he had captivating green eyes, a lazy, come-on smile, and kept his solidly built frame in shape by regular swimming and playing racquetball. Though stocky, he was also extremely agile, having achieved a black belt in karate before moving to Paris from New York.

Unfortunately, her fear of commitment had caused Sally to proceed with caution. For the past few months, however, she'd been seeing a psychologist, hoping that, given time, she'd be able to relax and enjoy the relationship.

Luckily, Georges was insightful. After seeing each other several times, he sensed her disquiet, and they'd discussed it. Since then, she'd been much less apprehensive and was now looking forward to being with him again.

Her heart sank when she saw the number of people at Immigration. Fortunately, the line advanced quickly, and the entire procedure turned out to be a breeze. With a "*merci beaucoup,*" she collected her passport and headed for the baggage claim carousels.

"*Cherie*?" a familiar voice said behind her.

She whirled. "Georges! How did you manage to get in here?"

"Ah, Sally, have you forgotten my powers of persuasion so quickly?"

"No," she laughed, returning the embrace. "Not at all. It's only that you never cease to amaze me. I couldn't be happier to see you, whatever it was you had to say to get in." *He really does have the most beautiful green eyes.*

"Anticipating your need for a more than average wardrobe, I thought it would be more comfortable if we had a car." He waved in the direction of a man wearing a long black coat and chauffeur's cap. "Jacques there will drive us."

"You do think of everything, don't you?"

"How was your trip? *Bon*?"

"It was, yes."

"And the gourmet food?"

She laughed at his look of disdain. "Actually, not bad. But the wine was good."

"Ah. Then all was not lost, eh?"

They collected her bags and left the terminal. Fifteen minutes later, they were on their way in the car.

"We'll get you settled," Georges said, "But then I must return to the gallery." He reached for her hand. "We'll have dinner together later, yes?"

"I'll look forward to that," Sally said, giving his hand a squeeze.

"*D'accord.* Suppose I come to collect you around six? That is not too early?"

She shook her head. "No. Six should be fine."

"*Bon.* That way, you can have the day to unpack and get some rest."

Despite it being the morning rush hour, the traffic into Paris was not bad, and before long, Jacques was pulling the car up in front of the address Sally had given him.

She'd chosen the furnished, one-bedroom apartment from an add in one of the college alumni magazines: "Left bank, third floor, elevator-building, one bedroom with bath, modern kitchen, beamed ceilings, wood-burning fireplace, windows overlooking the Seine and Louvre." Adding to its appeal was that it was within walking distance of the gallery Georges and his sister, Gabrielle, co-owned on Rue du Bac.

The men helped Sally with her bags, and when she put her key in the lock and pushed open the door, her uncertainty turned to joy. It was enchanting.

"*Bravo, Cherie*. It seems you've made a good choice," Georges said, coming along side and putting an arm around her.

"I did, didn't I?"

"Do you need help unpacking?"

"No thanks. You go ahead. I'll see you at six."

Instead of leaving, Georges went into the kitchen and opened the cabinets and refrigerator. "But you have nothing here. There is a *petite charcuterie* on the corner." He came back into the living room. "Suppose I pick up a few things—water, thé, café, bread, meat, yes?"

"That would be wonderful. I hadn't given it a thought."

"*Bon*. I won't be long," he added kissing her cheek. He turned to Jacques as he started toward the door. "*Allons*."

"*Merci beaucoup*, Jacques," Sally said with a wave.

"*De rien, mademoiselle*," Jacques answered, following Georges and leaving Sally alone.

She went to the sofa and collapsed on its cushions. *Paris. I'm really here and spending the next few weeks in Paris!*

She nestled deeper into the pillows in the corner but sat up once she began to drift off. *Best I keep moving.*

Collecting her luggage, she began to unpack.

Georges returned with the staples within the hour and helped Sally put them away in the small, but adequate, kitchen.

Slipping his arms around her, he gave her a hug. "Glad you're here."

"I'm happy I'm here, too," she said, smiling up at him.

Once he'd gone, Sally finished unpacking, and by one o'clock, had everything stashed away.

Her stomach growled, making her realize the last time she'd eaten was on the plane at five o'clock that morning.

She hurried to the kitchen and made herself a sandwich from the French bread, sausage and cheese George had left, adding a dollop of French mustard as a final touch. *Yum*! *I'm in heaven.*

She took a shower, set her alarm for five, and crawled under the gaily-colored patchwork quilt covering the bed. It was the last thing she remembered before falling into a deep sleep.

* * *

Back at the gallery, Georges and his sister, Gabrielle, were discussing what frames to use on the two pieces he'd brought back from Rebecca's when the call came through.

"I have a long distance call for a Monsieur Lartigue."

"This is he," Georges replied.

"Go ahead, Pittsburgh."

"Monsieur Lartigue?"

"*Oui?*"

"This is Doctor David Weiss, Monsieur Lartigue."

"I'm sorry, but I don't know any doctor by the name of David Weiss," Georges said. "Are you sure you have the right person?"

"My apologies. I'm one of the chief psychiatrists at Western Psychiatric Hospital in Pittsburgh, Pennsylvania, Monsieur Lartigue. My call concerns a patient of mine, one Miranda Sloane Lartigue, who, I believe, is, or was, your wife. Am I correct?"

A chill ran down Georges' spine. He'd intentionally postponed calling Brian that morning until he'd had a chance to arrange for the extra security.

"Monsieur Lartigue?"

Georges cleared his throat. Tried to get a grip. "Pardon, Doctor Weiss. You are of course correct. Miranda was at one time my wife."

Gabrielle mouthed, "Is there anything I can get you?"

Georges shook his head.

"Again my apologies for springing this on you over the phone, Monsieur Lartigue. However, there is no other way to inform you that your ah, Miranda is missing. By any chance, have you heard from her or have you any idea where she might be?"

"Why do you ask?"

"For the past two and a half months, Miranda has been a patient of mine, first in the hospital at Western Psychiatric, then, after her discharge, as an outpatient. Two weeks ago, she failed to show up for her appointments, and we haven't heard from her since. No one seems to know her whereabouts. Monsieur Lartigue, were you at all aware of Miranda's hospitalization, or the reason why it was necessary?"

"My wife, Miranda, disappeared following an automobile accident seven years ago and was officially declared dead. She and I, therefore, are no longer married." *Mon Dieu, I hope it's still true.* "Then, one morning last week, she appeared in my gallery."

"In other words, you have seen her?"

"Yes, but I've no idea where she is now. Her welfare no longer concerns me."

"Under the circumstances, I can certainly understand that, Monsieur Lartigue. But if at all possible, Miranda needs to be found. You see, she's afflicted with a condition known as dissociative identity disorder that, in her case, was precipitated by trauma. My concern is that if for some reason she becomes severely agitated, she could pose a threat, not only to herself, but possibly to others."

Georges' worst nightmare had just been born. "What do you suggest, doctor?"

"Since she's already made contact with you, she'll probably do so again. Therefore, it would be best if you were to familiarize yourself with her condition. Do you have a personal physician, Monsieur Lartigue, one with whom I might speak? That way, you'll have someone in Paris with whom you can discuss Miranda's condition and who can be there for you should you need him."

Georges reached for the Rolodex, his fingers flipping through the cards. "My physician's name is André Marchand. He can be reached . . ." He read off the number. "And, if Miranda comes into the gallery again?"

"If she appears normal, try to find out where she's staying. If possible, have someone monitor her movements. If she's distressed, try to keep her there and summon medical help."

"I'll notify Doctor Marchand and tell him to expect your call."

"That would be most helpful."

"In the meantime, can you brief me so I'll know what to expect should she reappear?"

"Dissociative identity disorder is what's known in layman's terms as 'split personality.' Some patients have as many as ten, even fifteen, different identities. As far as we've been able to determine, Miranda has only two. So far, they appear to be distinct from each other and do not conflict or interact, although she was hallucinating at the time she was brought in."

"Does anyone know where Miranda had been prior to her hospitalization, Doctor Weiss??"

"When was her accident?"

"April of 2003."

"Then I fear her history immediately following will always remain a mystery. I first saw Miranda when she was admitted to Western Psychiatric two and a half months ago. At that time, she was extremely agitated. But with proper medication—in her case lithium—she soon leveled out enough for us to begin probing into her background.

"What we were able to ascertain was that as of August, 2003, Miranda was in Pittsburgh, had obtained a social security number, found a job, was renting a room from a family, and living under the name of Jennifer Sloane, her 'other self.' Then, earlier this year, she suffered some sort of stress, and during the subsequent agitated period, she reverted back to Miranda Lartigue.

"Among her belongings were two checkbooks: one in the name of Miranda Lartigue linked to a Citibank account in New York—the last check being written in April of 2003—and the other, in the name of Jennifer Sloane, linked to a branch of Chase Manhattan in Pittsburgh. In addition, there was a Chase Manhattan Visa card and an expired American Express card in your name."

Georges recalled the number of charges she'd posted to the account the day of her accident. They'd appeared on the following month's statement, but he'd never paid attention to what they were for. *Could one of them have been for transportation or anything relating to her disappearance?* If so, it would have proved that she hadn't perished in the crash. At the time, the possibility had never occurred to him.

"I'll call Doctor Marchand later today," Doctor Weiss continued. "But let me give you telephone numbers where I can be reached—day or night."

Georges recorded them in the Rolodex. "*D'accord. Merci,* Doctor Weiss."

"You're welcome. Remember, do not hesitate to call if there's any kind of a problem. Good-bye for now, Monsieur Lartigue."

"*Au revoir,* Doctor Weiss." Georges reached for the directory. It was now even more imperative he obtain the security Brian had so wisely recommended he should.

CHAPTER TEN

After a frantic Wednesday, Rebecca and her sister were on the nine-thirty flight to Paris Thursday morning. The paintings destined for Georges were securely packed and traveling in a special compartment of the aircraft.

Rebecca fastened her seat belt, leaned back, and closed her eyes. "I never thought we'd make it."

"Nor did I," Adelaide said, shoving the last of her luggage into the overhead compartment and dropping into the seat next to her. "I threw together what I thought was appropriate, but I still have to go shopping. I brought nothing as dressy as what I'll need for this wedding."

"I packed two outfits but will probably come with you. After all, there's nothing like shopping in Paris."

"It's thoughtful of Georges to send a car," Adelaide said.

"Indeed it is."

"He's got great eyes," Adelaide continued. "Not only are they an unusual shade of green, they always seem to be twinkling. It puts me in mind of Puck."

Rebecca laughed. "As a matter of fact it does. It's misleading, too. He seems so serious, but I'll wager that under that façade is a person who enjoys everything there is to life."

"Sexy, too."

Rebecca threw her a look.

Adelaide shrugged. "Think about it. Then tell me if he isn't."

Rebecca thought about it. "But it's not any one thing that makes him so. It's the overall aura he projects."

"Exactly."

"Hmm. This trip may be more interesting than anticipated."

"And, if Tuesday was any indication . . ." Adelaide began. "Ah ha! Whose eyes are twinkling now?"

Rebecca waved a hand at her. "Addie, *really.*"

"Uh-huh."

But Rebecca refused to acknowledge her sister's smug, all-knowing look.

Halfway through the trip, Rebecca asked, "Addie, did you happen to notice the man sitting in the black sedan parked farther down the road this morning? He was there as we left."

"No. Can't say that I did. Why?"

"Seeing it there gave me the creeps because it reminded me of how I was followed and hounded with phone calls following Jeffrey's death. Remember? That's when I hired the private detective and upgraded the security systems."

Adelaide turned to her. "You think someone's following you again?"

"I'm not sure. But there was someone in a similar car parked in that same place the day I took David, Senhor Carlos, and Georges to the airport."

"What about the security system on the house in Las Vegas?"

"Clarissa told me that last week there'd been a power failure. The electric clocks stopped, and the red light on the main security panel by the front door was lit and beeping. Within minutes, the alarm company called and said someone would be out to check and re-set the system."

"She keeps the alarms on while she's there?"

"Those for the doors and windows, yes, but not those for the internal motion detectors."

"Did the alarm company ever say what caused the power failure?"

"They attributed it to a sudden power surge. Luckily, the system's breaker system shut things down which prevented a fire. As to the cause, they said they were as much in the dark as she was."

"Your house is pretty isolated. Did Clarissa say whether or not the house down the road was affected?"

"She asked the repair man, but he said it wasn't. Since the houses are about a quarter of a mile apart, each has its own power supply that branches off the main somewhere out along the highway. Perhaps it was just a coincidence, or else I'm paranoid. At any rate, it all gives me the creeps."

Adelaide reached over and put her hand on Rebecca's arm. "Try not to think about it while you're in Paris. Remember the mantra: I'm in Paris. I'm in Paris. I'm in Paris."

Rebecca laughed. "Thank heavens for you, Addie."

Upon their arrival at Charles de Gaulle Airport the following morning, they had to wait in line at customs for fifteen minutes. When at last they moved forward, Rebecca presented the declaration certificates that Georges had sent by Federal Express for the paintings. In no time their passports were stamped and they were waved through.

A slim, attractive, blue-eyed blonde approached and introduced herself. "Hello. I'm Georges' friend Sally Livingston. You both look weighted down. Here, let me carry something."

"Thanks, Sally," Rebecca said. "If you take my shoulder bag, I can carry the paintings."

As they passed through the doors into the main terminal, a man came forward, and Sally introduced them to Jacques, Georges' chauffer.

"We'll drop you at your hotel so you can check in and get settled," Sally said when they were in the car heading to Paris. "But then, Carrie and I would like to take you to lunch."

"What a lovely idea," Rebecca said, glancing at Adelaide.

"I'm certainly up for it," Adelaide agreed.

"Wonderful. Carrie will be pleased."

"At some point though, I need to shop for clothes."

"Do you have any particular shops in mind?" Sally asked.

"I don't. Can you make a few suggestions?"

"I'd be happy to. Fashion is my field. I'm a coordinator who works with several designer houses in New York. If you like, I'll go with you and present my business card. Who knows? It might help."

"Would it interfere with your plans if we go tomorrow?" Rebecca asked.

"Not if we go early."

Adelaide grinned. "Just name the time."

"Suppose I pick you up you at your hotel at nine thirty?"

"Perfect. All right with you, Becca?

"Yes, of course."

"Good," Sally said. "I look forward to it."

The car pulled up in front of the hotel Manoir de St.-Germain-des-Prés. The doorman opened the door and helped Jacques unload the luggage. He gestured to the packaged paintings. "Mademoiselle?"

Rebecca looked at Sally. "Are you taking the paintings to Georges now?"

"That was my thought."

"Wonderful. Then I won't worry about them any longer." She slid from the car and spoke to the doorman while Jacques helped Adelaide.

"Will twelve thirty be all right to meet for lunch?" Sally asked.

Adelaide nodded. "Sounds good to us," Rebecca said. "Thanks again for coming to pick us up."

"You're most welcome. See you at twelve thirty."

Rebecca and Adelaide had been in their room barely twenty minutes when the phone rang. Rebecca was the closest and answered.

"*Bienvenue,*" said a voice on the line.

"*Merci beaucoup*, David."

"How'd you know?"

Rebecca laughed. "Psychic, I guess." She decided against telling him she'd never forgotten the sound of his voice.

"Trip good?"

"It was. Thanks."

"Sally met you and all?"

"She did. Georges is a lucky man. She's a delight."

"Yes, she is. Is there a chance you might be free for dinner?"

"Tonight?" Rebecca blurted. At this rate she'd gain five pounds.

He chuckled. "Yes, tonight. Is that a problem?"

Rebecca rolled her eyes at her sister as Adelaide walked by. "Ah . . . no, no, not at all."

"Would Adelaide like to join us?"

"Wait, I'll ask."

She asked.

"Adelaide says she'd love to, but isn't three a crowd?"

"Well, it just so happens I have someone here whom you both know and who's interested in joining us."

Rebecca tried to think but her mind had shut down at the sound of David's voice. "I can't imagine who it could be."

"What if I were to tell you it was Paul Smith?"

"Paul Smith?"

Adelaide stuck her head out of the walk-in closet.

"Yes, remember him?"

"Yes . . . yes, of course I do. So does Adelaide," Rebecca said, looking at her sister.

"That way we'll be four."

She laughed softly. *This man is too much.* "What time? We're to have lunch with Carrie and Sally at twelve thirty."

"Is six too early?"

"No. No, six will be fine." Adelaide nodded from across the room.

"Good. Enjoy lunch, but eat light so you save room for dinner."

"Yes, sir!" Rebecca said looking up at the ceiling. "I'll certainly keep that in mind."

He laughed. "Good. See you at six."

Rebecca hung up and stared at the phone. Then with a whoop, she threw her arms in the air and fell backwards onto the bed laughing. "And here I thought I was leaving Las Vegas to sell the paintings and finally put my life in order!"

CHAPTER ELEVEN

"Nervous?" Adelaide asked as she and Rebecca rode down in the elevator.

"A little. But I couldn't be happier that we're doing this. Perhaps then I'll be more relaxed about going to the wedding."

They arrived in the lobby just as Sally, accompanied by a stunning blonde, walked through the front door. "Hello, Rebecca. I'm Carrie Norman."

Rebecca grasped the outstretched hand. "Hello, Carrie. How nice to be meeting you at last."

"And you must be Adelaide," Carrie said, turning to her. They shook hands.

"What a pleasure it is to be meeting Brian's fiancée."

"Why, thank you, Adelaide," Carrie said, obviously pleased.

"Shall we be off?" Sally asked with her usual buoyancy. "When Georges knew we were going to lunch, he engaged Jacques for the afternoon. Chez René is within walking distance, but the car will save us time."

Once they'd placed their orders and were enjoying a glass of chilled Sancerre, Carrie turned to Rebecca. "Brian and I were fascinated by David's story of how he and Georges came to be at your home. What made it so amazing was that you and David had met before."

"Yes. I'd just graduated from college and David was taking a break from his studies."

"Were you surprised to see him?" Sally asked.

"Surprised?" Adelaide interjected, "She fainted."

Sally looked at Rebecca. "Is that *true*?"

"I'm afraid it is," Rebecca answered, glaring at her sister. "I can only assume my reaction was because I'd just returned from a weekend in

Santorini which is where David and I met twelve years ago. Seeing him in my living room several days later was a shock."

"From what David told us, it was a shock to you both," Carrie said, laughing. "But Brian and I were delighted he had the presence of mind to invite you to the wedding. And," she continued, withdrawing two envelopes from her purse and handing one to each of them, "we hope you'll join us for the reception afterward."

Rebecca opened the envelope. Inside was an invitation to the dinner at La Tour d'Argent. She smiled. "Thank you, Carrie. I accept with pleasure."

"As do I," Adelaide said. "Thank you."

After lunch, they walked back to the hotel. On the way, Carrie fell into step with Rebecca. "I've been hoping for a chance to speak with you and want to thank you for the lovely note you sent following John's death. I know it couldn't have been easy."

Rebecca was trying to think of how to say what was foremost in her mind, but before she could reply, Carrie continued.

"I hope you won't mind if I ask you a question."

Rebecca braced herself. "No, of course not."

"In your letter you mentioned that your brother-in-law, Jim Broker, was not a very nice person, and might have been responsible for the major part of John's distress during the insurance investigation. Did you know about Broker's blackmailing him and Dan Jenkins?"

"No, not when I wrote the letter. Adelaide and I found out at the conclusion of the reinvestigation. But I knew Jim. He was a person no one crossed. While his employees adored him because he was a kind, considerate employer—and, thank goodness, a very good husband to my sister—he always made me uncomfortable, acting as if he knew something about me that I did not. In addition, I frequently caught him staring at me in a way that I found . . ." her eyes met Carrie's, "for a lack of a better word, lustful. Yet, I never knew him to have any other woman but my sister." *At last, an opportunity to exorcise past ghosts.*

Rebecca hadn't planned the one night affair with John the evening of her brother-in-law's party. When she'd offered to take him for a drive into the desert, her wish had been to put him at ease. Only when they doubled back had she thought of stopping at her house for a nightcap.

But as the evening progressed, she found herself drawn to him. She saw him as a lost soul. Her kiss on the cheek when they were about to leave and return to the city had been nothing more than a sympathetic gesture. She never dreamed he'd respond—let alone with such ardor—nor that she'd match his advances equally. It made her realize how much she missed Jeffrey. Carrie's voice brought her back to the conversation at hand.

"I . . . I'm sorry. What did you say?" Rebecca said, embarrassed as though Carrie had read her thoughts.

"You said you wondered if John's death could have had anything to do with you, and I said, 'perhaps partially, but only indirectly.' You see, Jim Broker found out about . . ."

Rebecca guessed. She had always suspected. "About John and me."

"Yes, and used it to blackmail John when he and Dan began uncovering information that, if exposed, could have torpedoed Broker Industries' chances of obtaining the extra life insurance."

Rebecca had never felt worse. *But I mustn't stop now*! She tried swallowing the lump in her throat. "Once John knew, why didn't he and Dan do something about it?"

"I think because John thought his indiscretion, if discovered, would be acutely embarrassing and damage his career. He held back information for fear of exposure."

If that were possible, Rebecca felt even worse.

"But the greatest offense," Carrie continued, "was that he and Dan not only agreed to act as counsels for Broker Industries, but accepted Jim's offer to be on the Board of another company that ultimately proved to be associated with Broker Industries. Both constituted a flagrant conflict of interest and were much more damaging to their careers than John's liaison with you. He's never said, but I think in deference to John, Dan was reluctant to inform the insurance company on his own about what they were uncovering."

Rebecca glanced at her. "But was John so devoid of hope that he saw suicide as his only solution? How horrendous that must have been for you!"

"More than that. I was on the way to our apartment with Bill Height, our attorney and John's dearest friend, when we heard the shot." Tears filled her eyes.

Rebecca stopped, clutching her throat. "You *heard* it? My God, Carrie. I can't imagine . . ." She couldn't think.

Pulling a handkerchief from her bag, Carrie blotted her eyes and snifled. "Sorry."

"To answer your question," she continued once they resumed walking, "I think John found himself in an untenable situation because he'd never be able to face his father. An only child, John was the focus of all the man's hopes and dreams. For John to have had to tell him everything was something he could not face."

And to think I was responsible. Rebecca's throat ached and tears threatened. "I . . . I'm so sorry, Carrie. If only I could undo everything."

"I didn't know about you and John until after his death," Carrie continued. "Then your letter arrived and I knew. Because I was hurt, I didn't want to believe it. That was when I went to Bill Height. He was the one who confirmed it.

"I wasn't surprised he knew. John held him in such high regard. I'm sure had John been able to talk about what happened, the person he'd have chosen to tell would have been Bill. We were all in college together. When John and I married, Bill was John's best man. Then when Bill married, John was his."

She glanced at Rebecca and coming closer, threaded her arm through hers. "But neither you nor I were destined to be John's keeper, Rebecca. Bill and I repeatedly tried to help . . ." She shook her head remembering. "Oh, how we tried. But John remained inconsolable."

"But if he and I . . ."

Carrie looked at her. "Had never met or gotten together? I don't believe that. It was timing. If it hadn't been you, it would have eventually been someone else. Our marriage had been ailing for some time, something that became evident once I met Brian. I tried broaching the subject, but John refused to discuss it—and then he met you. If John and I had been honest with each other, he would have told me about his affair with you. Then I could have stopped trying to save our marriage and told him of my attraction to Brian." She gave Rebecca's arm a tug. "But none of that happened, did it? We can never remake the past, can we?"

Two tears ran down Rebecca's cheeks. "No, sadly. We can't." She looked up. "Carrie . . ."

"In that case, let's put it behind us," Carrie said, giving Rebecca's arm another tug, "and concentrate on the future. Because, some time," she continued, looking ahead at the backs of Sally and Adelaide, "I'd love to hear more about you, your life, *and,"* she added with a smile, "what it is you've done to David. I've never seen him more delighted with the world as he's been since his return from Portugal."

* * *

Miranda saw them coming from a distance. She recognized Sally because she'd seen her picture in the fashion magazine, *W*. She didn't know who the others were, but the fact they were attractive didn't escape her scrutiny.

Her thoughts switched to her former sister-in-law, Gabrielle. *Bitch. Always fawning over her brother. Not only did she work with him at Sotheby's New York, she's now here in Paris working with him again*!

She looked forward to the next unannounced visit. The opportunity would arise. She only needed to be patient. With the 4,000 dollars Georges had given her plus money still in her Citibank account, she was set for a while—at least until the application for the Carte de Séjour went through.

Feeling better, she increased her stride, left the Boulevard St. Germain, and walked down Rue de Bac.

Moving along, she thought about where the time had gone since she'd last seen Georges. His comments the day of her surprise appearance had made her even more aware of the void those lost years represented. *Where the hell had he been?*

She had a vague recollection of a car flying through the air. Try as she would, however, she could not remember more. When she did try, her head would begin to throb and she'd become confused. It was then she'd hear the voice the doctors called her "other self."

So, for now, her thoughts were interrupted as she saw Georges come out of the gallery with a tall, handsome man sporting a stunning smile. Her interest was piqued.

Hello. Where have you been hiding?

She stopped and watched them walk away. *Enough. Besides, I'm starving.*

Reversing direction, she turned back toward her hotel.

Earlier, before Miranda spotted him, Brian had strolled into Gallerie des Artistes to visit Georges. Seeing him in his office, Brian had walked back and knocked on the door.

Georges looked up. "Ah, there you are."

"Have you been trying to reach me?" Brian said, dropping into a chair.

"Not really, but I am happy to see you."

"Has something happened?"

"It has." Georges told him about the call from Doctor Weiss.

"Have you taken my advice about security?"

"*Oui,* but only just. Unfortunately, the trip to Portugal delayed my doing that."

"Larry called again an hour ago."

"Yes?"

"He says you have nothing to worry about and confirmed your marriage officially ended with the judge's declaration of death. There'd only be issues if you decided to go for a divorce because it would then involve the matter of estate. But, take heart. Even if Miranda is somehow able to reverse the declaration, it will not reinstate the marriage."

"So I'm no longer married even though she's alive?"

"That's right."

Georges' relief was obvious. Resting his elbows on the desk, he closed his eyes and put his head in his hands.

After a minute, Brian asked, "How about going for a drink?" He glanced at his watch." I know it's only three o'clock, but under the circumstances, I think the situation warrants it, don't you?"

Georges straightened, and making little come-on gestures, got up and headed for the door. "*Allons.* Gabrielle can close up. Let's go to my apartment. I've an ample supply of both wine and scotch. At least there, we can relax and talk without interruption."

"I'm all yours," Brian said, following him out the door.

CHAPTER TWELVE

That evening just before six, Paul and David arrived at Adelaide and Rebecca's hotel. While they waited for them, Paul told David about his previous introduction to both women.

"Obviously, both are very beautiful. But the way they conducted themselves following the murder of Adelaide's husband and the reinvestigation of his firm, Broker Industries, left Brian and me with lasting impressions.

"What still puzzles me, though, is how someone as lovely as Adelaide could have married someone as . . . as depraved as Jim Broker. He had hidden cameras installed throughout his house, corporate headquarters, and heaven knows where else. He then went about creating situations—that often included drugs and/or sex—and the individuals being filmed were compromised without their knowledge. The guy was a voyeur . . . a bloody pervert! What I'd really like to know is, whether he did it strictly for prurient interests or to use for blackmail to insure certain matters would go his way? Damned if we ever knew."

"Perhaps it was both," David suggested.

"Maybe. He kept the films under lock and key in the library at his home."

"Do you think Adelaide ever suspected?"

"Frankly, I don't think she ever had a clue."

The conversation ended as Rebecca and Adelaide walked out of the elevator.

Rebecca spotted them immediately, taking note of how marvelous David looked in his dark navy suit, white dress shirt, and pink and navy, club stripe rep tie. It reminded her of how handsome he'd been the first time she laid eyes on him. She also noticed the warmth that suddenly flowed through her.

"Hello, Paul," she said, extending her hand. "What a pleasure it is seeing you again." She remembered his height, boyish features, and thick, brown hair. *He too is a good-looking man. Unfortunately, I'm prejudiced.*

"Hello, Mrs. Lawler. Believe me, the pleasure's all mine."

She turned and smiled at David who stood to one side. "Hello again, David."

He grasped her outstretched hand and grinned. "Hello, Rebecca." She was wearing a long-sleeve black outfit with a top shot with silver threads that glinted in the light as she walked, her high-heeled black sandals made clicking noises on the marble floor. But the attention-getters were her shapely, sheer, black-stockinged legs visable beneath her knee-length jersey skirt that swung slightly as she walked, exposing a little of the leg above the knee.

Rebecca watched Paul's expression as he looked at Adelaide. She was dressed in a two-piece dark blue, silk-jersey outfit that matched her eyes. A turquoise and diamond pin peeked out from under the shawl draped across her shoulders, and matching earrings flashed bits of light with every move of her head. With her lustrous black hair stylishly cut, Rebecca thought she looked quite gorgeous.

Paul cleared his throat. "Hello again Mrs . . . ."

"Adelaide," she said. "Hello, Paul. Hello to you too, David." She shook his hand and looked back at Paul. "At last I have the chance to tell you how grateful I am for all that you and Brian did for me earlier in the year."

"My pleasure . . . Adelaide."

She laughed. "Better. *Much* better."

"Are we ready?" David asked.

"Yes," everyone agreed. David placed a hand under Rebecca's elbow. "Allow me."

The doorman held the door while they climbed into the waiting limousine and, without further direction, the driver pulled away.

"Do I dare ask where we're going?" Rebecca inquired, her eyes bright with expectation.

"Yes, I'm dying of curiosity," Adelaide chimed in.

Paul shrugged and looked at David. "Are we telling?"

David shook his head. "Why not wait and see? It won't be long."

A few minutes later, they drove down a ramp leading from the Place d'Alma to a pier where a there was a boat waiting.

Rebecca looked at David. "The Bateau-Mouche?"

"Thought you'd never ask," he said.

"Leave it to you," she said, sending him a big smile.

Adelaide and Paul were deep in conversation, but stopped once the car came to a halt.

"Are we here?" Paul asked.

"We are," David answered. He issued instructions to the driver. Then, with Paul and Adelaide bringing up the rear, he grabbed Rebecca's hand and walked up a small gangplank onto the Bateau-Mouche.

David told them he had requested a table on the port side because when the boat slows toward the end of the Île de la Cité, you get the best view of Notre Dame, "illuminated by lamps hidden in strategic places."

The dinner was delicious, each course accompanied by the perfect wine. Food and wine aside, this evening the ambiance held court.

The four of them talked animatedly, but David's eyes were fixed on Rebecca. As the boat cruised the Seine, the lights along the way alternately illuminated and cast shadows across her face and hair which she'd braided with black ribbons and wrapped around her head. David listened intently, hoping to discover what she'd been up to during the past twelve years. She still retained the quiet intensity that he occasionally found disquieting. But now, she possessed a maturity that, in his eyes, made her even more beautiful.

He learned that she and Adelaide were born in Vienna but moved to the United States when their father changed jobs. At the time, Rebecca was ten.

"If you remember," she told him, "the summer you and I met, I'd just graduated with a Fine Arts Degree from the University of California. After Greece, I worked for two and a half years at the Museum of Contemporary Art in San Francisco." She paused to drink some water.

"Don't stop," David said. "I'm a captive audience."

She laughed, "I was thirsty."

"Following my marriage," she continued, "Adelaide talked me into the co-ownership of a refuse removal company headquartered in San Francisco. Making her COO was one of the numerous things Jim Broker gave her as a wedding present. Soon after, he offered me the position of

Director of Acquisitions for his firm which meant that I purchased art as an investment for the corporation. I met Jeffrey right after that. He was eight years older, but we were well suited and very happy until . . . until he was killed."

"He was *killed?*"

"Yes. A little over three years ago . . . by a hit and run driver in Madrid."

David put a hand on her arm. "I'm so sorry, Rebecca."

"Thank you, David."

They finished their entrées.

"And now," Rebecca said, sitting back and reaching for her wine glass, "it's your turn to tell me about you. As you might imagine, I'm very curious."

He laughed. "I wish I had something amazing to tell you, Rebecca, but I don't." He sipped some wine.

"Before we met," he said, "I'd attended Middlebury College for two years, but, as you know, suffered from wanderlust and couldn't settle on a subject that interested me. So, with my parents' blessing, I took that break. Before going to Greece, I spent eight months driving rigs cross-country."

Rebecca stared at him. "You actually did that?"

He laughed. "Yes. I had a ball and did a lot of thinking. Added to that, I was paid exceedingly well. I quit just before I came to Greece with the idea that I might return someday and drive them again." He steadied a look on her. "Then that summer I met you . . ." their eyes locked and Rebecca's heart skipped a beat. "Once you left," he continued, quickly looking away, "I decided it was time I went back and finished my degree, although in what, I still had no idea. Two years later, I graduated from Middlebury . . . in Fine Arts."

"Fine Arts? You too?"

He laughed. "Yep." They waited while the waiters cleared the table and set it for dessert and champagne.

"Then what?" Rebecca asked.

"Fortunately, it wasn't that long before a friend of mine told me he'd rented some space in SoHo and wanted to open an art gallery. He asked if I was interested in becoming a partner. I had no money to speak of, but I helped him renovate the place. At his request, I stayed on to make frames, cut mats, etc. In the evenings, I built scenery for one of the local theaters, and within several months, I began designing their sets."

"And you find none of this amazing?"

He blushed, shifting in his seat. "Not really. Eventually," he continued, "I became co-owner of the gallery. But after five years, I branched out and became an independent art consultant. Though I acquired several substantial clients, I continued to run the sales through the gallery. Around that same time, I learned about the art the Nazis confiscated. Fascinated, I went on to develop the expertise needed for establishing provenance. It was due to my work and study in that area that Brian introduced me to Georges Lartigue."

They watched the waiter flame and serve their baked Alaska.

"Doesn't this look fabulous," Adelaide beamed.

Rebecca took a bite. "It is fabulous."

Mouths full, David and Paul nodded in agreement.

Adelaide and Paul resumed their conversation. Glancing at David, Rebecca caught him studying her.

"Yes?"

"Uh, sorry." He was embarrassed. His thoughts had drifted to their night together on the beach in Santorini. He reached for his champagne.

"Do you still have your Greenwich Village apartment?" Rebecca asked.

"No. A year and a half ago I purchased a loft in SoHo, drew up plans for the interior, hired a contractor, and helped with its construction."

"I bet it's beautiful. Describe it for me."

"Well," he said with his customary grin, "it's a loft, which means it's basically two huge rooms that I've partitioned. I have a kitchen, bathroom, a living room—that includes my work space—and a bedroom."

"It must have great light. Have you hung a lot of art?"

He nodded. "Selectively. I also have several unique pieces of sculpture."

"What color are the walls?"

"I mirrored the one over the living room fireplace," he said, distractedly making circular patterns on the tablecloth with a fork," but painted the other two and the ones surrounding the windows opposite, a soft, gray-white. Those in the kitchen I painted a light mustard yellow to compliment the rust-colored Mexican tiles on the floor. As for my bedroom and bathroom, those walls are . . . silver."

"*Silver*?"

He nodded. "Yes, silver."

Rebecca threw her head back and howled, "Wow." Paul and Adelaide looked at her.

"Are we still raving about the dessert?" Adelaide asked.

"No!" Rebecca said. "David's apartment."

"That good, huh?" Adelaide asked.

"I've been there with Brian," Paul said. "Believe me, it's a showplace. His bed is half the size of the room, with a steel headboard and a shiny gray duvet for a bedspread."

"Satin's the word, Paul, "David said. "A *satin* duvet."

"Okay, *satin* duvet," Paul concluded.

"Way to go, David!" Adelaide cheered.

"Addie!"

"Gee, you guys, you make it sound like some kind of sex studio," David said, color rising to his cheeks.

"At least it's private and has class," Rebecca said.

He looked at her. "Hey, Rebecca, I thought you were on my side."

She gave him a glorious smile, and reaching across the table, put a hand on his arm. "Oh, but David. I am." Their eyes held.

David covered her hand with his. "I'm happy to hear you say that."

Adelaide and Paul grinned at each other.

A waiter approached. "Café mésdames *et* monsieurs?"

"Anyone up for a walk?" David asked, as they disembarked the Bateau-Mouche and approached the waiting limousine. What he wanted was some private time with Rebecca so he could tell her that tomorrow, Elise Crawford, his live-in lady friend, was arriving to attend the wedding. Having cajoled Rebecca and Adelaide into coming, he was now uncomfortable as to how his invitation would be viewed.

"A walk's fine with me," Rebecca said.

"Paul? Adelaide?" David asked.

They exchanged glances. "Sure, we're up for it," Paul replied.

"Great," David replied and spoke to the driver. As the car pulled away, they followed it up the embankment.

For a while, they walked along the Quai d'Orsay in silence.

David soon turned to Rebecca. "Any plans for tomorrow?"

"Yes. Sally's taking Addie and me shopping. What about you?"

He remained quiet for so long, that Rebecca touched his arm. "David, is anything the matter?"

He now wished they'd taken the limousine back to the hotel and gone for a nightcap. "Rebecca, there's something I need to tell you."

She fixed him with one of her stares, and his courage faltered even more. He felt responsible for her coming to Paris and hoped what he had to say wouldn't put a damper on the visit. Not that he imagined Rebecca harbored any special feelings for him. Yet . . .

"A little over a year ago I began sharing my apartment with," he cleared his throat, "Elise Crawford." He was pacing himself so he wouldn't upset her. But she replied before he could go on, and her comment was not what he expected.

"Oh, David. How nice for you both."

"The thing is," he continued, puzzled as to why he felt rebuffed. "Brian and Carrie invited her to the wedding before I came to Portugal."

"Under the circumstances, it would have seemed odd if they hadn't."

"Yes, it would." He took hold of her hand. "Thanks for understanding."

She squeezed his hand in return. "Thank you for telling me. It was most considerate."

"I just didn't want it to be a surprise and have you wonder why I talked you into coming." Why had he?

"Perhaps because that day at lunch in Portugal we were all having such a good time that we got caught up in the moment."

"Then you're not sorry?"

"Sorry I came to Paris? Good heavens, no. If anything, I should be thanking you."

He looked at her, and the smile she gave him lit up the evening. His spirits soared. With a grin, he slid his arm across her shoulders and pulled her against him.

CHAPTER THIRTEEN

The shopping spree with Sally the next morning was a delight. The fact that she was an insider connected to the higher echelons of fashion only added to the feeling of inclusiveness.

Having paid homage to the boutiques of Sonia Rykiel and Givenchy, they were now at Oscar de la Renta on the rue du Faubourg St.-Honoré. Adelaide watched Rebecca as "Madame" presented one spectacular outfit after another. She herself had chosen a deep burgundy, silk-jersey dress. The skirt had been cut on the bias and fell in soft folds that rippled as she walked. With it, came a sheer, long-sleeved beaded jacket that hung to the waist. It offered just the right amount of coverage, for the bodice had only narrow shoulder straps.

She studied Rebecca wondering whether it was the late hour of the night before or the several mile walk in high heel sandals that made her seem reserved, similar to the way she was on her return from Greece after college.

Yes. It's the same today. Could it possibly have something to do with David? She decided it did.

They lunched at Sébillon before returning to pick up their clothes at Oscar de la Renta where a few minor alterations had been made to their clothes. From there, they hopped a taxi, stopping at Stéphane Kélian in a quest for shoes. Finished by three, they thanked Sally and returned to their hotel room. On arrival, Rebecca hung up her things and flopped on the bed, elevating her feet. "Tired?" Adelaide fished.

"A bit," came the reply.

"It was fun last night, wasn't it?"

"It was great."

At this rate, Adelaide was never going to learn a thing.

"Did you and David get caught up on old times?"

Rebecca turned on her side, propping her head up with a hand. "What is it you'd like to know, Addie?"

"Oh, nothing in particular," she lied.

"You and Paul seemed to have gotten on."

"Yes. We had a wonderful time. He's quite nice. Attractive, too."

Rebecca rolled onto her back. "David's live-in friend, Elise Crawford, is coming to the wedding."

So that's it. "Oh?"

"Yes. He wanted to tell me in advance so I wouldn't be surprised or upset he'd invited us to come to Paris."

"Upset? Then he doesn't know how much you love Paris."

"Oh, Addie, you know what he meant."

Adelaide sighed. "You're right. I do. How do you feel about the news?"

Rebecca stared at the ceiling. "I'm surprised he's never married."

Never one to ignore a chance to play the devil's advocate, Adelaide said, "Well, I can think of two reasons. One, he has a preconceived idea of what his wife should be like and, two, he hasn't met the one who can match his specified ideal."

Rebecca's head snapped around.

Score! Was that hope I saw in her eyes? Satisfied, she switched subjects. "So while you're there giving my edifying pronouncements some thought, I'm going to remove my gorgeous things from their protective bag and look at them."

"Good idea," Rebecca said, slowly coming to her feet. She walked to where hers hung on a rack near the entrance, unzipped the bag, and removed the contents.

"You really picked a winner, Becca," Adelaide, said. "I don't ever remember seeing an ensemble made of so many unusual colors. Just count them." She ran her fingers over the tight pleats of the strapless bodice. "There's plum, olivine, chartreuse, dark brown, and ochre. And the way the folds in the silk chiffon skirt move when you walk, it's an eye-catcher."

Rebecca lifted a section of the skirt and let it float back into place. "You're right. It is beautiful. But you have to admit the plum-colored jacket adds the finishing touch with the way the edges of the neck and wrists are trimmed with tiny beads the same colors as the dress."

"With the ruby and diamond earrings Jeffrey gave you, you'll be sure to knock 'em dead.

Adelaide hung her dress in the closet and collapsed into a chair, "So, what shall we do this evening for an encore?"

"How about," Rebecca replied, lying back again on the bed, "we each soak in a perfumed bubble bath, order wine and something special to eat from room service, and watch a romantic movie on television with lots of sexy scenes in it?"

Adelaide sent her a look. "You mean watch a porno flick?"

"*Adelaide . . .*"

"But you said . . ."

"*Addie . . .*"

Adelaide's eyes twinkled. "Afraid you'll get frustrated?"

With a roar, Rebecca grabbed a pillow and threw it at her sister, who saw it too late and caught it in her face. Pillow in hand, she slowly rose from the chair.

But Rebecca was quicker and, squealing with delight, dodged around her, fled into the bathroom, and locked the door.

"You'll have to come out at some point," Adelaide taunted, "and I'll be waiting because I'm a *very* patient person."

An hour or so later, Rebecca, her hair wrapped in a towel and wearing one of the luxurious terry cloth robes the hotel supplied, quietly turned the lock and opened the door . . . and laughed. For there, curled up in the chair with her arms around the offending pillow, was Adelaide, sound asleep.

CHAPTER FOURTEEN

Georges woke in a cold sweat, his breath coming in short gasps. *Merde!*

Looking around, he was relieved to see he was in the king-sized bed in his apartment. He closed his eyes and waited for his heart rate to return to normal. It was, he realized, the second time in a week he'd dreamt about Miranda. In this one, however, she was about to torch the gallery with him, Sally, and Gabrielle in it. He prayed the private investigator he'd hired would soon locate her.

As to what he'd do with the information once he had it, he wasn't sure and selfishly wished Brian wasn't about to leave for Italy on his honeymoon. Since Brian was the only one who knew about his relationship with Miranda, he would miss his counsel if things began to heat up. Of course, if worse came to worst, he could always call his physician who, thanks to Doctor Weiss, knew the whole story.

He glanced at the clock on the night table. Seven A.M. He and Sally had gotten in at eleven thirty the evening before. After a run-through of the wedding ceremony at Église de la Madeleine, they'd joined Brian, Carrie, David, Elise Crawford, and several others for a lavish dinner at nearby Lucas-Carton—known for its superb menu and precisely chosen wines. Today was the wedding.

Marriage. *Mon Dieu!*

Panic seized him again, and he decided to get up and go to the gallery. He pushed aside the sheet, and, sitting on the edge of the bed, thought about the two paintings he and David brought back with them from Portugal. They'd returned from the framer the day before just as he was leaving, and he hadn't had time to check them. So far, the background material, proof of purchase, and lists of previous owners for each was in order. Rebecca's husband's grandfather had acquired them in the early 1930's before the Nazis came to power.

The provenances of the Meidner drawing and the Cézanne and Beckman paintings also checked out. Jeffrey's grandfather had purchased them from a dealer in Madrid in 1930 and 1931, respectively. That left the Kandinsky and the Kirchner in Lisbon that Senhor Carlos was bringing on Wednesday.

Georges' thoughts switched to the paintings that had hung in his parents' home in Brussels and belonged to his grandmother's family. At his request, his mother had forwarded him the list and documentation that his grandmother had kept. In the hope of tracing at least one, he'd begun research and found names of nineteen dealers and collectors who, while living or working in Belgium from 1939 until the end of the War, trafficked in stolen art. One, by the name of Mader, had been head of the dreaded *Einsatzstab Reichsleiter Rosenberg*. Yet, to date, it was the ERR'S meticulous inventories that continued to be the best resource for finding stolen art.

He yawned and stretched, then lay back on the bed. Somewhere in the back of his mind a shower beckoned, and it occurred to him that, if he had any intention of getting up, he'd better do so.

Two hours later, he finally took that shower.

* * *

At three forty-five that same afternoon, Rebecca and Adelaide mounted the stairs of the Neo-classical Église de la Madeleine. A man, dressed in a suit, raincoat, and hat, stood to one side staring at them and Rebecca's nervous system went on full alert. But when he opened one of the magnificent bronze doors for them and nodded a greeting, though her heart was pounding, she managed a smile and said, "*Merci, Monsieur.*"

He lifted his hat. "*De rein, Mademoiselle.*"

Once inside, they paused to let their eyes grow accustomed to the lowered light.

Rebecca looked around. "It's so beautiful," she whispered.

The splendid interior was aglow with light from multi-armed brass chandeliers. Backlights and candles highlighted the gold leaf outlining the colored marble and mosaics adorning its surfaces and illuminating the awe-inspiring altar of white marble angels hovering about *La Magdalene.* The historic Cavaillé-Coll cathedral organ quietly played Mozart.

"I think we might be blocking the way," Adelaide whispered.

They stepped aside as a hushed voice behind them inquired, "Are either of you sitting with anyone?"

Looking around, they saw Paul Smith accompanied by an attractive sandy-haired male.

"No," Adelaide said, "we're not."

"Would you like to join us?" Paul asked.

She glanced at Rebecca who nodded. "Yes, thank you. We would."

Paul's companion offered his hand. "By the way, I'm Stan O'Neil."

"Oh, sorry, Stan," Paul said. "Guess I got distracted."

"I can certainly understand why," Stan said, smiling at the two women.

"We've been admiring this magnificent church," Adelaide whispered. "It has to be one of the most beautiful I've ever been in."

"It is beautiful, isn't it?" Stan agreed, studying the interior.

"Rebecca, why don't you and Stan lead the way?" Paul suggested.

"Please, Rebecca, after you," Stan said, making a subtle forward movement with his hand.

"Now that you've gotten past 'Mrs. Broker,'" Adelaide said to Paul who was walking beside her down the aisle, "how about going one step further and calling me, Addie?"

He looked at her and smiled. "All right, Addie, you're on."

Rush-bottom, ladder-back chairs flanked the center aisle and stretched in front of a flower-laden bower of calla lilies, baby's breath and fern that spanned it. Matching bouquets decorated the steps leading to the altar. White satin ribbons adorned chairs reserved for family. Rebecca chose seats on the left side, one row behind the flowered arch.

"Would you prefer to sit on the aisle?" Stan asked.

"No thank you. The view's quite good from here."

Soon Brian and David, looking handsome in their cutaways, entered from the right and took their positions.

Brian acknowledged several guests, but David's eyes roamed the crowd until he found Rebecca. Upon doing so he winked.

Once the organ burst forth with Jeremiah Clarke's "Trumpet Voluntary in D Major," everyone stood and looked toward the back of the church.

Sally came first, dressed in a long sleeved, blush-colored, silk shantung suit with a button-front jacket and slightly flared, calf-length skirt.

Carrie—elegant in a creamy beige, silk charmeuse, long sleeved, fitted jacket and ankle length gored skirt—followed several paces behind on the arm of her father. Her blonde hair had been loosely braided and molded into a chignon.

Each wore high-heeled sandals that matched their dresses, and each carried a bouquet of ivy and roses several shades lighter than the dresses. Both wore headbands trimmed with ivy, the difference being, Carrie's had a nose-length, diaphanous veil.

All eyes followed them as they proceeded down the aisle. Rebecca watched Brian as he looked at Carrie and it squeezed her heart. She thought of Jeffrey. *How I miss being loved.*

As she listened to them promise to "love, honor and cherish," tears filled her eyes and bits of moisture clung to her lashes. Sniffing, she opened her purse in search of a handkerchief.

"Will this help?" Stan asked, handing her his.

She smiled. "It will. Thanks." She blotted her eyes. "I—I'm sorry it's only . . ."

"No need to apologize. It's an emotional moment. My throat's gone tight as well."

Following the exchange of rings, Brian lifted Carrie's veil, and for one long moment, they gazed at each other while a hush fell over the room. At last, with hands on either side of her face, Brian kissed her with such obvious tenderness that Rebecca doubted there was a dry eye in the church.

Suddenly the service was over. Carrie took her bouquet from Sally. With a hand tucked in Brian's arm, she smiled up at him as they walked up the aisle past family and friends while the organ played the overture to Henry Purcell's "Fairy Queen."

"Will you look at this view!" Adelaide exclaimed, once they were outside standing on the portico. Rue Royale and Place de la Concorde stretched out before them, the auto headlights and street lamps sparkling in the dusk like clusters of diamonds on dark velvet.

"And look," Rebecca said, pointing, "there's the Hôtel des Invalides on the hill across the Seine."

Georges walked up to them. "Do you need a ride to La Tour d'Argent?" Receiving no immediate response, he added, "Come. There's plenty of room. I have a limousine. Be my guests and ride with Sally and me."

With little resistance, they followed him down the steps into the waiting car.

CHAPTER FIFTEEN

The reception at La Tour d'Argent was held in one of the restaurant's private dining rooms. Large oval tables were set with silver candelabras, white linen cloths, tall crystal goblets, and gleaming sterling flatware. Arrangements of fern, baby's breath, and small white calla lilies were centerpieces. Silver urns containing massive bouquets of magnolia leaves and large white calla lilies, rested on stands near the entrance and on either side of the head table.

On arrival, each guest was offered a flute of champagne and invited to take a handful of rose petals from a silver basket held by a tail-coated waiter.

"Talk about a view!" Adelaide exclaimed, admiring the expanse of windows.

"Incredible," Paul agreed. "Where else could you get a birds' eye view of Notre Dame, Île de la Cité and Île St-Louis all together?"

"And from such elegant surroundings," Adelaide added, looking around the room.

Rebecca held up a hand full of petals. "Don't forget to take some of these."

Moments later, accompanied by strains of the wedding march from Wagner's *Lohengrin,* Carrie and Brian walked through the doorway into a flurry of petals, handshakes and hugs. Carrie handed her bouquet to a waiter, and the maitre d' served them champagne.

In addition to Carrie and Brian, seated at the head table were David, his friend Elise Crawford, Georges and Sally, and Brian and Carrie's closest friends, Bill and Jan Height. The bride and groom's parents, their children, and families, were at two other tables, while Carrie and Brian's friends were at another. A pianist provided music.

Paul and Stan had just seated Rebecca and Adelaide when a lovely brunette arrived.

"Hello. I'm Vicky Reynolds, Carrie's friend from New York, and this is my husband, Jim," she announced, placing a hand on his arm.

Everyone introduced themselves while waiters held their chairs.

"Carrie was so pleased that you both were coming to Paris," Vicky continued, once she was seated.

"So were we," Adelaide said. "How could anyone turn down that kind of invitation?"

"She also told me that you and David, Rebecca, had met in Greece."

"That's true. But it was a long time ago."

"Rebecca had just graduated from college," Adelaide said, with a know-it-all smile that wasn't lost on Rebecca."

"And you never saw each other again? "Vicky asked.

"Until a week ago," Rebecca answered.

"Oh! Carrie never mentioned that. What a marvelous story that has to be."

"Yes," Rebecca said with a laugh, "it's actually quite a remarkable one."

A first course of crayfish bisque arrived accompanied by a perfectly chilled 2006 Sancerre.

"Mmm. This is delicious," Vicky said after tasting the bisque.

"As is the wine," Jim said, sampling it.

"Jim and I've only been to La Tour d'Argent twice before," Vicky continued, "and everything we've eaten has been exceptional. I have to say, I don't agree with the professionals who claim the restaurant no longer lives up to the gold star ratings of its past."

"Did you know that because of their value, they keep over a half a million bottles of wine under 24/7guard in the wine cellar?" Paul asked.

Adelaide stared at him. "Really? It would be fun to know which is the most expensive."

He grinned. "Let's ask. Perhaps they'll tell us."

"What did you make of the lobby?" Jim asked. "It's a virtual museum. One could spend hours just looking at the memorabilia in the cabinets alone."

"To say nothing of another few figuring out who the celebrities are in all the pictures," Stan said. "And did you see the great bar? You could do all your snooping while getting pleasantly buzzed."

Jim laughed. "Now there's a thought."

Paul finished his bisque. "I read that there's been a restaurant on this site since the 1500s. The building apparently stands on the site of a 400-year-old inn that was frequented by Henry the IV."

Adelaide sent him a look. "Where did you pick up these choice tidbits?"

"Online, for the most part. I tend to be curious."

The main course was the restaurant's much celebrated pressed duck or *caneton*, served with cooked spinach over which were julienned strips of carrot. The accompanying wine was a 2000 Bordeaux Grand Reserve.

"What's this?" Rebecca inquired, picking up the piece of paper the waiter had just placed beside her plate.

"La Tour has it's own duck farm," Stan told her. "Every one of the ducks is registered and has a number. When you order *caneton*, the restaurant presents you with a certificate printed with the number on your particular duck. Yours is on that piece of paper."

"Amazing," Rebecca said, placing it on the table next to her wine glass. She tasted the duck. "Oh my! The duck's fantastic but umm, the gravy's sensational."

"They make it from pressed duck bones," Stan said, sampling a piece of the meat.

Rebecca made a face. "Did you think I really needed to know that?"

He laughed. "Sorry. I had no idea you were so squeamish."

"I'm not, really. It's just that your explanation produces a rather graphic image."

"Leave it to our host," Jim said, "the wine complements it beautifully."

Throughout dinner, guests made toasts, most notably Bill Height, Brian's brother Larry, and Carrie's brother, Greg. Brian's sister, Kate, also rose to the occasion. She wished "the brother who so often took my side, tended both my bruised ego and scraped knees, and his lovely wife Carrie, all the happiness life has to offer." And finally, Carrie's father—not only a professor of art but also a recognized artist himself—gave "a toast to my lovely daughter, the princess of my life, and my newly acquired son-in-law, Brian, her handsome prince."

When the time came to cut the wedding cake, Brian and Carrie walked to the table where the three-tiered confection was displayed, its top covered with sprigs of ivy and pale yellow roses made of icing.

As everyone applauded, the bride and groom cut the first slice and fed pieces to each other, managing to get icing on their faces and hands. They solved the problem with several licks and nibbles, ending with a kiss that raised cheers as champagne corks popped. The wait staff moved in with moist towels, and the maitre d' supervised the serving of the guests. Arms around each other, Carrie and Brian returned to their table.

Once they were seated, David rose and gave his toast.

"Today, I have the distinct honor of being my brother Brian's best man, and I sincerely hope what I have to say approaches the level in which I hold him in regard.

"Until the age of thirteen, my idolatry focused on my oldest brother, Larry. But when Larry went off to California to pursue higher knowledge in the academic halls of Berkeley, my adolescent awe turned to Brian, who, to my good fortune, stayed on the East Coast and attended Columbia.

"I was far from a model teen, yet despite his work load and all that he elected to do, Brian somehow managed to be there for me always ready to listen, advise, or let me fall on my ass as the case might be." He paused while everyone laughed.

"It was therefore with deep regret," he continued, "that I, due to a sense of total inadequacy, was unable to give him the support he needed following a personal tragedy several years ago."

Rebecca and Adelaide exchanged glances.

"But now a new light has entered his life, one that shines with special brilliance. For Carrie, also no stranger to tragedy, radiates the kind of strength that only comes from surviving great inner turmoil. No two people ever deserved to be together more than these two exceptional individuals; and today, it has not only been my pleasure, but my privilege, to bear witness to the crowning glory of their commitment." Turning to them, David raised his glass. "May your love endure for all time." And, leaning down, he kissed Carrie's upturned cheek dampened by tears.

"Hear, hear," everyone shouted, standing and raising their glasses in toast while Brian rose and gave David a back-slapping embrace.

Rebecca had been so moved by David's speech, that she didn't realize Vicky had spoken to her until, while reaching into her purse for Stan's handkerchief, she heard Adelaide say, "I don't think my sister heard you, Vicky."

Rebecca looked up after blotting her eyes. "I'm sorry, Vicky. I guess I got carried away by David's toast."

"Not to worry. I share your feelings completely. All I said was that I understand you're involved with art?"

"That's true," Rebecca said, surprised. "How did you know?"

"Carrie told me. Did you know Carrie's a painter?"

"How marvelous. In what medium does she work?"

"She prefers watercolor and is very good. Sally and I tried to get her to exhibit, but she says it's impossible while she's still working."

"What does she do?"

"She works for an organization that plans benefits to raise money for grants that they award aspiring artists."

"Is that how she and Brian met?"

"No. They met at the fifteenth wedding anniversary party of Sally's cousin."

"Brian was a widower, wasn't he?" Rebecca asked, remembering her talk with Carrie.

"Yes. His wife, Melissa, had been a very close friend of Sally's."

Just then, Brian arrived and pulled up a chair. "Hello, again, Mrs. Lawler, Mrs. Broker."

Adelaide made a face.

"You're right. I guess that is a bit formal under the circumstances." He grinned. "Hello, Rebecca. Hello Adelaide."

"Addie," Adelaide corrected.

He nodded. "Yes, and you, too, Addie." He looked at Rebecca. "Carrie and I were amazed to hear David's story about meeting you again after so many years."

"She fainted, you know," Adelaide said.

Brian chuckled. "Really? Seeing my kid brother again was that bad, huh, Rebecca?"

"On the contrary. I'd just returned from Santorini, which is where David and I'd met. It triggered memories of our time there together, and I was a bit overwhelmed to find him standing in my living room several days later." She shook her head in wonder. "I don't ever remember fainting before. Tell me, Brian, does David often have that affect on women?"

"Touché, Becca," Adelaide said as Brian howled with laughter.

"No," he answered, still laughing. "I can't say that I know anything about that. But Carrie and I were very happy he invited you and Addie to the wedding."

"And very pleased you accepted," Carrie said, arriving on the scene with another couple in tow.

Brian stood and wrapped his arm around Carrie, pulling her close. Carrie smiled at him, and he placed a kiss on the tip of her nose.

"Rebecca, Adelaide," Carrie said, "I'd like you to meet our good friends, Jan and Bill Height."

"A pleasure," Bill said, shaking hands.

"Yes," Jan said. "How nice to meet you."

Knowing Bill had been the one who'd confirmed her one-night affair with John to Carrie, Rebecca's stomach did cartwheels, but she still managed a smile.

As if sensing her unease, Carrie sat down next to her.

Bill looked at Stan who sat with his arm across the back of Rebecca's chair. "And how is this boss of mine treating you ladies?"

"Gallantly, it would seem," Adelaide replied, glancing at Stan.

They chatted a few minutes longer until Brian put a hand on Carrie's shoulder. "We'd better finish making our rounds."

"And if we don't see you again later," Carrie said, standing, "I certainly hope we will soon."

"Come to Portugal," Rebecca suggested.

Brian grinned at Carrie. "We just might do that."

"Georges has my telephone number and address," Rebecca said. "Perhaps he and Sally could come too."

"Sounds wonderful. We'll definitely give it some thought," Brian said. Smiling at Adelaide, he gave Paul's arm a playful punch. "I hope you're taking care of this lovely lady."

Paul nodded. "Absolutely."

"No complaints from this department," Adelaide confirmed.

"Good. Glad to hear it." Brian and Carrie started to leave, but just then David arrived.

"Some of us thought we'd go dancing at La Coupole. Any takers?" He looked at Rebecca.

She loved the idea but couldn't very well go unescorted and was happy when the others accepted.

"Georges said he can take eight of us in his limo," David continued. "The rest can ride in the bridal party's two cars."

"Does that mean you and Brian are coming?" Adelaide asked Carrie.

"I guess it does. I wouldn't miss it."

"All set then?" David asked, putting a hand on Rebecca's shoulder.

Everyone nodded.

"Great. See you out front."

By one in the morning, Rebecca had danced with almost everyone she'd met and, without a second thought, had removed her jacket and stepped out of her shoes.

She was at the table talking with Bill and Jan Height when David came over and took hold of her hand. "Excuse us," he said and maneuvered her onto the dance floor.

The disco music had slowed. After pulling her close, David caught a whiff of Rebecca's perfume. He fought the impulse to nuzzle her neck. *Whoa! Am I nuts?* The last thing he wanted was to embarrass Elise and make a fool of himself. He relaxed the embrace.

He'd watched Rebecca throughout the day. Given the knockout dress she was wearing, it had been impossible not to. He wasn't quite sure how to say what was on his mind without sounding presumptuous, but he knew he had to see her again. *This isn't eleven years ago, I'm neither unemployed nor a college dropout.*

"What are your immediate plans, Rebecca?"

"Georges and I have an appointment at Hôtel Drouot on Tuesday to see about placing the two smaller pieces at auction. I also want to be here when Senhor Carlos brings the other two paintings on Wednesday. Since Addie wants to be back in Las Vegas within two weeks, we'll probably return to Portugal on Thursday. And you, David, what are your plans?"

He pulled back and looked at her. "I don't suppose you'd allow me to visit you in Las Vegas sometime?"

Before she had a chance to reply, he added, "My business often takes me in that direction. Having seen a portion of the Lawler art collection in Portugal, I'm quite interested in seeing the rest."

When she hesitated, David thought he'd overstepped and hastened to assure her, "Of course, I'd stay somewhere in town."

She smiled. "It isn't that, David. It's just that I told Georges I'd leave my schedule open in case he wants me to meet him in London to take two paintings to Christie's for auction. I wouldn't want to miss you."

He drew her against him. "Not a chance, Rebecca, not a chance."

The evening ended just before two. Brian and Carrie had already left, and now, the rest of the bridal party and few remaining guests trailed out the door toward the limousines.

Rebecca smiled at Elise with whom she'd enjoyed talking earlier. "How are your feet now?" she asked, her own shoes still off despite the chilly pavement.

Elise held up a hand from which hers were dangling, and they laughed.

The ladies entered the limousine first. The men followed, sitting on the foldaway seats. Only when she'd sunk into the deep leather seat next to Adelaide, did Rebecca realize how tired she was.

Stan looked at her and smiled. "Comfortable?" he asked.

"Very," she answered with a sigh. Once Stan discovered she'd be in Paris for a few days, he asked her to join him on a visit to Pompidou and the Louvre followed by dinner. Since Adelaide and Paul would be on an all-day visit to Versailles, Rebecca had no wish to spend the time alone, especially in Paris, so she'd accepted.

"I can't believe it's over," Sally said. "It seems that only yesterday Carrie and Brian's lives were in turmoil."

"*Et maintenant*," Georges said, "now they will be able to spend their entire future together."

Knowing how dear they were to Georges, Sally reached over and placed her hand on top of his. "I know. Isn't it wonderful?"

Adelaide and Rebecca were the first to be dropped off. Since David was blocking their exit, he got out to assist them.

"I'll be in touch," he told Rebecca, squeezing her arm before reentering the car. Paul and Stan escorted Rebecca and Adelaide into the hotel.

"Suppose I pick you up on Monday around one?" Stan asked Rebecca, kissing her cheek.

"One is fine," she answered. "Have a good day tomorrow."

"I'll probably spend it relaxing with my feet up reading the paper."

"What, in Paris?"

Stan laughed. "And I suppose you're going to hike across town?"

"Believe me. It's tempting, but no," she laughed. "I'll walk somewhere for sure, but may start the day with a massage and sauna."

"An even better idea. Until Monday then."

With that, they were gone.

CHAPTER SIXTEEN

The following week, four events occurred that would affect Georges Lartigue's life. Three impacted Rebecca.

Tuesday, she and Georges went to Hôtel Drouot at 9, rue Drouot. Following their scheduled appointment, they attended an auction already in progress. Marveling at the pace, Rebecca watched the various ways participants—many of them dealers—placed bids or unobtrusively signaled the auctioneer.

"That was fascinating," she said when they were leaving. "I'm still amazed at how easy it was to arrange for both the Cézanne painting and Dégas sketch to be auctioned next week. But when you have a moment, I'd like you'd go into more detail about finding someone to be my representative when the pieces go to auction. The publicity that is sure to accompany the Kandinsky and Kirchner continues to make me uneasy." She refrained from telling Georges that her reluctance had to do with the questions she had about Jeffrey's death and the way she'd been hassled afterward. *They even had my cell phone number.*

As a result, it had taken more than her usual courage to start out on this venture, but she was sure it was what Jeffrey would have wanted; that alone had stiffened her resolve.

"No problem, Rebecca. It's done every day. If you wish, we can discuss it with them right now."

"That would be wonderful. The sooner all this is settled, the happier I'll be."

Afterward, they went to meet Sally for lunch at Café Runtz located not far from Drouot.

On their way in, Rebecca noticed a man in a black coat, smoking a cigarette watching them from across the street. She stiffened. *If I'm right, it's the same man who was outside Drouot this morning.* She shook her head. A minute later she looked again. He was no longer there. *Now I'm beginning to imagine things!*

As they entered the restaurant, Rebecca took in the dark woodwork and red and white-checkered curtains. "Just look. How wonderful!" Etched partitions separated tables with brass gas lamps. Large pots of ferns supplied a hint of greenery, while mirror-covered walls reflected a multitude of black and white photos taken of those who'd performed at the nearby Salle Favart or Opéra Comique.

"You're right. It is wonderful," Sally said. "And the black and white photos remind me of Sardi's, New York." She wrinkled her nose. "Something smells fabulous, too. I'm starved."

Rebecca inhaled. "Umm . . . sausages and sauerkraut."

"And beer," Georges added as the owner/chef's wife, Madame Le Port, showed them to a table.

"What prompted you to become involved in art?" Rebecca asked Georges, once they were seated and had ordered.

"When I was ten, my parents took me and Gabrielle to the Museum of Modern Art in New York. It was there that I saw my first abstract. It was a Georges Braque and I was hooked."

"Were you a Fine Arts major in college?"

"*Non.* I majored in Business Administration with a minor in Fine Arts. Both before and during my studies at Columbia University, I worked for my father in his import-export business. Though my primary interest lay in art, I knew the value of having a business background. After my parents moved back to France, I became an appraiser at Sotheby's in New York. It was there that I learned about the Nazi looting during the War, and because of personal experience, I made tracing stolen art a priority."

Madame LePort supervised the arrival of their food. "Mmm, at last," Sally said, eyeing her order of sucré-salé, or quiche and green salad that came with a glass of the house's white Riesling, a 1992 Gustave Lorentz in Bergheim.

"Umm. Glad I ordered the same thing," Rebecca said, all smiles. She watched as Georges was served his order of choucrote, or sauerkraut, with apples and sausage.

"That looks marvelous, too," Sally said, peering at it over her wine glass.

He smiled "But what makes it even better, *cherie,* is this," he gestured as Madame Le Port brought him a large glass of beer.

"*Cette biere est trés, trés speciale,*" she said as if on cue. *"C'est regionale de la maison de Schutzenburger."*

Georges sampled it. "Bravo, madame. *C'est delicieux. Merci."*

"De rein, monsieur. Bon appetite!"

For a while, everyone was quiet, enjoying their food.

Sally broke the silence. "Did Georges tell you his mother's family lived in Vienna and were among those who lost a substantial amount of art during the War?"

Rebecca swallowed a mouthful of salad. "Members of your family were collectors, Georges?"

"On my maternal grandmother's side," Georges said, helping himself to a piece of bread and buttering it. "Mother's parents, her two brothers, sister and their assorted families were Austrian Jews who belonged to the upper crust of the Viennese middle class. In addition to being large collectors and patrons of the arts, they regularly supported young artists such as Oskar Kokoschka, Gustav Klimt and Egon Schiele, who were then leading modernists.

"What has never ceased to amaze me, however," he continued, "is that despite what was happening in Germany, none of the family made plans to escape before the Germans crossed the Austrian border in March of 1938. They were therefore trapped, when Himmler flew to Vienna in the middle of the night and sealed the borders."

"Knowing how much I loved Vienna," Rebecca said, "and how I despaired when we moved, I can understand their hesitancy."

"You lived in Austria?" Georges asked.

"My father was transferred to Vienna shortly after my parents were married. It's where Adelaide and I were born."

"Vienna certainly was and is again a wonderful place," he agreed. "But in the late 1930s and early 1940s, it was very dangerous to live there, especially if one was a Jew. Just after the *Anschluss,* the Nazis passed

Ayranization laws, which meant that all property and assets belonging to Jews had to be registered with a variety of offices, and either sent or taken there by the owners. What happened more often, however, was that the SS simply invaded homes and removed anything and everything—art, jewelry, furniture, gold . . ."

"Which is what happened to Georges' grandmother's family," Sally said.

George nodded. "*Oui*. In addition, all those with substantial art collections like my great grandparents, were required to fill out separate applications for the expropriation of any art they were leaving behind. Giving it away," he snapped his fingers, "just like that! *Outrageous*, *non*? Between 1938 and 1939 there were 16,500 applications alone. Imagine! It gives you some idea of the size of the task the Nazis had set out to accomplish."

"Indeed," Rebecca agreed. "What the Nazis confiscated and put in storage defies imagination."

"And if it hadn't been for the benign-looking Rose Valland, the curator of the Jeu de Paume," Georges interrupted, "much more art would have been lost. In secret, she not only copied the negatives of everything that was coming in and its destination once it was removed, but kept the resistance up to date on it as well. In return, the resistance kept her apprised of what was going on at the Louvre. As a result, her records are as detailed as those of the ERR."

"The ERR used salt mines as repositories," Rebecca said to Sally. "There were four hundred *tons* of art from Berlin's museums alone found in one mine at Merkers."

"Four hundred *tons?"*

Rebecca nodded as she finished her quiche. "Yes, tons."

"Along with enough gold bullion to represent a significant portion of the Third Reich's gold reserves, the manuscript of Beethoven's Sixth Symphony, the gold and silver shrines with the relics of Charlemagne, the bust of Nefertiti . . . I could go on and on," Georges said, making waving gestures with his hand.

"By 1946," Rebecca continued, sitting back and sipping her glass of wine, "the Allies had discovered over one thousand places where the Nazis had stored or hidden art treasures."

"Fortunately," Georges said, "these same repositories were also used to store and protect the contents from German and Austrian museums, King Ludwig II's castle Neuschwanstein, being one."

Sally shook her head and stared at them. "The scale of the plunder is almost too difficult to grasp."

"Except when you stop to realize the Nazis had four years," Georges added.

"Were any of your grandmother's family ever able to leave Vienna?" Rebecca asked.

"Finally, but only after agonizing delays from being sent from one agency to another. In the end, they bought their way out of the country. Fortunately, they had money and didn't end up like those less affluent, or those whose names were on the Nazi's list of 'political undesirables.' Those poor souls were either murdered outright or summarily rounded up and deported to one of the thousand plus concentration camps."

"Where did your family go after Vienna?" Rebecca asked.

"Spain, initially."

"Really?" Jeffrey's grandparents lived in Madrid. His grandmother still does."

"Are they natives to Spain?" Georges asked.

"Only his grandmother. Ernst Lawler, Jeffrey's grandfather, was born in Germany. His father, Jeffrey's great grandfather, Gustav, was also born in Germany. Gustav was the one who worked for Alfred Krupp in the early 1900s and was there in 1939 when Hitler celebrated his fiftieth birthday.

"Jeffrey said his grandfather had no patience with the philosophies of the budding Third Reich and thought Hitler was nothing more than an upstart nobody. It was Ernst who became the family's first art connoisseur. In the late 1930s, he moved the family to Spain where he started his own business."

"If Jeffrey's grandmother's still alive," Sally said, "how old must she be?" She paused. "Sorry. I didn't mean to be rude. Must be the wine."

"You're not rude," Rebecca said. "She and the family are quite proud of her age. She's ninety-eight going on ninety-nine and continues to stay healthy and retain an active mind."

Sally smiled. "Wouldn't it be nice if we were all that fortunate?"

"Indeed it would," Rebecca agreed. She looked at Georges. "Don't let me rush you, but once you've finished your lunch, I'd love to hear the rest of your story."

He swallowed the last piece of sausage and pushed his plate aside. "Where were we? Ah, *oui*. I was speaking of Grandmother's paintings.

"There were ten from her family's collection in the house in Brussels, but they were left behind in 1940." He went on and told them what he'd told Brian. "Those are the paintings I've been trying to locate and would love to find, especially one: a Gustav Klimt portrait of my great grandmother, Emilia Wegenstein, or *Emma* as the painting's titled."

"Have you made any progress?" Rebecca asked.

"Some, and I continue to be hopeful. In the last ten to fifteen years, there's not only been a steady increase in the number of organizations formed for the restitution of Nazi-plundered art, more and more information is becoming declassified and available. Initially, I was registered with two organizations: the London-based Art Loss Registry and the Commission for Looted Art in Europe, or ECLA. Since the 1998 Conference on Holocaust Art, however, each country now has at least one commission dealing with looted art. Switzerland has ten. Interpol finally became involved and now has a list our things.

"Several years ago, my hopes were raised when I learned that in 1969, officials of the Austrian government had published a list of one thousand confiscated objects found in 1953 by U.S. forces which were stored at a monastery in Mauerbach."

"Yes, I remember reading about that online when I was working at the Museum of Contemporary Art in San Francisco," Rebecca said. "The article had been in the 1984 issue of *ARTnews* and was titled 'A Legacy of Shame.' It said that the Austrian government had made little attempt to trace any of the owners."

"Not only did they make little attempt," Georges said, "but they had guaranteed the Jewish community that the owners could not be found or traced, despite substantial documentation in the Federal Monument Office." He chortled a laugh. "I couldn't help wondering if the guarantee had anything to do with the fact that the then president of that office was a man by the name of Walter Fodl, the same Walter Fodl who was instrumental in helping Nazis loot art works from Eastern Europe during the 1940s."

"And who obviously had firsthand knowledge of every thing that had been stored," Sally said.

"I'm sure," Rebecca agreed. "But then, right after that, the Austrian government announced they were going to have an 'heirless' benefit sale of these items and began making arrangements to transfer them to the Jewish community."

"Luckily," Georges said, picking up the conversation, "in the Jewish Community was a scholarly young woman by the name of Sophie Lille overseeing the transfer. While examining the art, she became fascinated with the marks and stamps on the backs and discovered some indicated the pre-war owners. Others had the original collectors' stamps. Several bore stickers with the letter *J* for Jew. She began an extensive search, and, finding there were many ownership records readily available in the Monument Office files, she shamed the Austrian authorities by publishing a fourteen-hundred page book with the information. She then went to work trying to locate the families."

"That's right," Rebecca said. "The English title of her book is *What Once Was."* She looked at Georges. "Did it help you find anything of your grandmother's?"

"*Non.* But I learned a great deal about how provenance research works. Each experience makes the search more compelling, more fascinating, and, much too often, more frustrating."

"Why did the Austrian government wait until 1969 before doing anything about restitution?" Sally asked.

"Ah, the way things were left after the war was very complicated, *cherie*, and the job, enormous. So many people died in the gas chambers. Too often heirs did not know what art their families had possessed. Even when they did and tried to establish a claim, they had to go through an arduous process of proving they were the rightful heirs before the statute of limitations on claims went into effect. To add to the difficulties, Austria considered itself a victim of the War, and felt it was under no obligation to return anything."

Sally gaped at him. "A *victim*? What do you mean, victim?"

"Austria viewed its position the same way the Allies did—as an occupied country that they had liberated."

"Even though Austria fought alongside the Germans?"

"*Oui.* You see, Austria thought of the German occupation as an annexation, and the Allied liberation as a breakdown of German rule. Up until recently, the country thought it unnecessary to make restitution to those it viewed as 'enemies of the Third Reich.' That, for the most part, included Jews."

"And lest we forget," Rebecca added, "Austria was Hitler's birthplace and where he intended to install one of his monuments, the art museum at Linz that he claimed was going to be a masterpiece to rival any other." She looked at Sally. "Did you know Hitler was an artist?"

"No!"

"Yes. Hitler was a fairly decent watercolorist who, at the age of 19—along with Egon Schiele and Oscar Kokoschka—applied for entrance into Austria's Academy of Fine Arts. As luck would have it, Hitler was rejected. But Schiele and Kokoschka were accepted and went on to become two of the most famous German Expressionists. Later, Hitler discovered that not only were several Jewish jurors on the Academy's panel, there were Jewish artists in many of Austria's art schools."

"Is that what precipitated his anti-Semitism?"

"No, it began earlier and was insidious. Outraged at what was being passed off as 'Modern Art,' Hitler was convinced the Expressionists were mentally deranged and destroying Germany's image as a leader in the art world. That, plus his rejection, led to an obsession that ultimately resulted in the systematic plunder of what he believed to be 'degenerate art.'" She reached for her wine glass.

"As decrees were issued," Georges said, picking up the conversation again, "many 'degenerate' artists were prevented from buying supplies. Should any member of the Gestapo or ERR arrive at a studio and smell turpentine, the artist risked arrest. Finally, due to lawsuits and international pressure, Austria at last acknowledged its part in the persecution of the country's Jews and, in 1994, created a state commission to deal with the matter."

"Why am I not particularly impressed?" Sally asked.

"I understand that," Georges said. "But if history is any example of progress, we know it to be slow."

"I guess that's true," Sally said, finishing the last of her wine.

"Café?" Georges asked Rebecca.

"I'd love a café au lait."

"*Cherie?*"

Sally nodded. "A café au lait would be lovely, thanks. I have one more question. What is the Monument Office?"

"Today, it's where the lists of unclaimed, confiscated art are kept," Georges said. "In 1940, many curators and museum directors were concerned about the fate of art work and historical artifacts that would be in the path of advancing armies, or could fall victim to bombing.

"As a result, special committees comprised of individuals with a knowledge or background in art were formed and strategies on saving and protecting priceless pieces of art and cultural monuments, developed. Then, with the blessing of President Roosevelt and General Eisenhower, lists of these monuments and art works were issued to advancing allied military forces, accompanied by an order that saving lives took precedent.

"As the War progressed and the Allies reclaimed portions of the European continent, additional soldiers with a knowledge of art volunteered to find and protect cultural monuments and rescue and store moveable items. These men became known as the 'Monuments Men.' They collected, tagged, cataloged, and ultimately returned enormous amounts of confiscated property. That project alone took six years. More qualified individuals were assigned the prodigious job of onsite restoration that continues today."

"All you have to do is look at photographs of the devastation to marvel at how European cities, reduced to rubble, ever managed to recover," Rebecca said. "On top of that, 600,000 pieces of art had been stolen from private collections, churches, synagogues, and museums before being stored in numerous locations."

"That's the reason World War II is referred to as the 'greatest theft and greatest genocide,'" Georges added.

Rebecca looked at him. "While your family led interesting lives, their lives were very uncertain and difficult."

"That is true, but your life has been interesting too."

"Indeed it has," Sally agreed, "with the wonderful places you've lived and the unusual jobs you've had."

"You're right. Fortunately, it was neither uncertain nor difficult, and like you said, I have lived in some wonderful places."

"When did you and your family leave Vienna and return to the United States?" Georges asked.

"We moved to California in 1987 when I was ten." She laughed. "And now you know my age."

Georges waved a hand at her. "Age? What is age? Age is not important. Just look at you—you're not only beautiful, you're knowledgeable and talented as well." He winked at Sally.

Smiling, Sally put her hand over his. "Where Rebecca's concerned, I have to agree with you."

"Hey, no fair, you two. You're embarrassing me," Rebecca said, heat rising to her face. "Nevertheless, thank you for that. Thank you also, Georges, for taking me to Drouot."

"*De rien*, Rebecca. My pleasure."

* * *

The next event occurred on Wednesday with the arrival of Senhor Carlos, the second Kandinsky, and the Ernst Kirchner.

Rebecca held her breath as Georges and Gabrielle removed the frames. There was a torn label with the remains of a pre-war stamp of ownership on the Kandinsky, but nothing on the Kirchner.

"It seems we have *un petit problem*," Georges said.

"Yes," Senhor Carlos agreed. "I noticed that, too."

Everyone looked at Rebecca

Rebecca's mouth had gone dry. *What else is there to do but admit knowing about it?* "I suspected as much with the Kirchner but hoped I was wrong and that we'd find something—even a Nazi inventory stamp—hidden behind the wide frame despite its lack of documentation.

"I apologize for not mentioning it but was afraid if I did, neither of you would agree to help me. I really am very sorry. Deception is not part of who I am."

"What will you do now?" Sally asked.

Georges heaved a sigh. "We become detectives, *cherie*." He smiled at Rebecca. "Who knows, between the two of us, we might even uncover something about my family treasures. Tomorrow I'll begin laying out a plan," he looked at her, "but you must understand that it will take time."

"Believe me, I'm in no rush. I do want you to know how much I appreciate all your help, especially given the fact that I misled the two of you," she added.

"When are you returning to Portugal?" Georges asked.

"Tomorrow, on the noon flight, but I'll come back or meet you in London if you decide to go to Christie's. Just let me know."

"*Bon*. We'll see how things go. But it's most important we stay in touch."

"Definitely. And you must let me know if I can do anything to help with the research." A sense of guilt washed over her. "I fear I've left you with a dreadful project."

"As it happens, I just finished a search for the Louvre. Now with this, I no longer have to worry about ennui, *n'est-ce pas?*"

Rebecca smiled. Grateful, she said, "Thanks. Now, I really owe you."

"Want to go for some lunch?" Sally asked, glancing at the Calder clock on the wall.

"*Non*," Georges said, "you and Rebecca go along. Senhor Carlos and I will get something once we've finished here."

Georges and Gabrielle walked them to the door. "How long do you plan to stay in Portugal?" Georges asked.

"Ten or twelve days. Then Addie and I will return to Las Vegas. You have that number as well as my cell. We must talk often but I don't want to bug you."

He shook his head. "*Jamais*, Rebecca, never. Bon Voyage. As for you . . ." he said turning to Sally and unobtrusively giving her buttocks a pat, "I will see you later. Enjoy lunch."

The third event occurred at precisely two thirty that afternoon when Miranda—having managed to escape the scrutiny of Detective Hulot, the security guard Georges had posted outside, strolled into the gallery. Sally was in the back repositioning canvasses while Gabrielle was up front with a customer. She glanced up and gasped as Miranda walked in.

Miranda remained quiet with a smirk on her face.

"May I help you?" Sally asked, hesitantly coming forward. There was something about the woman that made her uncomfortable.

Gabrielle glanced at her customer. "Excuse me a . . ."

"Yes, you can help me. Thank you," Miranda said, her voice cutting through the quiet atmosphere. "I'm Mrs. Lartigue, and I came to see my husband. Is he here?"

Sally froze. "Your *husband?*"

"Yes. Georges. I believe you two are acquainted."

"Miranda," Gabrielle said. "Please come into the office."

The customer looked at all three. "Perhaps I'll come back at a later time."

"Of course," Gabrielle said. "I'm so sorry."

Sally was totally still, her expression full of shock and misery. Then, before either Gabrielle or Miranda could say or do anything, she marched past them into Georges' office, grabbed her purse, and fled, tears spilling down her cheeks.

Georges and Senhor Carlos were a block away on their return and had just crossed the street when they saw Sally running in the opposite direction.

"*Cherie*?" Georges called. "Sally ! *Mon Dieu!*" Fearing the worst, he ran toward the gallery.

"Monsieur Lartigue," Detective Hulot called as Georges sped past, "is something wrong?"

When Georges did not reply but continued running, Hulot turned and followed. Senhor Carlos brought up the rear.

"Gabrielle," Georges shouted as he entered the gallery. He stopped in his tracks. "YOU!"

Miranda laughed. "Yes my darling, none other."

Detective Hulot looked from one to the other. "Monsieur . . . ?"

"Yes," Georges hissed, "*she*'s the one."

Hulot took one step toward her.

"I wouldn't do that, Monsieur. You see, I'm Monsieur Lartigue's legal wife. Did you know that? And as such, I have every right to be here. If you so much as touch me, I'll have your license. I am an American citizen, a guest in your country, and have committed no crime. In other words, the American embassy would look very carefully at any charges I might bring against you should you make any attempt to physically abuse me, and that includes restraint."

Detective Hulot looked at Georges. "Is what she says true, Monsieur? She is your wife?"

"*Was* and only recently escaped from a psychiatric facility in the United States. Gabrielle, please phone Doctor Marchand."

Miranda snickered. "Oh, so that's your game? My dear husband, by the time the doctor or anyone else gets here, I'll be long gone." She headed for the exit, walking past Georges, Senhor Carlos, Gabrielle, and Detective Hulot.

And Georges realized two things, that he'd made a dreadful mistake by not telling Sally, and that he had to be the one to go to Miranda, not wait for her to come again to him.

Detective Hulot had been watching Georges expectantly. As Miranda reached the door, he started to follow.

"*Arretez*," Georges said. "Let her go."

And with a triumphant look, Miranda strolled out.

At four o'clock that same afternoon, the fourth event occurred. The private investigator Georges had hired, came into the gallery to say that a Mrs. Miranda Lartigue was registered at the hotel Champ de Mars on rue du Champ de Mars.

CHAPTER SEVENTEEN

Sobbing, her mind a blur, Sally ran blindly, crisscrossing the narrow streets in the area neither thinking nor caring where she was going as long as it was away—away from the gallery, away from Gabrielle, and away from the person who called herself Mrs. Lartigue.

Before long, she realized she was in front of Hotel Manoir de St.-Germain-des-Pres, Rebecca and Adelaide's hotel. On impulse, she entered and approached the desk, hoping the sunglasses would mask her distress.

"Would you ring Rebecca Lawler's room for me please?"

"Of course, mademoiselle. Who shall I say is calling?"

A new surge of hysteria threatened, but she bit down on her lip and it passed. "Sally Livingston."

She heard the call connect. In the next minute the concierge said, "Madame Lawler says to go right up. Suite 1107."

"*Merci, monsieur.*"

"*De rien*, mademoiselle."

Tears filled her eyes on the elevator but she managed to hold them in check. It was a different story when she saw Rebecca standing in the doorway of her suite.

Erupting into sobs, Sally ran toward her. Alarmed, Rebecca wrapped an arm around her and pulled her inside.

"Did I hear you say 'Sally?' "Adelaide said, coming in from the bedroom. "Oh, dear."

Sobbing, her face in her hands, Sally sat on one of the settees while Rebecca sat next to her, a box of tissues in one hand and Sally's sunglasses in the other.

After several minutes, Sally paused long enough to take a deep breath. "I . . . I'm so sorry. I didn't mean to intrude. It's just that I . . . I . . .," but her sobs took over again, and she was unable to complete the sentence.

"I think you could use a drink," Adelaide said, going to the mini-bar. "What's your preference? Nod when I've hit the right one: scotch, gin, vodka . . ."

"Is there s-some wine?" Sally gulped, her voice muddled with tears.

"Wine it is," Adelaide said. "Red or white?"

"W-White please."

"Becca? Some wine?"

"Please."

"Three wines it is." Adelaide uncorked the bottle and poured. "Here's to better days," she said handing them each a glass.

Sally's eyes were red and swollen, but her sobs were diminishing to sporadic gasps. She took a sip of wine.

"Do you want to talk about it?" Rebecca asked.

Sally shook her head, then nodded furiously.

"You don't have to," Rebecca cautioned.

Sally nodded again. "I-I know."

"Take time and drink some wine first," Adelaide suggested.

Rebecca got up and turned on the radio. "Perhaps some music will help."

Fifteen minutes later, Sally had finished half of her wine. Though she was no longer crying, her intermittent gasps continued. "I-I don't know where to b-begin."

"Would it help if I asked questions?" Rebecca said.

"I th-think so."

Rebecca took a deep breath. "Would it have anything to do with Georges?"

Sally bit down on her lip and squeezed her eyes shut.

"Jackpot," Adelaide said under her breath.

Rebecca sent her a glance.

"Sorry," Adelaide murmured.

"He's *married,"* Sally exploded.

"Who? *Georges?"* Rebecca asked.

"Yes. And all the time Gabrielle *knew."*

Rebecca looked at Adelaide and back at Sally. "But there *has* to be an explanation. There *has* to. I can't believe Georges is the kind who would cheat on anyone, let alone intentionally deceive them. Besides, he adores you."

"N-Nonetheless he is *married!* Th-That horrible woman came into the gallery after Georges and Senhor Carlos l-left for lunch. I had a strange feeling about her right from the start and knew something was wrong when G-Gabrielle gasped at the sight of her. And then she called her by name!" More tears.

"Did this woman say anything?" Rebecca asked.

"Oh yes! Loud and clear, '*I'm* Mrs. Lartigue and I'm here to see my h-husband.'" Sally paused to blow her nose. "At first I couldn't think of whom she meant because what she was inferring was so . . . so unbelievable. I said, 'Georges?' and she said, 'Yes' and something about us knowing each other." She let out a sob and vigorously shook her head. "It was awful, just awful."

Rebecca passed her a tissue. "I can imagine. But in order to be absolutely sure, you really must ask Georges. As bad as it must seem, there has to be an explanation."

"And h-here I'm at last beginning to overcome my fear of getting involved." She blotted her eyes.

Rebecca glanced at Adelaide. Sally added, "It's a l-long story. I was only involved once . . . with Brian Neville." She looked at them. "I know how that must seem."

"Seems pretty good to me," Adelaide said. "Brian's divine."

Rebecca sent her a look.

"Oops. Sorry."

"It was before Georges or I knew Carrie," Sally continued. "Did you know Brian's wife, Melissa, d-died as a result of a bomb attached to the starter in his car?"

Rebecca looked at Adelaide. "No!"

"'M,' as we called her, and I were very close, and after her death our shared grief drew B-Brian and me together. I dropped the relationship after a y-year and a half without an explanation. It hurt him and I vowed never to do anything like that again."

Silence.

"It may be difficult to believe now," Sally continued, "but back then, I was shy and fearful of commitment. Knowing Brian as I did at first made our relationship easy and natural. As time went on, however, our mutual attraction overwhelmed me and I panicked. I terminated our relationship a few days later. When I found myself attracted to Georges, I sought the advice of a psychologist."

"It 's obviously helping," Adelaide said.

Choked up again, Sally could only nod. But after a minute, she gasped, "*Yes*. B-but don't you see, that's why it's so aw-awful!"

Adelaide poured more wine.

"Sally," Rebecca said, "why not stay for dinner and we'll order from room service?"

"But aren't you leaving tomorrow?"

"Yes, but I'm almost packed. When do you leave?"

"I can't stay here now!" New tears spilled onto her cheeks, "I—I just can't. But the thought of having to pack up all my things . . ."

Rebecca handed her another tissue. If it was possible, she felt almost as miserably as Sally. "Oh, Sally, I do sympathize, I really do. But at some point, you are going to have to let Georges explain before you walk out of his life forever."

She glanced at Adelaide. "I don't suppose you'd consider coming to Portugal with Addie and me? We'll be there for another twelve days, and you're more than welcome. It would do you a world of good and give you the time and space you need to think. Besides, we'd love it."

"I can vouch for its healing properties," Adelaide said. "It worked wonders on me in the aftermath of Jim's death and the scandal that followed."

Sally thought about it. Other than the apartment she was renting, what did she have to lose? Under the circumstances she couldn't remain in Paris and the thought of going back to New York distressed her even more.

"In fact," Rebecca said, "I might even come back to Paris with you. Georges may have news on my paintings by then. I could help you pack and accompany you to New York on the way to Las Vegas."

"You could see David," Sally said.

Adelaide beamed and nodded.

Rebecca ignored them both. "What do you say? We'll call the airline, have an early supper and afterwards, you can go to your apartment and start packing your things. If you'd like to come back and spend the night, that's fine, too. Otherwise, we'll pick you up tomorrow on our way to the airport."

Sally smiled for the first time that afternoon. "Thank you. I'd love to come to Portugal. And if you don't mind, p-perhaps I will come back and sleep on your couch. The thought of being alone tonight is . . ." She closed her eyes and swallowed.

"Wonderful," Rebecca said.

"Actually the couch is a bed. We'll have it made up for you," Adelaide said.

"However," Rebecca added, "there is a condition."

"Yes?" Sally said, looking apprehensive.

"Someone, either you or I, have to call Georges."

"I-I can't manage that at the moment, Rebecca. So, if you would call him for me, I'd be truly grateful."

"But you do understand why?"

She nodded. "Yes."

"And at some point you'll let him explain?"

"I will. Perhaps even while I'm in Portugal. I just need to get away."

Rebecca leaned over and gave her a hug. "Great. Now, let's call the airline.

CHAPTER EIGHTEEN

That Friday, five days following their return from France, David arrived home to find Elise in the bedroom packing.

"Elise, what's going on?"

"I'm leaving, David."

"Leaving? But, why? Can't we talk about this? Were you planning to walk out without so much as an explanation? Am I not entitled to at least that?"

She put the last two items in her suitcase, and turned to face him. "Yes, you are, and no, I wasn't going to leave without an explanation." She started to sit down on the bed.

"Please. Can we go into the living room?"

They left the bedroom. Elise took a seat on one of the two couches. David chose the chair next to it. Elbows on knees, he leaned forward and clasped his hands. "Now, tell me what this is about."

She leveled a look at him. "You really have no idea do you, David?"

He shook his head. "No, I don't."

She took a deep breath and let the air escape slowly. "I'm leaving because I feel our relationship is no longer viable, and I think it's better to terminate it now than to go on and have it die a miserable death with neither of us having any regard for the other."

He was afraid of the answer, but went ahead and asked, "Just when did this change in attitude occur, Elise?"

"In Paris, David. In Paris." She paused. "I always knew there was something that kept you distant . . ."

"*Distant?* You can hardly call . . ."

Elise held up her hand. "Let me finish. I'm not talking about the physical side, David. I mean emotional distance. You might never have been aware of it yourself, but it's there nonetheless, and not until Paris, did I realize that it was not some *thing,* but some *one,* that caused the remoteness. Face it, David. You're in love with her and probably have been from the time the two of you met. If you're smart, you'll tell her before you lose her again. Rebecca's not only beautiful, she's extremely nice, and I'm surprised she's never remarried.

"We had a lovely time talking at the reception and again later at La Coupole, but there's something about her—a balance—a composure that leads me to believe the average male holds no appeal for her and probably never has. However, you, David, are anything but an average male. Take my advice and get together with her."

He studied his hands, feeling like a heel to have caused this wonderful woman such distress. He looked up. "I don't deserve you, Elise."

She waved a hand at him. "Don't belittle yourself, David. Yes, you do. Actually, you're one hell of a guy. It's just that it didn't 'click' for us. For me, it has to 'click.'"

He wanted to touch her, hold her close and tell her how sorry he was, but he had the feeling it would do no good and only add insult to injury.

"Would you consider at least having dinner with me or, failing that, a drink?"

She reached over and squeezed his hands. "What would that accomplish, really?"

He shrugged, feeling miserable.

"No," she said, standing, "it's better I leave now."

"Want me to go with you?"

She managed a smile. "No, thanks. But I'd appreciate it if you could help me into a taxi."

He looked at his watch. "You'll never get one at this hour on a Friday. Besides, I've a better idea. I'll call my car service. All right with you?"

"Great. I forgot it was Friday and never gave the hour a thought."

He called for a car and helped bring her things to the front door. "We have a bit of a wait. Are you sure you won't reconsider and have a drink?"

She hesitated, "Oh, all right. Make it a white wine. Thanks."

He went to the bar, uncorked a chilled bottle of Chardonnay, poured it into two glasses, and handed her one.

She studied her drink. "I'm not sure there's a toast for a time like these."

David tilted her chin so she'd look at him. "I'm so sorry. Truly sorry."

She rose on her toes and kissed him. "I know. So am I." She took a sip of wine.

He could see she was fighting tears and shook his head. "I never meant to hurt you, Elise. It devastates me that I have."

She put a hand on his arm. "I know it wasn't intentional, David. Nevertheless, you did. Yet looking back, I don't know how it could have been avoided."

He sighed. "Unfortunately, I think I do. I was so amazed at seeing Rebecca again after twelve years, that I got carried away. Forging ahead, I suggested she and Adelaide bring the paintings to Paris and go to the wedding. At the time, it seemed like a great idea, especially since they both knew Brian."

"But all that's past history now, isn't it?"

He stared into his glass. "You're right. It is."

"Regardless, thank you for your honesty."

They sat on the couch. This time she didn't object when he wrapped his arm around her and pulled her close.

In silence, they drank their wine and watched the sky grow dark through the tall windows opposite as dusk descended and enveloped Manhattan.

"I'll turn on some lights," David said rising, but he was interrupted by the buzzer announcing the arrival of the car.

They walked to the door, and David helped her slip into her coat.

It took several trips, but at last the car was packed.

"It's a good thing you never got rid of your apartment," David said, in an attempt to say something positive.

"Well, we agreed that living together was an experiment, remember?"

Hands in his pockets, David studied the ground and nodded. "Yeah, I do." He looked at her. "You're sure you don't want me to come help unload?"

"No. The doorman and evening crew will do that."

"And if they don't?" He hated her leaving like this. The worst of it was he was responsible.

Her lips trembled but she managed a smile. "Not to worry, they will."

"Do you have any food in the apartment?"

"Have you forgotten, David? I'm a woman of the twenty-first century. The magic words are, 'frozen' and 'microwave.'"

He forced a laugh. They continued to stand looking at each other as if neither wanted to be the first to say the final goodbye.

David moved to embrace her, but she held up her hand.

"Better not."

He could see tears glistening in her eyes.

"Goodbye, David."

He swallowed and voice thick with emotion, said, "Goodbye, Elise."

She entered the limousine, he closed the door, and the car slowly pulled away. Her head was visible through the rear window, but she did not look back.

He watched the car, carrying the person whose life he'd shared for the past year, thread it's way north along the narrow street toward Houston until, turning the corner, it was lost from sight.

He felt wretched.

CHAPTER NINETEEN

After Sally fled and Miranda had left, Georges was desolate and realized he had been a fool.

Added to that, a colleague from Lisbon had had the dreadful misfortune to witness a part of what Georges considered the seamier side of his past.

But Senhor Carlos had proved to be a professional in every sense and had remained detached throughout the drama. They'd retired to Georges' office immediately afterward, and it was there that the private investigator found them and delivered his report on Miranda's whereabouts.

Now, desperate to locate Sally, Georges tried to think where she might have gone. First he tried her cell phone, then her apartment. Having no success, he called Rebecca's hotel. But her line was busy and, after several attempts, he left a message with the hotel concierge requesting that Rebecca call him on his cell phone immediately.

Senhor Carlos then suggested that he and Georges walk back to his hotel, The Four Seasons Hotel George V, on the Champs-Élysée, and indulge in a sauna, massages, drinks and dinner.

That was exactly where Georges was, in the midst of a massage, when the call came through from Rebecca.

"I'm so glad you were there for her, Rebecca."

"So am I."

"Will she talk to me?"

"Not at the moment, but she promises to call you before the end of next week."

"Ah . . ."

"I've assured her there's an explanation."

"Of course there is. Despite that, I should have told Sally about my previous circumstance as soon as Miranda reappeared on the scene.

It's a long story, Rebecca, and I feel I owe Sally the first explanation, *comprends*?"

"Heavens yes. I never meant to imply you should tell me, Georges."

"I understand that. Please forgive me if I gave you the wrong impression." He paused. "Rebecca, will you call me from Portugal and let me know how she is?"

"Certainly. I'd be happy to."

"*Merci.* You are an angel."

Senhor Carlos left the next day, and, by some miracle, Georges managed to get through Thursday. Midway through Friday, however, he succumbed and phoned his long time friend Denise Boucher and made a date to get together Saturday evening.

He and Denise had met during his first year in Paris. Their mutual attraction had been immediate. Shortly thereafter, they'd become lovers.

Georges was twenty years her junior, but no one would have guessed. Stylish and petite, Denise looked young enough to have been in her mid to late thirties. To Georges it didn't matter for whatever their age, he'd always enjoyed the company of women. But his marriage had left him bruised, filled with self-doubt, and overly cautious when it came to the opposite sex. Denise, however, had been the exception, and Georges remained convinced that her maturity was responsible for the difference. A *grande dame* in every sense of the word, she restored his confidence. By introducing him to well-connected friends in the art world, she had helped him get back on his feet and open a gallery. Their passion had abated some time ago, but their abiding friendship had not. And so here he was, seeking her friendship and the wisdom of her council once again.

Looking as beautiful as ever with her natural honey-blonde hair coiffed into a French twist and wearing a Chinese silk kaftan with brightly colored flowers outlined in gold thread, Denise greeted him with open arms.

"It's been awhile, *mon cher*," she said as they walked arm in arm to where champagne and caviar waited in the living room.

"*Je connais*, I know," he agreed as he settled into a chair, happy to be in her company.

"So your lady love has flown?" Denise asked, sitting after pouring them each a glass of champagne.

"*Ah, oui,* but I'm hoping it's only temporary."

Denise spread several crackers with caviar. After adding bits of chopped onion and hard-boiled egg, she offered him one. Then, resting back, she sipped the wine and looked at him over the rim of her goblet.

"Do you wish to say why she has seen fit to run off?"

Georges hesitated until, after downing half of his champagne, he told her the story.

Denise topped off his glass. "It was unwise not to have told her, but I'm sure you know that now."

Georges shrugged. "Please try to imagine my shock when Miranda walked in that evening. After the three horrid years we spent together, and then believing her dead . . . As she sat there on my desk, I prayed it was only a dream and that I'd wake and find her gone. The thought of telling Sally, hurting her . . ."

"Or losing her."

"*Oui*, or losing her, was," he made small circular gestures with his hand, "was too . . . too . . . You see, even now I cannot find the words to describe how I felt! Then Miranda's doctor called, and I was sure that with help I'd be able to arrange it so Miranda would go away, Sally would never have to know, and I would have protected her."

"For how long, *mon ami*? One month? Two?"

"Ah . . ."

Denise relaxed into the deep cushions of the couch, and, resting her head against the back, studied him. "Love of my life, you are what is called a truly nice man—a rare breed these days. What makes you vulnerable is that you happen to like women. Many men love women, but you not only love them, you *like* them, and there is a difference. All the better for us dames, *n'est-ce-pas*, but not always so good for you, yes?"

He nodded as he watched the bubbles in his glass rise to the top. "*Oui*."

"She will come back, dear heart."

He looked up. "If only I could be sure."

"Put it from your mind for now. You told me you're working on a special project involving Nazi confiscated art. Concentrate on that, *mon amour*, and when she's ready to listen, *tell her*. Then before you know it, pouf, your Sally will again be at your side."

Denise's comments lifted his spirits. He so desperately wanted to believe her, and he inwardly knew he did because past experience with her advice had taught him well.

"And now," Denise said, sitting up, "let us go in and have dinner. I have reason to believe Gaston and Marie have outdone themselves in your honor."

"*Je t'aime*, Denise."

She smiled. "I know, and that is good because I shall always, always love you."

They stood. Georges took her hand, and raised it to his lips. Then, with arms around each other, they walked into the dining room.

CHAPTER TWENTY

When Rebecca and Adelaide arrived in Faro with Sally, Ricardo met them at the airport. Within minutes, they were on their way to Casa des Palomas.

To her relief, Rebecca noticed that the black car and its occupant were no longer on the lower road, but once they drove up the driveway and paused to open the gate, an identical car with two men pulled up alongside. Near panic, Rebecca leaned forward. "Ricardo . . ."

He swiveled around to look at her. "Is all right, Senhora. These men talked to Maria and me. They want to make the appointment to see you."

And before she could reply, one—dressed in a white shirt, striped tie, navy blue blazer and tan trousers—got out of the car and approached, holding up an open wallet. In it was a card identifying him as Bruce Ross. But it was the symbol and heading on the card that caught Rebecca's eye. Dominating the upper left corner, was a blue and white image of the earth partially surrounded by an olive leaf wreath. A vertical sword stood behind it with a set of golden scales dangling from a hilt that had several letters on it too small for Rebecca to decipher what they were. Centered on the card in large letters, however, was the word "INTERPOL." She lowered the window.

"Senhora Lawler?"

"Yes."

Bruce Ross introduced his partner, Justin Benares.

"I apologize for the intrusion," Ross continued, "and realize you've just returned from a trip, but we've been trying to reach you for over a week to make an appointment. Eventually, Maria and Ricardo spoke to us. It's important that we talk. If now is inconvenient, perhaps we can decide on a time when we can come back. Otherwise, if you could spare a half hour or so, we'd very much appreciate it."

She glanced at Adelaide and Sally, then back at Ross. "Yes, of course." *Just as soon as I recover from my heart attack.* "Please, follow us in."

Upon entering the house, Adelaide ushered the men into the living room while Rebecca excused herself and took Sally to the guest room. "Don't worry about me, Rebecca," Sally said once they were there. "I'll sit on that lovely terrace outside and relax while you speak to those men."

"Shall I have Maria bring you something?"

"No. I'm fine for the moment, thanks. You go ahead."

"Hopefully, this won't take all that long. All right then, see you later."

Joining the others, Rebecca asked for Adelaide to stay. Once everyone was settled and Maria had brought in a beverage tray, Ross turned to Rebecca.

"Mrs. Lawler, do you mind if we record this interview?"

"Not at all."

"Thank you."

Benares placed a recording device on the coffee table.

Ross cleared his throat. "Again, my apologies for approaching you in this manner. Unfortunately, I think we also upset your housekeeper earlier in the week. Thankfully, Ricardo came to the rescue. They're quite protective of you. You're very fortunate."

"I agree. To be honest, I'm not all that surprised to see you given the way you've been keeping me under surveillance."

Ross and his partner shared a look. "Surveillance? When did you first notice?"

"Before my sister and I went to Paris there was someone sitting on the lower road in a black car similar to yours. It upset me because it reminded me of the way I was harassed after my husband's death. Then, recently, I was followed in Paris."

"And you feel sure that you're the one being targeted?"

"There's no one else living along this strip of road. I keep wondering if it has anything to do with my recent activities involving some paintings I inherited from my husband. He and I were making plans to sell them when he was killed."

"I don't want to alarm you, Mrs. Lawler, but at the moment, Interpol is not the one watching you." He glanced at Benares who'd pulled out his iPad and was running his fingers across its surface.

"However," Ross continued, "both Interpol and the CIA were doing so for a while after your husband's death. They stopped once those responsible for the harassment were apprehended."

"You and the CIA helped with that?"

"For a time, yes."

"Then I owe you both a round of belated thanks. The threats had become frightening."

"Yes, we were aware of that." Ross reached for his coffee cup and drained it before returning it to the coffee table. He looked at Rebecca. "Mrs. Lawler, I hope what I have to say won't come as a complete shock, but I know of no other way to put it. Were you aware that your husband was working as an undercover agent for Interpol?"

She felt the blood drain from her face. "*Excuse m*e? Working for *Interpol* did you say?"

"Yes."

"*Undercover?*"

"Yes."

I can't believe this! She shook her head. "N-no. I had no idea." *Why didn't he tell me?*

"But how is that possible? He was a project manager for my brother-in-law's firm." She didn't know if what she was feeling was only due to shock or also due to a sense of betrayal.

"He was under contract as a civil servant."

"As of when?"

"As of 2006. Considering he was a substantial art collector with international connections, we had reason to believe that he could be helpful to us in the Art Crimes division. It's our opinion that he was finalizing a report when he was killed."

Rebecca's shock was complete. "Then you don't think his death was an accident?"

"Let's just say we're not satisfied with the findings."

"Mr. Ross, Jeffrey's death was anything but an accident. He was murdered." She reached for a glass of water and realized her hand was shaking. She swallowed several mouthfuls.

Ross looked at her. "You okay?"

"Yes. At least I think so. It's just that . . . all this . . . your news has come as a shock. A huge one, in fact."

"I am sorry. I thought Mr. Lawler might have said something to you. Since he didn't, I can only assume it was for your protection. I don't mean to frighten you, but if the individuals who were after your husband thought you knew any of the details, it could have proven as fatal for you as it did for him."

"So you *do* think his death was intentional."

"The evidence we have points in that direction, yes. Unfortunately, we need additional proof. We aren't dealing with the average thief, Mrs. Lawler. Those involved in this business are cold, calculating professionals who've been in the system for years, scamming, making deals and doing business with the worst—the majority of them in the guise of legitimate businessmen. Nothing or anyone is going to interfere with their success. There's way too much money involved.

"Before he died, your husband hinted that he'd almost completed a list of dealers and their associates who continue to traffic in confiscated art. Several have roots dating back to the early 1940s. For, it was in the 1940s that the Vatican Ratlines were established to help move refugees from the War from place to place. Now, recent information confirms that the former Ratlines—or avenues similar to them—are operational and part of a sophisticated criminal network."

"For the purpose of?"

"Illegal commerce . . . counterfeiting; smuggling—gold, diamonds, drugs, art, both originals and copies; pornography—most of it involving children. It all depends on the fluctuation and demand of the mainstream market. Millions of dollars flow back and forth on a regular basis. Did Jeffrey ever mention knowing anything about illegal trafficking in art, or say anything about having a list of dealers who dealt with it?"

"No. But now that I think about it, there was something. When his grandfather died, he left Jeffrey quite a few paintings. Then just before Jeffrey was killed . . ." Rebecca went on to tell them how Jeffrey discovered Bruno Lohse's name among his grandfather's things. "Jeffrey could never figure out what had triggered Loshe's name in his grandfather's mind."

"Since your husband's grandfather had been an art collector for some time," Bruce Ross offered, "he had to have known that Loshe was an art historian and leading confiscator who, working under Goering, was appointed to a unit whose specialty was seizing Jewish assets of Jews living in occupied countries. He was a witness at the Nuremburg trials before being extradited to France where he appeared before a military tribunal. He was acquitted. Although initially barred from working as an art dealer, in the 1950s, the German hierarchy gave him permission to continue as such in Munich.

"Following his death in 2007, however, authorities discovered he'd hidden over a dozen masterpieces, each worth millions of euros, in a Zurich bank. Perhaps your husband's grandfather came across something he thought had been confiscated?"

Could it have been the Kirchner? Ernst Lawler had purchased it through the Mendes Galleria. It was on one of their sales slips that he'd written Lohse's name. "Possibly. Does the name Dietrich Radtke mean anything to you?"

"May I ask how you know Dietrich Radtke?"

"He worked as a consultant at the Mendes Galleria in Madrid during the time Jeffrey's grandfather purchased graphics and paintings from the gallery. Radtke's name was on the majority of the sales slips. It was Radtke who Jeffrey was on his way to meet when he was killed."

"And you think there might be a connection?"

"I do. Yes. Obviously, you know of him as well."

"The Mendes Galleria was once on our watch list."

"I see." Rebecca reached for the pitcher and poured herself another glass of water. "Mr. Ross, as pleasant as it is, I'm sure your visit is more than just a social call. There's something you wish me to do, isn't there?"

"You're very astute. As it happens, there is. We'd like you to try and find a list or any other documents Jeffrey might have been keeping on this issue. We know he'd begun compiling a roster of dealers who'd been involved in the barter/trade industry initiated by Goering and Lohse. Most of the original owners and dealers are dead, but Mr. Lawler said he was planning to follow up on the younger ones to see if any were still in the business of buying and selling art."

"I'm returning home to Las Vegas in another week. Jeffrey kept an office in the house there. I'll make a point of going through his things: business notes, files, briefcases . . . even his clothes." *They're still in his drawers and closet because I've been unable to face the thought of sorting through them.*

"That would be extremely helpful. I trust you've come across nothing here?"

"There are files and a safe, but I had reason to go through them just before our trip to Paris. Had there been something, I would have found it." *Though, now that think of it, I've never gone through Jeffrey's clothes here either.*

"Then I guess that's about all for the moment." He looked at his partner. "Find anything more on who's doing the surveillance?"

"Only that it confirms it isn't us. It's now been made a priority."

"Good." Ross looked at Rebecca. "Is there anything you'd like to ask us before we leave?"

"I can't think of anything at the moment."

"Should you happen to," Both men stood and produced business cards, "this is where we can be reached," Ross said. But before he handed his to Rebecca, he turned it over and wrote something on the back. "I'm giving you the name of one of several CIA agents working with us in Nevada. As it happens, this one's the same agent who looked after you before." He handed her the card.

Rebecca scrutinized the name. "Jack Deevers."

Ross tapped the card with his finger. "Now, be sure to call him and establish contact once you get back to Las Vegas. In the meantime," he reversed it, "please stay in touch and don't hesitate to call either of us at any time should you need to. All the numbers are there," he added, again tapping the card.

Rebecca got up and walked over to her handbag. Reaching in, she withdrew a business card. "And here's my card," she said, handing it to Ross. "My phone numbers and two addresses are on it."

Ross glanced at it and extended his hand. "Thank you for taking the time to speak with us on so short a notice, not to mention the circumstances."

"Yes, Mrs. Lawler," Benares said, pocketing the recorder and coming over to shake her hand. "Much appreciated."

Rebecca followed them to the door. "It was a shock to see you initially but reassuring to know you're around."

"Don't forget, now," Ross said, before getting into the car. "News or no news, we expect to hear from you," he glanced at Benares, "shall we say, once a week?"

Rebecca watched them leave. *It seems my goal of selling the paintings has just moved into second place. The primary goal now is to avenge Jeffrey's death.*

CHAPTER TWENTY-ONE

During her stay in Portugal, Sally had spoken to Georges on several occasions. On the last, she agreed to meet with him once she and Rebecca returned to Paris.

He'd told her a little about Miranda—enough so that she'd know he was not married at the time he and she met. As for a more in depth explanation, he begged to speak with her vis à vis, and she agreed to do so on the evening she returned.

When they met for dinner, Sally could not dismiss the leap of joy she felt upon seeing him, his hair tousled, striding toward her.

He came to a halt a few feet in front of her. Once she saw his pained expression, she all but leaped into his arms.

He buried his face in the crook of her neck. "Oh, Sally. Sally. How do I tell you how sorry I am?"

"No, Georges, no. I'm the one who needs to apologize. I never should have fled without first hearing you out. It was just . . . just that . . . she . . . that woman was so . . ."

"*Ah, bien,*" he said planting a kiss on her eyelids. "How well I know. We'll go inside this wonderful restaurant and have a lovely dinner. It's quiet in there and where I told Brian about Miranda the evening she came to the gallery."

"Brian knows?"

"*Oui*. I told him because I needed him to ask his brother Larry, who's a New York attorney, to check the legality of my marital status once Miranda reappeared. But come," he said putting his arm around her as they walked into Le Poquelin. "Let's let Monsieur Lassé seat us. And then, I will tell you all."

Sally and Rebecca left for New York the following Tuesday. That same morning, Georges corralled Detective Hulot from his post outside the gallery, and they taxied over to Miranda's hotel, the Champ de Mars.

While Detective Hulot presented his I.D. to the concierge, Georges introduced himself and asked that they be announced.

The man looked from Hulot to Georges. "You wish me to ring Madame Lartigue, monsieur?"

The sound of the name reverberated through Georges' nervous system. It hadn't occurred to him she'd use it to register. He steadied himself. "*Oui.*"

The concierge rang Miranda's room. After a minute's conversation, he said, "Madame Lartigue asks what this is in reference to."

Georges managed to keep a lid on his frustration. "Tell Madame Lartigue that *Monsieur* Lartigue is here with the security guard from his gallery and wishes to discuss her disruptive behavior last week at the gallery. Tell her, if she refuses, she will leave me no choice but to summon the *gendarmes.*"

The desk clerk blinked, stared at Georges, and hastened to relay the message.

Addressing them once again, he said, "Madame says you may go up, monsieur. She's on the fourth floor in room 407."

"*Merci,*" Georges said, sorry he'd had to involve the poor man.

They arrived on Miranda's floor to find her peeking out from behind the door with the chain still on.

"Whatever it is you have to say can be said with you standing in the hall," Miranda told them.

"Miranda, if you do not wish me to summon Dr. Marchand, who'd most certainly arrive fortified with others from the medical community and place you in the center of quite a stir, remove the chain and let us in!"

For a moment, nothing happened. Then she closed the door, slid the chain off, and pushed it open.

The two men entered. Georges went to a chair on the far side of the room and sat without invitation. Miranda took the only other chair. Detective Hulot remained standing near the door.

"I don't know what you intended when you came into the gallery last week," Georges said, "but I have a pretty good idea."

"So? I'm free to go where I want."

"Fine. However, you should know that I've told Doctor Weiss you've been 'found.' Whatever he sees fit to do about it, is now between him and my physician, Doctor Marchand."

"Why should that matter to me? Yes, I was under Doctor Weiss' care, but as an outpatient . . . free to move about and go anywhere I liked. So, as far as I can see, telling Doctor Weiss I've been 'found,' as you put it, means little because none of you can touch me. I'm here on my own volition, minding my own business, and supporting myself with my own money."

Georges raised an eyebrow. "Oh?"

"Yes. For your information, I still have your check, intact—you know—*un-cashed*?"

Georges feigned surprise. "Bravo! A first, I'm sure. But getting back to Doctor Weiss and Doctor Marchand, they *can* touch you because you were never officially discharged. As a result, you remain the patient of a doctor affiliated with a major psychiatric hospital in the United States. If you're smart, Miranda, you'll make an appointment with Doctor Marchand and not wait until he has to come to you. Because if he does, you can be sure he won't come alone."

"Just what does this Doctor Marchand have to do with me*? I* certainly don't know him."

"He's Doctor Weiss' contact here in Paris. He also happens to be my physician."

With a look that bordered on satisfaction, Miranda smiled and said, "I see. And, does dear Doctor Marchand know I'm your wife?"

"Miranda, this may come as a shock, but we—that is, you and I—are no longer married. Do you understand? *We* are no longer *man* and *wife*, *comprends*?"

She gave him a haughty look. "I don't believe you. Nothing's changed. Besides, I still have a copy of the marriage license."

He struggled to remain calm so as not precipitate one of her rages. It wasn't easy.

"Tell me, do you have any memory of your car accident?"

She frowned and looked at her hands, then stood and started to pace. "Of course. What about it?"

Georges knew from his conversation with Doctor Weiss that she had to be lying. Nevertheless, he went along with the guise. "*Bien*. Where did you go afterward? Can you tell me, eh?"

Silent, but now visibly agitated, she continued to walk about.

"Did you know that the police dragged the river for you and, finding nothing, put out a tri-state alert? *Non,* right?"

Silence.

"Exactement! And, that, Miranda, is the reason that seven long years later, a New York circuit court judge declared you dead, *finis,* and, with that, put an end to our marriage . . . if you could have called it that," he added, under his breath.

She stopped, placed her hands on the back of her chair and leaned forward, eyes flashing. "You sit there telling me the police put out an alert and even dragged the river for me, but you, you! What did *you* do? Anything?" And to his silence, added, "Ha! See there? You did *nothing.* You abandoned me . . . just like my father. Typical."

It was no use. The word rational was simply not in her vocabulary. "Miranda,"

Her near hysterical laugh filled the room. "You say we're no longer married because *I* disappeared? Well, Georges," she said, pounding a finger rhythmically against her chest, "here I am—*in* the flesh. What would that circuit court judge have to say now, hmmm? Tell me. And if you persist in saying we're no longer married, I may have to return to the United States, hire an attorney, and investigate."

His heart sank because he knew she could do exactly that. He also realized that he'd just accomplished what he'd set out to avoid—pushing Miranda to the limit. Had he not fallen into the age-old trap of intimidation and revenge, he could, had he been more careful, have prevented her from considering such action.

Hoping to appear detached, he said, "By all means, Miranda. If you have the funds, go!"

Her look of triumph chilled his bones. And when she said, "Ah, but since I'm very much alive and, in my mind, legally married, *dear husband,* it will be you, not I, who'll be paying my legal fees," he snapped, his tolerance pushed beyond restraint.

"You deceive yourself, Miranda. Any judge will uphold the court's prior ruling once he's heard the testimony of Doctor Weiss. And, believe me, my attorney will make certain the good doctor gives a full report." He stood. "Hulot?"

Hulot opened the door as Georges started toward it.

"*Go to hell, Georges Lartigue,*" Miranda shrieked at his departing form. "Do you hear me? *Go to hell.* You haven't seen or heard the last of me. Only I will determine the when and where. Only I . . ."

Fortunately, her comments were cut short when Georges, following Hulot into the corridor, closed the door and said, "Ah. *C'est fait!* Done. Blessed silence at last."

The silence was short lived. For Miranda, still screaming, now vented her fury against the door.

As they walked away, Doctor Weiss' words echoed in Georges' ears, "My concern lays with the fact that if under any sort of circumstance Miranda becomes excessively agitated, she could pose a threat, not only to herself, but possibly to others."

And he wondered what he'd just done.

CHAPTER TWENTY-TWO

At two that Wednesday afternoon, David Neville opened the door to his apartment, and, jostling luggage, walked in and tripped on his roller-blades.

Shit. By now you'd think I'd have learned.

He kicked them to one side, dropped his bags and, switching on the lights, closed the door.

It was good to be home. The early morning flight had been late getting in from San Francisco, and he was exhausted from the two-week marathon of visiting artists, clients, and galleries on the West Coast.

He tossed his jacket on a chair and went to get a beer. On the way, he changed his mind, and detoured to the bar where he collected a cocktail shaker, glass, and bottle of Absolut Vodka. *Tonight warrants a martini.*

Going into the kitchen, he put the glass in the freezer, filled the shaker with ice, added three drops of vermouth, three-and-a-half ounces of vodka, and, popping on the top, he set it aside while he went to cut a piece of lemon rind. Except, there was no lemon rind, because there was no lemon—another thing Elise used to remedy. She'd been gone almost a month, and he'd counted every damn day of it.

Yes, he missed her and still felt terrible about the way things had ended. But he couldn't pretend what he didn't feel, and he wasn't ready to marry. Somewhere in the back of his mind had been the thought that given time living together that might change. Still, sixteen months later, it still hadn't. And then, Rebecca reentered his life.

Guess I'll have to settle for olives.

He retrieved the chilled glass from the freezer, deposited two rinsed olives in it, picked up the cocktail shaker, and shook it until the outside was frosty. He poured the liquid into the glass and took it into the living room where he picked up the remote. Setting the martini on the coffee table, he collapsed on the couch and turned on the television.

At last. He took a sip of his drink, closing his eyes and savoring its flavor as the cold vodka slid over his tongue. *Mmm, good. It's even better with lemon rind.* He glanced at the pile of accumulated mail and decided it could wait.

David's thoughts switched to Rebecca. Despite what Elise had said, he'd resisted contacting her. He couldn't overcome his reservations about turning to another woman as soon as one walked out the door. He took another sip of his drink.

It's true I already knew her . . . well, not exactly. Then there was Paris. What about Paris?

There was no denying he and Rebecca had had a great time—the Bateau-Mouche, dancing at La Coupole. Yes, the attraction was certainly there.

And, hadn't he felt a twinge of jealousy when he'd noticed Stan paying attention to her and how she was enjoying his company? Perhaps Elise was right. He should call her. He was never going to resolve anything this way.

He took a third sip of his drink, set it aside, and looked at his watch. Five minutes to three in the afternoon. And in Portugal? What was the time difference, five, maybe six, hours?

Another martini and I'll collect my bags and fly there.

He got up and grabbed his iPhone from his jacket. Seated once more, he checked the number and dialed Portugal.

After five rings, he heard Maria answer. "*Esta Alo*?"

"*Boa noite*, Maria. This is David Neville in New York."

"*Boa noite*, Senhor Neville. Senhora Lawler not here."

"She's not? Where is she? Can you tell me, *per favor?*"

"*Sim,* yes. She left for Paris with Senhorita Sally on Sunday."

Paris? Senhorita Sally? What the devil had Sally been doing in Portugal?

"So, Senhora Lawler is now in Paris, Maria?"

"*Nao,* Senhor Neville. She now in New York."

"New York?"

"*Sim*. Yes, Senhor Neville. New York."

"Do you happen to know where she's staying in New York?"

Silence. Then, "Moment, senhor."

He heard papers rustling. "Not sure, Senhor. Please to call Senhora Broker."

"Senhora Broker? All right, I'll do that. *Obrigado*, Maria. Thank you. *Adeus.*"

"Adeus, Senhor Neville."

Well, that's news. He decided to call Georges. He first tried the gallery.

"*Bonsoir. Gallerie des Artists.*"

"Gabrielle? It's David Neville."

"Oh, Monsieur Neville. How are you?"

"Fine, thanks. Is Georges there by chance?"

"*Non*. He left for Berlin this morning."

"Berlin?"

"Yes, in regard to two of Mrs. Lawler's paintings."

"Why Berlin?

"He said he wanted to see if he could discover what was on display in a gallery of the Kronprinzenpalais right before the start of the War."

"Really? And Mrs. Lawler and Miss Livingston?"

"They were just here but left for New York yesterday."

"I see. Do you know when Georges plans to return?"

"He said that this was only a preliminary trip and that he'd be back tomorrow."

"Good. I'll call back then. Thanks, Gabrielle."

Guess I'll call Addie.

With the glass in one hand, David touched in her number, but got a machine. So he left a message.

He took a swig of his drink, set the glass down, and dialed Paul Smith's office.

"Paul Smith."

"Paul, it's David."

"David, how are you?"

"Trying to locate Rebecca."

"Have you spoken with Addie?"

"Just tried Portugal, Paris, and Addie. But I had no luck, so I decided to call you."

"Well, from what Addie told me, I think Rebecca's supposed to be here in New York."

"That's what Gabrielle said, but no one seems to know where she's staying. Do you?"

"Gee. Let's see if I can remember . . . the Waldorf? No. Helmsley Palace? No. Pla . . . Got it! The St. Regis."

David laughed. "Thanks, Paul. Appreciate it."

"Sure thing."

He got the number of the St. Regis from information, dialed it, and was soon connected to Rebecca's room. One ring, two, three, four . . . "Hello?"

"Rebecca?"

"Yes?"

He lowered the volume on the television. "It's David Neville. How are you?"

"David! How nice to hear your voice. I'm fine, thank you. And you?"

Feeling like Superman. "I'm fine, too. What brings you to New York?"

"Actually, I'm only passing through. I leave for Las Vegas in the morning.

"Are you busy tonight?" *I must be mad.*

"As a matter of fact, I'm having dinner with Stan O'Neil."

Great. "Okay. How about breakfast tomorrow . . . or lunch? What time is your flight? Perhaps you'd like a ride to the air . . ." He heard her laugh. "Sorry."

"My flight's at ten," she answered, still laughing.

Damn. "I could still give you a ride."

"That's most thoughtful, but I've already hired a car."

Shot down again. "All right, suppose we regroup. When can we get together?"

"Do you still intend to stop in Las Vegas sometime?"

He sat up straighter. "Yeah, that is, if it's still all right with you."

"When do you think you'll be going out that way?"

"I just got back from a trip to the West Coast, and don't have anything on the immediate horizon. Why not just give me a date?"

"All right. I have my calendar right here. Let's see . . . I may have to meet Georges in London on Tuesday, but should be home by Thursday. How about a week from this coming weekend? That'll make it Saturday, the twenty-fourth. Is that too soon to travel again?"

"Not at all."

"In fact, if you can get away on Friday, there's a concert that evening if you'd like to go."

"Wonderful. Are you going too?" He teased.

"Of course, I'm going! And, I just remembered something. It's a special performance; you'll have go black tie."

"Black tie? That's all? Should make for an interesting evening." He heard her laugh.

"There you go again. You know what I mean."

He decided not to push it. "Yes, Rebecca, I know what you mean. I'm pretty sure the date's okay. Hold on." He pulled up his calendar. He was free.

"The date's fine. I'll call once you've gotten back to Las Vegas, and, let you know the time of my arrival. By then, I should know where I'll be staying. Can we have dinner before?"

"Yes, but instead of going out, we'll have an early dinner at home. I love to cook and have been told I'm fairly good at it."

His mouth began to water. "I'm not surprised."

"Will you be bringing Elise? I've only the one extra ticket, but I'm a subscriber to the Philharmonic so it shouldn't be difficult to get another."

He paused. "Elise and I are no longer together."

"Oh. I'm so sorry, David. She was lovely."

"She still is. I'll fill you in when I get there. Give my best to Stan tonight."

"I'll do that. Until the twenty-fourth then. It will be good to see you."

"Likewise. Until the twenty-fourth."

Elated, he hung up and reached for his cocktail.

Well, what do you know? Elise might have been right, after all.

CHAPTER TWENTY-THREE

After Georges and Detective Hulot left Miranda, Georges asked Hulot to take up vigil near her hotel rather than near the gallery, "and do not hesitate to follow her—wherever she goes."

Hulot had done so. The next Monday, he phoned Georges to say that Miranda had checked out of her hotel and gone to Charles de Gaulle airport. It was from the airport that Hulot was calling.

"She's booked on an Air France flight to New York leaving at noon?" Georges asked with a sinking feeling in his gut. He knew for sure the reason she was going.

"*Oui,* Monsieur Lartigue, but I was unable to discover where she is staying once she gets there."

"Ah, well. Bravo, Hulot. *Merci, bien.*"

Georges went to the gallery but waited until noon before putting a call through to Doctor Weiss. It was six a.m. in the U.S. so he left a message with his service. Doctor Weiss returned his call within the hour.

"And when you left her, you say Miranda was extremely agitated?"

"Yes, and I fear I'm responsible. It's pretty much a fait accompli that she's going to New York to engage a lawyer. By proving she's very much alive, she hopes to invalidate the declaration of death that brought an end to our marriage."

"Does she know of an attorney?"

"I doubt it."

"It's going to take time and certainly won't be easy. Between lodging and attorney's fees, it could become expensive."

"I reminded her of that. But since she insists we're still husband and wife, she thinks I'll be obligated to pay her expenses."

"And it was a New York circuit court judge who signed the declaration?"

"Yes. I filed for it in 2003. The matter will have to go through the New York State Court of Appeals; any lawyer will want to know where she's been since. It will bring up her medical history and the fact that she was a patient in your hospital."

Doctor Weiss sighed audibly. "This has all the earmarks of becoming a crisis. But there's no way we can force her to return unless . . ."

"She's in a severe state of distress and poses a threat to herself or to others," Georges finished for him.

"Correct."

"Perhaps there's a way to avoid such a situation." Georges said. "Suppose I can arrange for someone to be there when Miranda's plane arrives and monitor her movements after that?"

He waited for Dr. Weiss to consider what he'd said before adding, "And perhaps you can arrange for medical backup in New York in case it's needed."

"Yes, I can certainly do that."

"I know a private investigator who might be able to help us find the right person to follow her," Georges offered, praying Brian was back from his honeymoon.

"Excellent. All right, Monsieur Lartigue. Give me an hour or so while I see what arrangements can be made with Payne Whitney, and I'll get back to you."

Despite the early hour, Georges phoned Brian at his office. He was in luck. "*Bienvenue, mon ami.* Welcome home. How's the married man?"

"Georges! I'm fine, thanks."

"And Carrie? The trip?"

"Both wonderful. And you? Despite the cheer, I have the distinct feeling something's troubling you."

Georges was only too glad to unburden himself.

"Ah," Brian said when Georges finished. "So the lady continues to plague you. At this point, I think you should consider discussing it with Larry. In fact, his advice is that you should get yourself a good attorney and take defensive action. Sue Miranda for desertion. I know there's the bit about a property settlement with divorce and someone needs to be appointed to act on her behalf should she die, but Larry says it seems to him the most definitive way of putting an end to the problem."

Georges listened but knew Miranda well enough to know divorce would not free him. She would continue to cause disruptions in his life whenever she had the opportunity. A divorce might even elicit a more violent response from her. Who could he appoint to act for her in the case of her death? He shuddered. "I'm doubtful a divorce would be any more effective than the ruling in place now."

"But she'd at least have the satisfaction of a monetary settlement."

"Ah, and therein lies the problem. Satisfied, you say? *Non.* Miranda has no knowledge of the word."

"Of course I'm not a lawyer, but if as you say the declaration remains in effect, there's no way you'd be expected to pick up her tab."

"I promise to think about it. In the meantime, could you find someone to check on her?"

"You mean tail her?"

"*Oui.* She's due to arrive in New York later today, around one p.m. your time."

"Unfortunately, I'm locked into another case, but there is someone here who'd be perfect, that is, if the substitution meets your approval."

"If the person meets yours, he'd certainly meet mine," Georges said.

"He's a she."

"*Comment*?"

"The person I have in mind is a woman, very capable, and, in this case, probably better. Having a female for a tail should be less obvious and arouse fewer suspicions."

"Bravo," Georges said.

"Her name is Odile Allard. She's attractive and definitely has the upscale sort of style that'll blend in."

"Will she be able to meet Miranda's plane?"

"You bet. Just give me the particulars."

Georges did and said he'd call back once he had the backup information from Doctor Weiss.

"When you call, ask for Odile. I'll have briefed her by then and will tell her to expect your call."

"*Merci, merci beaucoup*. I can't tell you how indebted I am."

"*De rien*, as you so often say," Brian answered. "And now, let me run so I can put your plan in motion."

Georges lowered the phone, placing it in its cradle. *Merde. Just as I made plans to meet Rebecca in London.* He picked up his iPhone and dialed her Las Vegas number.

* * *

Fortunately for Georges, Miranda's arrival in New York went off as planned: Odile Allard spotted Miranda at the airport and had maintained successful surveillance since. In addition, Doctor Weiss had lined up a physician at Payne Whitney whom Miranda could see in a crisis and whose specialty was dissociative disorders.

She'd checked in at the Milburn, a pleasant, comfortable, affordable accommodation located at 242 West 76th Street in Manhattan. As if to answer to Georges' silent query as to how she planned to pay for it, his bank statement arrived showing that his four thousand-dollar check had been cashed the day before Miranda left.

It was a relief to know she wasn't in Paris, but despite that, he remained anxious.

While George worried in Paris, Miranda struggled in New York.

Determined as ever, she refused to admit that finding a lawyer was difficult, time-consuming, and costly, all of which did nothing to dispel the resentment she harbored against Georges.

By the middle of the following week, she'd exhausted the resources of the Manhattan Yellow Pages, spent hours on a hotel computer, made dozens of phone calls and completed three of six planned visits to branches of Legal Aid.

Back in her hotel room, staring at the last two legal help sources on her list, her frustration with Georges peaked. *I wouldn't have made this fucking trip in the first place if it hadn't been for that bastard. The plane ride over was enough to finish me.*

Miranda had been on an aisle seat midway back in economy class. Next to her was a noisy, rambunctious seven-year-old boy who belonged to a very large woman occupying the seat nearest the window.

As if that wasn't bad enough, once the meal was served, the child had a temper tantrum and his entire entrée flipped off his tray table onto Miranda.

With tears of fury brimming in her eyes, she looked down where the remains of chicken dijon sat in her lap, its gravy soaking into her skirt.

Screaming obscenities, she unfastened her seat belt, and grasping both his and her entées, she pivoted and slammed them down onto the head of the child. Folding her table, she stood and watched as the food slid off her skirt onto the floor. Then, marching up the aisle randomly punching seat backs, she gesticulated wildly and screamed to the flight attendants that under no circumstances would she return to that "fucking seat."

This, of course, caused pandemonium As several attendants hurried toward the bawling child and hysterical mother in an attempt to restore some kind of order. Others tried to pacify Miranda by taking her to a bathroom and giving her a smock to wear while they attempted to clean her skirt. Afterwards, they took her to one of two available seats in business class. Once she was settled, another attendant retrieved her purse and carry-on luggage.

By the time they arrived in New York four hours later, Miranda had reasonably recovered, had her skirt back and a voucher from the airline to have it professionally cleaned. But an airline official met the plane and appearing solicitous, escorted her off the plane then stood by until she'd cleared customs.

CHAPTER TWENTY-FOUR

On Friday, the twenty-third, David was on a morning flight to Las Vegas. He'd spoken to Rebecca and knew she'd had a very nice time with Stan O'Neil, but it was a comfort to learn she was looking forward to his arrival.

He'd booked a room at the Las Vegas Hilton. His plan was to taxi there from the airport, then rent a car at the hotel. That way, he could get to Rebecca's without imposing on her to chauffeur him back and forth.

He looked at his watch. *We should be landing in another half hour.* He had to admit that the thought of seeing her again excited him. *Had she changed? Changed? In four weeks? How would she look? Good, of course, how else? How . . .*

Stop. This is crazy.

He picked up the *Time* magazine he'd been reading and leafed through it, looked again at his watch, and then out the window.

It interested him that she had subscription tickets to the Las Vegas symphony. A client had mentioned the opening concert when he was in Las Vegas on business a couple of years ago.

In New York, he and Elise had frequented Lincoln Center for a concert, the ballet, or even an opera, all of which he'd thoroughly enjoyed. Brian, however, remained the family connoisseur.

He'd brought Rebecca a present, a thank you for the invitation and the concert ticket. He'd purposefully walked through Tiffany's one day on his way to see a client. He hadn't been there fifteen minutes when he saw the earrings.

Set in gold in the shape of teardrops, the smoky topazes were surrounded at their base by small, yellow sapphires that fired sparks of light from all angles. The topaz reminded him of Rebecca's eyes. How could he resist? The announcement that they were about to land interrupted his reverie.

Forty-five minutes later, he walked off the plane and headed for the exit where he could get a cab, but something out of the corner of his eye caught his attention. Turning his head, he saw Rebecca—her hair swept up, and dressed in tan slacks and a dark brown turtleneck sweater—running toward him waving. *Damn! If that isn't a beautiful sight!*

"David!" she called drawing up short of colliding with him. "I thought the least I could do was be here to welcome you."

His grin was a mile wide. "What a great surprise! I feel very welcomed." He couldn't resist the urge to kiss her but for now chose her cheek.

"I know you said you wanted to rent a car at the hotel; I'll drive you there and wait while you check in. Afterwards, you can follow me home. Is that all right?"

He laughed. "You expect me to say, 'no?'"

"Now that I'm here, you'd better not." For a minute they stood looking at each other. "It's really great to see you, David." Then before he could think of a reply, she said, "Ready?"

"I'll never be more so."

He liked her car—a dark green, Mercedes E350 cabriolet convertible, top down, its insides covered in tan leather. When they pulled away from the parking lot at McCarran Airport, Rebecca noticed the black car that had followed her there was again on her tail, two cars back. But it kept going once she turned into the driveway of the Las Vegas Hilton.

They pulled up in front, but before David got out, he said, "C'mon, Rebecca. You might as well come with me and see what I've gotten myself into. We can ask the doorman to watch the car."

The room was on the tenth floor. Rebecca checked it out while David took a minute to leave a few things. After he collected his toilet case and suit-bag, they returned to the lobby where David rented a car.

"Do you have a cell phone with you?" Rebecca asked.

"I do."

She took a small pad from her purse and handed it to him. "Write down your number. Once we get beyond the strip, I'll call you and give you a guided tour."

"There's that much to see in the desert?"

"You're so bad," she said, giving him a poke.

Twenty minutes later, they were heading west toward the less populated area Rebecca referred to as "the desert." Within minutes, his cell phone rang.

"The road lined with palm trees that's coming up on your left is Addie's driveway.

"Adelaide's *driveway*?"

"You'll find Jim Broker did things in a big way. We're going over there tomorrow evening for dinner, if that's all right with you."

"Why would I mind? Besides, you now have me so intrigued, that I'd be disappointed if we didn't."

"I was concerned since it's the place where Brian had his accident. Of course, everything damaged by the fire has been restored."

He was now even more interested. "Not to worry, Rebecca. It's not a problem."

"I think Paul's coming this weekend, too."

"Really? I had dinner with him Monday. Funny he didn't mention it."

"I believe it was a spur of the moment thing. Once Addie knew you were coming, she decided to ask him. Well, here we are," she said, turning onto a side road that, once it forked, became a driveway that wound through landscaped grounds as it approached a handsome, Mediterranean-style building.

Rebecca stopped in front. David parked alongside her.

"Home, sweet home," she said, getting out of the car and coming over to him. "Are you hungry?"

He could think of several answers, but decided to keep to the point. "Yes, as a matter of fact." He opened the trunk and retrieved his things.

"Well, then," she said opening the front door, "come in and we'll scrounge up some lunch."

"Scrounge? I thought you said you were a good cook?"

"I'm saving *that* for dinner. Lunch is a scrounge."

He grinned. "It's your call, senhora."

He followed her inside, looked around, and stopped short. "For lack of a better word, 'wow.'"

The artwork on the walls of the foyer alone was amazing and included a large Picasso ceramic and a de Kooning abstract.

"I'll give you a tour later," Rebecca said, glancing over her shoulder as they walked through the dining room toward the kitchen. Seeing him carrying his suit bag and case, she came to an abrupt halt.

"Forgive me. I guess seeing you has me a bit flustered. I completely forgot you were carrying your things for the evening. Come, I'll take you upstairs so you can put them in one of the guestrooms."

They retraced their steps through the marble tiled foyer, up the wide, curved staircase to the first room down a long hall off the landing.

In the middle of the room to the left was a queen-size, four-poster bed with a matelassé coverlet, crocheted canopy and matching bed skirt. An antique wooden chest sat at the foot. Nomadic rugs lay scattered on the wide-board floor. Paintings and pictures of Portugal and the Aegean decorated the walls.

"You can hang your things in here," Rebecca said, opening a door to a walk-in closet, "and there's a bathroom in here," she gestured, opening another door and turning on the light. A multi-jet glass-enclosed shower filled one third of the room.

He chuckled. "Thanks. I think I can manage with this."

Rebecca crossed the room and opened a window while David left his case in the bathroom. Removing his tie and jacket, he put them on a hanger and hung them and his suit bag in the closet. Unbuttoning his collar and cuffs, he rolled the sleeves while walking over to peer out the picture window at the far end of the room. Below lay a midsize sculptured swimming pool surrounded by a flagstone patio on which attractive, dark green outdoor furniture was scattered. A manicured lawn bordered by landscaped trees and bushes lay beyond.

"Okay," he said at last, "I'm ready to scrounge."

Under the protection of an umbrella-covered table overlooking the pool, they lunched on chilled gazpacho and poached chicken sandwiches on peasant bread spread with a salsa-infused mayonnaise.

"Do you still swim?" Rebecca asked between bites.

"Does doggie paddle count?"

She choked on a laugh and, putting her half-finished sandwich on her plate, reached for her napkin. "David Neville, can't you ever be serious?"

He sobered and, raising a hand, reached over and lifted a stray strand of hair from her face. "The fact is, Rebecca, I'm not sure I dare."

Their eyes locked and she went completely still. Then, with one smooth motion, he lowered his hand and caressed her cheek.

Before he could withdraw, Rebecca took it and held it against her. "I'm sorry. I didn't mean to be . . ."

"Shhhh," he said, raising their joined hands and pressing his lips against the back of hers. "No apology necessary."

David's face lit up and he smiled, relieving the tension. "To answer your question, yes, I still swim, but haven't in awhile because I don't often get the chance. And you?"

Rebecca relaxed visibly, and he lowered their hands to the table. "Yes. I try to swim in the morning before breakfast, both here and in Portugal."

"Is it your favorite sport?"

"I don't know if I'd call it my favorite, but it's a convenient way to exercise. I used to run but no longer seem to get the time. So, I swim."

"Ever rollerblade?"

"No, but I've always thought it looked like fun."

"Tell you what," David said, "since you now owe me a visit, plan on coming to New York. We'll go to Central Park, and I'll show you how to rollerblade."

Her eyes lit up. "Sounds like fun. All right. It's a deal."

By mid-afternoon, after a tour of the house, they were relaxing with a glass of iced tea in the sun-filled solarium adjacent to the living room. Rebecca was curled up on a green wicker chaise that had the same flowered pillows as the rest of the furniture. David sat across from her on the wicker couch.

"Your home is a virtual museum, Rebecca. I'm impressed with how you've managed to mix contemporary abstracts with classic European paintings. You should invite Georges for a visit. He'd love it."

"Perhaps once the issue of my paintings is out of the way," . . . *and I've discovered who's responsible for killing Jeffrey* . . . "I can again look forward to being a hostess. Unfortunately, I can't think of planning anything until some provenance problems are solved."

"I didn't realize you were having problems."

"Yes, with the two paintings I took to Senhor Carlos' gallery in Lisbon."

"Before I forget again, how did you and Georges make out in London?"

"Georges had to postpone the trip." *I don't think it's up to me to tell David about Miranda.*

"Is he planning to reschedule?"

"Yes. I'm just not sure when."

"I tried calling him last week after I got back from the west coast. That's when Gabrielle told me he was in Berlin."

"That was just an overnight trip. He's since gone back."

"What made him suddenly decide to go?"

"He told me he began thinking about the records and photographs Rose Valland took of the looted art the ERR brought into the Jeu de Paume during the War. Many were works by the Expressionists that, we now know, were on their way to being destroyed, traded for the more desirable paintings of the European masters, or sold and sent out of the country. Thinking he might learn something about the Kirchner and the Kandinsky, he spent hours on the Internet pouring over Dutch, Belgian, French, and German museums' inventory lists, paying special attention to those museums that exhibited German Expressionist art. One such museum was Berlin's Kronprinzenpalais, Germany's first museum of contemporary art. Right after that, he decided to go."

"As I'm sure you know, Germany was the pioneer in the avant-garde long before Paris, London, and New York."

"Yes. It certainly was. I thought Georges said he'd be back yesterday, so when I didn't hear from him, I called Gabrielle. She hadn't heard from him either, but was under the impression that, if he discovered something, he'd stay a day or two longer. She said she was sure he'd call eventually."

"Is there reason to worry?"

"I don't know. I don't think so. Then again . . ." Rebecca thought about her recent report to Bruce Ross. In it, she introduced Georges, telling him of their travel plans. Ross knew about their having to cancel London, but at the time, she hadn't known about Berlin. Ross told her that by knowing their plans, he hoped to pick up a trail that could lead to those dealing in the counterfeiting and illegal sale of art.

"Perhaps I'll call Gabrielle again before dinner.

"Georges had hoped to reschedule our London visit for next week, but Addie and I must go to California. We need to visit our parents, and she has to attend her corporation's annual board meeting. Since time is precious, I told him to make the arrangements and go without me. He has someone in mind who can do the biding for us so it's not imperative that I be there."

"Does Addie's corporation have a name?"

"Carting Plus. Good one for a company involved in refuse removal, wouldn't you say?"

He nodded. "Seems pretty specific to me. Is Carting Plus the one you and she co-owned?"

"Yes. I stepped down just before Jim was killed."

"You were a co-owner of Carting Plus, an art consultant for Broker Industries, and commuting between two houses." He shook his head, laughing, "No wonder you retired."

Rebecca sighed and put her head back against the pillows. "I thought that by doing that, I'd have more time to organize my life and stay put for a while." She looked at him. "But that doesn't seem to be happening, does it?"

Though she was smiling, there was a wistful tone to her voice that made David want to pull her into his arms. Instead, he stood and stretched. "You up for a swim?"

Staring at him, she slowly got up off the chaise. "You mean to tell me that after all that doggie paddle stuff, you actually brought a *swim suit*? Why you . . ." And, erupting in laughter, she balled her fists and lunged at him.

The move took him by surprise but he recouped enough to catch her arms, pinned them behind her, and pulled her against him. He couldn't have planned it better. "Briefs," he said.

She stopped wriggling but the pins in her hair had started to come lose. "*What*?"

"Briefs. I brought swim *briefs,* not a *suit.*"

She resumed wriggling. "Of all the . . ."

He bent and planted a kiss on her half-open mouth, catching her mid-sentence. For a moment, he became aware of nothing but the position of their bodies.

A minute later, he lifted his head and looked into two very dreamy, hazel eyes. *Does she feel it too—that slow, increased heat of desire?*

He noticed her eyes begin to focus and he grinned. "You haven't answered my question," he said, his voice husky. "Are you up for a swim?"

Eyes locked with his, her voice barely above a whisper, Rebecca said, "David Neville, I told you once before, you're incorrigible."

In the next instant, she wriggled away from him, sprinted across the living room toward the stairs, and shouted, "The last one in doesn't get a prize!"

Well, I'll be damned. The little vixen.

Delighted by the challenge, he tore after her, taking the steps two at a time.

CHAPTER TWENTY-FIVE

At five-thirty that evening, David, in dress clothes, descended the stairs. Just as he reached the first floor, Rebecca called out, "Put some music on will you please, David? The audio system is in the tall Spanish Oak cabinet in the living room on the right."

"You got it," he answered.

He thought the room was the most attractive one in the house, reflecting Rebecca's talent with color and texture. He especially liked the large, open fireplace opposite the entrance that now had a pleasant fire going. Flanking it, were two multi-cushioned couches covered in floral orange fabric that matched the drapes on either side of the French windows. A wide bench of the same dark wood as the stereo cabinet, served as a coffee table. Chairs in coordinating fabrics dotted the room, several bracketing tables. An off-white Berber rug covered the cream-colored Mediterranean tile floor and, as in the rest of the house, paintings hung in here—one, a large Picasso in shades of off-white, beige and black. Indirect lighting gave the room its soft glow. Table lamps supplied light near the couches and chairs.

Opening the stereo cabinet, David glanced toward the end of the room where, under a trio of leaded glass windows, was a large, rectangular Spanish Oak table. Photos in silver frames were grouped at one end, while a decorative, silk-embroidered shawl, spread across the opposite corner, provided a splash of color. He smiled. *Nice touch.* Scanning the CDs, he chose two by Frank Sinatra.

"I'll be down in a minute," Rebecca said. "Go fix yourself a drink. The bar is in the library."

"Can I get something for you?" David asked, coming into the foyer.

"There's white wine in the cooler at the base of the bar. If you open a bottle, I'll have a glass of that."

"One white wine it is."

He entered the dining room and from there walked into the library. The built-in bar, with indirect lighting and mirrors reflecting the crystal barware on the shelves, was expertly fitted in between the book cases on the right-hand wall. Various selections of alcohol lined the perimeter of the base on either side of a small central sink.

He pulled a bottle of Kendall Jackson chardonnay from the cooler beneath. He peeled away the seal, removed the cork, and poured a glass for Rebecca. Noticing the bottles of single malt scotch, he opted for a snifter of Laphroaig. Although scotch was not his usual preference, he couldn't resist.

Hearing Rebecca's footsteps, he collected their drinks and headed toward the sound, entering the foyer as she descended the last of the stairs. *What a vision.*

Her hair was pulled up into a soft double twist, and she was wearing a "shimmer-gold" ruffled poncho over a long-sleeved black pants ensemble. Gold, high-heeled sandals and yellow diamond earrings—a Christmas gift from Jeffrey—completed the outfit.

He said the first thing that entered his mind, "You're beautiful."

She beamed, and he recanted, "No, I have that wrong. You're exquisite."

She stared at him open mouthed, but in the next minute, smiled and relieved him of her drink. "Thank you, David." Her eyes sparkled. "And you sir, look very handsome."

He bowed and offered his arm. "Shall we retire to the parlor?"

"But of course," she answered, hooking her arm through his.

Rebecca chose a seat on one of the couches, set her glass on the coffee table, and patted the cushion next to her.

David pulled her gift from his pocket as he sat down.

"Rebecca," he said, marveling at his level of nervousness.

She relaxed against the cushions, her face lit up in a smile. "Yes, David?"

He withdrew the box from Tiffany. "I have a little something for you . . . a small thank you for inviting me this weekend and taking me to the concert."

She looked at him, at the box, and back to him. "Oh, David. There was no need."

He placed the box in her lap. "I saw these and couldn't resist. I hope you like them."

For a minute, she just sat there. At last she untied the ribbon, removed the small velvet box from within, opened it and gasped.

"Oh, David. They're gorgeous!" And in a hushed tone added, "Just gorgeous." When she looked up, her eyes were moist. "I don't know what to say."

"Then you like them?"

She shook her head. "Like them? I," and leaning forward, she kissed him on the lips.

He sat on his hands.

She removed her earrings. "Would you like to put them on for me?"

He stared at the box. "But they're for pierced ears."

She laughed. "So were those I was wearing. Look," she said, leaning forward so he could see her ear, "just poke the post through that tiny hole in my earlobe. Then push on the back."

Finally, "Okay. If you say so."

Removing one of the earrings from the box, he followed her instructions. Encouraged by his success, he did the same with the second. They looked spectacular.

"Come," she said, taking his hand and pulling him along. "Let's go into the library. There's a powder room in there with a mirror."

Opening the door of the small bathroom, she switched on the light. Immediately, the sapphires flashed their fire.

"And the verdict is?" David asked.

She turned and threw her arms around him.

He couldn't have been more delighted. The display of emotion was better than any words. He encircled her in his arms. "I'm happy you like them."

But once her scent began to envelop him, he eased back, not wishing to further test his resolve by remaining the way they were, packed into the small space. "Shall we go back to our drinks?"

"Good idea," Rebecca said, waiting for him to step out of the room so she could follow. "Thank you, again, David. The earrings are really beautiful."

They ate dinner by candlelight in the dining room, and David joined Rebecca in a glass of sauvignon blanc. Using Rebecca's recipes, her housekeeper, Clarissa, prepared and served sherried consommé, veal scallops sautéed with tarragon, broccoli soufflé, and mixed green salad. Miniature cannoli with chocolate sauce and coffee was the dessert.

They spoke of many things. David told Rebecca about Elise, eliminating her comments about the reason for the breakup. Before it seemed possible, it was time to leave for the concert.

It turned out to be an all Tchaikovsky program featuring a guest violinist who, for the final selection, played the renowned violin concerto that brought the audience to its feet. By the time they arrived home, it was after eleven.

"Would you like a nightcap?" Rebecca asked, once they were in the house.

"Not alone. Will you join me?"

"All right. I'll have a very small brandy."

He poured their drinks and returned to the living room. Rebecca paused by the stereo and replayed the Sinatra CDs.

They sat together on the couch for a while, sipping brandy and listening to the music.

"You could stay here, you know," Rebecca offered, looking at him with her head tilted back against the cushions.

"What, and miss another wonderful stay at the Las Vegas Hilton?"

"I thought of mentioning it when I invited you, but felt it might sound presumptuous."

He cocked an eyebrow. "Presumptuous? How?"

"You know, widow entices good-looking, unmarried male, type of thing."

He grinned, shifted position, and slid one arm across the couch in back of her. "Yes? Go on."

She poked his side. "I doubt I need to. But considering you rented the car and reserved a hotel room, it would be a waste not to use them."

"I've wasted more on less."

"I mean it, David. You're more than welcome to stay."

It was certainly tempting, but he decided to adhere to the plan. "Next time, for sure, that is, if you'll invite me again so there'll be a next time."

Rebecca took a sip of brandy. "You know, once the paintings are sold, I'd like to host a celebration. Since you, Georges, Sally, Paul, and Addie have been in on it from the beginning, what would you say to my inviting everyone here? Georges could see the rest of my collection, Addie and I'll cook up something special, and we'll eat, drink champagne and celebrate. Who knows? I might even hire a few musicians and float gardenias in the pool. Of course, it could be Easter before anything like that happens."

He lowered his hand and gently massaged her neck. "How about you, Addie, and Paul coming to New York, I'll invite Georges, Sally, maybe even Brian and Carrie, and I'll host the celebration for you there?"

"That's very nice of you, David, but here, no one would have to stay in a hotel. Between Addie's house and mine, there'll be plenty of room. I may even let you cook—with my help, of course." Eyeing him, she sipped her brandy.

"Oh, ho! So you doubt my ability in the kitchen, do you? Okay then, what say we make a deal?"

"Such as?"

"If everyone agrees to have the party here, you must come to New York for a visit first so I can prove I can cook."

Her eyes twinkled. "Come for a visit?"

He nodded. "Yes."

"A visit to New York, or to you?"

He pulled his arm off the back of the couch and took her hand. "What do you think?"

She tried to hide a smile. "I can go to New York anytime, David."

He tugged her hand. "To visit *me*, Rebecca, *me.*"

Feigning surprise, she said, "Oh? And I'd be staying?"

He played along. "Again, with me, in my apartment. You know, the one with the satin duvet on the *large* bed in the *silver* bedroom?"

She laughed out loud. "Can I let you know? In the meantime, I'll mention it to Addie when we go over there tomorrow." She looked at him. "It's all a bit premature, after all. To date, not one painting has been sold."

"Okay. Then for the moment, we'll just think about it." He looked at his watch and finished his brandy. "Time to call it a night."

On their way out of the living room, Rebecca glanced at him and asked, "Now, you're sure you wouldn't like to stay?"

He stopped and reached for her, drawing her close and placing a kiss on the top of her nose. "Of course, I would. But I think we both know that in spite of everything, it's better that I leave."

She shook her head and tried to pull away. "I didn't mean . . ."

"I know you didn't, Rebecca, but let's face it. It's not as if we're complete strangers, and, at the moment, it's better for me this way." He lifted her chin and brushed his lips over hers. "Trust me."

After a minute, she nodded. "It just seemed it would be easier for you because of the hour. Although, you're right." She touched her ears. "And thank you again for my beautiful gift."

He smiled. "You're most welcome." He released her and walked toward the stairs. "I'll run up and get my things. Be right back."

When he returned, she followed him out to the car and waited while he threw his clothes in the back. With hands on her shoulders, he drew her toward him. "And thank *you* for a memorable day and evening."

"Then you enjoyed the concert?"

Surprised by the question, he replied, "Yes, very much. Why do you ask?"

"It's been my experience that those who live in cities, like New York or Boston, consider symphony orchestras in smaller cities to be of lesser quality."

He slipped his arms around her and gave her a hug. "Well, I'm not one of those individuals. What time tomorrow?"

"How's ten? I'll fix us brunch."

"You're on." He gave her a quick kiss and, entering the car, he closed the door and rolled down the window. "Sleep well," he said. After firing up the engine, he slowly pulled away.

The car that had followed them earlier was nowhere to be seen.

CHAPTER TWENTY-SIX

"Did you know the Bellagio has a fine arts gallery?" Rebecca asked, the following morning over brunch.

"I did, yes."

She took a sip of coffee. "I wasn't sure what you might want to do today. Is there anything you'd particularly like to see? Of course, we could stay here, lounge around the pool, sleep, or read, if that appeals to you. We aren't due at Addie's until five."

"Actually, I thought I'd like to visit the fine arts museum over on West Sahara Avenue, if that's agreeable."

She selected a piece of French toast, sprinkled it with powdered sugar and helped herself to the fig-peach syrup. "Indeed it is. The newer building is spectacular, and the exhibits are always excellent. At the moment, I think they're featuring works by a local sculptor. Did you know the museum is affiliated with the Smithsonian?"

He reached for the coffeepot and topped off their cups. "Really? No, I didn't."

"It has been for several years. We can leave after we finish here. If we're hungry later, we can grab a bite while we're out."

"Sounds good to me."

They were back by two-thirty and opted for a swim. Drinking iced tea and relaxing on poolside chaises afterwards, David asked, "Do you have a preference between your home in Portugal and this one?"

"I suppose I'm more accustomed to being here. It is, after all, the house Jeffrey and I moved into once we were married and where we spent most of our time. But alone, I tend to rattle around in this big a house. Then recently . . ."

David looked over. "Yes?"

That slipped out. I hadn't planned to mention it. Too late now. "The last few weeks I've been receiving phone calls that end in hang-ups whenever Clarissa or I answer." *At least Ross and Deevers know.* Deevers had given her a hand-held panic button that, when pressed, sent a signal to both his personal receiver and a central station in Las Vegas.

"Could be a coincidence," David said. "If they continue, keep a record of the date and time each call comes in."

"Good idea. I'll tell Clarissa to do the same. Even though we screen calls, to have it ring so frequently is terribly annoying. We now keep it on mute and are only aware of the answering machine picking up. There's never a number listed, just, 'Unknown caller,' or, 'Unavailable.'"

"What's the climate like here?" David asked several minutes later.

"It gets unbearably hot in the summer, but the other months are nice. The best are those in the spring and fall. Jeffrey and I bought the villa in Portugal as a vacation house. Over the past few years, however, I haven't been able to get there as often as I'd like."

"You have incredible taste, Rebecca. Both homes are beautiful, each distinct from the other. You just seem more relaxed and at home there."

She laughed. "How insightful you are, Mr. Neville."

"Am I right?"

"Perhaps. What was extremely worrisome here, was when the President approved using Yucca Mountain as the dumpsite for radioactive nuclear wastes. By overriding the state's veto, he gave the go-ahead for a construction and operating license for the dump. Everyone was up in arms because the mountain has cracks in it from the atomic blasts of the 1940s. In addition, the area's earthquake susceptible. The waste could easily leak into the groundwater here and down stream. Getting the waste here, poses another problem for it would mean shipping it through a number of states. Thank heaven the U.S. Court of Appeals threw out the EPA's flawed radiation release regulations! The question is, for how long?"

David finished his iced tea. "Did the court's decision have any effect on the rate of development in the area?"

"Yes. It increased it significantly. I'm keeping my fingers crossed that it won't affect me this far out, at least not for a while. I mean, where would I go and what would I do with all the art?" She shook her head. "Thinking about it only bedevils me. So, I continue commuting between the two houses and try not to worry about it."

"Sorry. I didn't mean to open Pandora's box."

She reached out and put her hand on his arm. "You didn't, David. It's just that since Jeffrey's death, I often find myself in limbo."

"When did he die?"

"Three years ago."

"Which is really not that long ago." He put a hand over hers and gave it a squeeze. "Cut yourself some slack, Rebecca. As they say, 'go with the flow.' If it isn't pertinent, don't dwell on it. When the time comes to decide, you'll know what to do."

She sent him a smile and rotated her hand to better grasp his. "Thanks. I appreciate the vote of confidence."

They sat holding hands and gazing at each other for several minutes until the electricity between them escalated, and they released each other simultaneously.

Heart beating wildly, Rebecca tried easing the tension. "Have you always looked at things so logically?"

He choked out a laugh. "It's a cover."

"What?"

"A cover. You know, so that no one can guess what's really going on inside. Then, too, isn't it always easier to look at another person's problems more objectively?"

"See? There you go again. You are logical. Insightful too."

"I think you're giving me more credit than I'm due. But," he grinned, "thanks."

It was so pleasant sitting there that Rebecca was almost sorry they were going to Addie's. She looked at David. "Do you have your watch?"

He reached for a small leather case and withdrew it. "It's ten to four."

She got up and started to remove her sunglasses. "I guess I'd better go shower and get ready."

He stood. "Not a bad idea." But when Rebecca glanced at him, he cocked an eyebrow and added, "Yes? Something on your mind?"

She shook her head, wrinkling her forehead. "Why? No—only a shower. Was there something on yours?"

With a whoop, he made a lunge for her and scooped her up in his arms. With her kicking and wriggling and trying to hold onto her sunglasses, he carried her toward the outdoor shower.

"Where are you going?"

"Why I thought you said you wanted a shower," he answered, shifting his grip to open the shower door. Setting her down, he turned on the water.

"It's COLD," she howled.

"Oh. Sorry." He adjusted the temperature. Then, reaching for the soap, he began rubbing it over her arms and shoulders. Sputtering, she tried pushing him away so she could get out from under the downpour.

"Now I'll have to wash my hair," she wailed.

"Be my guest," he said, offering her the soap. He spotted the shampoo. "Or is this, perhaps, what you had in mind?"

Seeing him standing there with his wet hair plastered over his forehead, made her laugh. She handed him her dripping sunglasses. She took the shampoo from him, unclipped her hair and stood under the water. When it was thoroughly soaked, she added shampoo and handed the bottle back to him. She worked it into a rich lather, piled it onto the top of her head, reached around her neck and began untying the straps to her bikini top."

"What are you doing?" David asked, obviously on full alert.

She looked at him innocently. Completing my shower."

"Rebecca!"

"Yes?" She undid the back.

"I'm outta here," he announced, pushing against the door and all but leaping onto the patio. He was just closing the door as the top came off in her hands.

"Quitter," she shouted. "But if you don't want me walking around naked, I suggest you hand me a towel from one of the chaises."

Silence.

"David?" She removed the rest of her bathing suit, rinsing it and her hair thoroughly. "David?" Still no answer.

She turned off the water, rung out her hair, then her suit. There was only one thing to do. "Ready or not . . ."

She opened the door . . . and laughed.

There he was with a napkin tied over his eyes, arms spread wide holding a beach towel. "I felt it wouldn't be right to abandon you."

She walked over to him, turning around and letting him wrap the towel around her. Then, for a minute . . . just a minute . . . he held her against him.

"Thank you, David," she said as he released her. "Now. What about you? Are you still planning to shower?"

"Just waiting for you to finish," he said, removing the substitute blindfold. Grabbing the other towel from the chaise, he walked into the shower. After hanging the towel on a hook, he turned on the water and began tugging off his briefs.

"David!" Rebecca shouted.

"Can't hear you," he said, water pouring over his head.

"Close the door," she yelled, laughing.

"What?" he shouted, removing the last of his clothing as the door banged shut. "Thank you," he hollered, and started singing the Rolling Stones number, "Satisfaction."

She let out an agonized cry.

"How come you didn't sing in the shower?" he yelled.

"Because I can't carry a tune. That's why," she shouted back.

"Liar. You told me that as a child you were very musical and imagined yourself a famous dancer." He resumed singing.

"Dancing has nothing to do with being able to sing."

"I didn't say anything about being *able* to sing, I only asked why you *didn't* sing."

"All right. I'll hum something for you later."

"Can I make requests?"

"I'm leaving now," she shouted between bouts of giggles.

As she walked away, she was engulfed with nostalgia, remembering another time, another place, when a young, handsome, blonde, male—his legs coated with black sand—followed her up a narrow stairway to her hotel room where she let him use the shower.

CHAPTER TWENTY-SEVEN

At four forty five that same afternoon, Rebecca turned off the main road onto the palm-lined driveway of the Broker estate, noticing that the black sedan following her did not. *Whoever it is obviously knows about the Broker security system.*

Once past the guardhouse and through the gate, she nosed the car in the direction of a garden of leafy shrubs and bushes. Circling it, she pulled up in front of a set of wide marble steps that led to the canopied porch of a modern, multi-winged mansion.

She glanced at David and killed the motor. "No need to comment. Your expression says it all."

He looked at her and grinned. "Is 'holy cow' acceptable?"

She laughed. "Yes."

"Addie lives here by herself?"

"She does now. At first I thought being alone in so much space might bother her, but since we returned from Portugal, there's been so much to do both here and at Broker Industries that she hasn't had time to think about it.

"After Jim's death, and when it became clear he'd been blackmailing John Norman and his partner Dan Jenkins, the same insurance company that had approved increasing Jim's life insurance only two weeks before, obtained a warrant to examine the private film collection he kept under lock and key here at the house. Not only were there DVDs further compromising John and Dan, there were fifty or more that Jim could have used to blackmail the many others he'd used as subjects. Though the fire destroyed about a quarter of them, enough films remained to suggest what he'd had in mind. Added to that, evidence of multiple construction contract violations and irregularities were found in the company's records."

"You mean the SOB shorted and downgraded building materials and benefited from the profit?"

"No. According to Adelaide, it had more to do with bid rigging, inflated contingency funds, and paybacks. Once they realized they'd been compromised, John and Dan feared the consequences of reporting it." Her thoughts switched to her conversation with Carrie. "Instead of requesting an audit, they never said a word to anyone. Unfortunately, that, coupled with charges of 'conflict of interest' leveled against them for giving legal counsel to Jim, was their undoing—especially John's. Within the next two months, he committed suicide."

David did a double take. "Carrie's former husband, John Norman, committed *suicide*? Jesus. I had no idea. Some guy, your former brother-in-law."

After a moment's silence he asked, "In Paris you told me Jeffrey was a project manager for Broker Industries."

That was his real job. "Yes, that's right."

"Did he ever say what he thought about Jim?"

"No. Jeffrey never brought work home." *It's no wonder I never knew anything about Interpol.* "But I wasn't surprised to learn about the films. I never trusted Jim to begin with."

"Yet, Addie married him."

"Yes."

"Do you think she ever suspected?"

"I'm not sure I'd know. Addie has a wonderful way of compartmentalizing things. She and Jim always appeared happy together. But then again, he was always on his best behavior around her. He was also very good to her. In a way, they led separate lives. Being the co-owner of a company in San Francisco, Adelaide was often away in California. Jim's business often took him there, too, so they eventually bought an apartment in the city."

David reached for her hand. "I'm sorry for your loss, Rebecca, and didn't mean to open old wounds."

"Thank you, David. It's only natural for you to ask."

To shake the gloom and return to the present, she threw him a smile and said, "Getting back to Addie, I was relieved to learn she'd lured two of her trusted attorneys away from Carting Plus to help her sort out things here and at B.I. They're also reviewing Jim's will that includes substantial property and monetary assets. Put all together, it's an enormous job. At least now, along with Tom Hutchins, the excellent counselor Bill Height recommended, she has a qualified team of experts working on her behalf."

"Seems she'd have to."

"I don't think she and Paul have anything going," Rebecca continued, "but it's certainly nice to have him as a friend."

She leaned over and kissed David's cheek. "I can't thank you enough for inviting us to come to Paris, David. It did her a world of good."

He released her hand and slid his arm across the back of the seat. "And her sister? What did it do for her?"

Obviously flustered, Rebecca remained silent, gazing into his eyes.

Just then, the front door opened and Adelaide and Paul burst forth.

Immediately, Rebecca straightened. But one look at her sister told her the heat she felt in her cheeks was visible.

"Come in, come in," Adelaide said, hurrying toward them, eyes dancing. Paul followed, grinning from ear to ear.

Rebecca and David left the car and jogged up the steps.

After several hugs and handshakes, they followed Addie and Paul into the expansive terrazzo-floored foyer. A large crystal chandelier hung from the center of the ceiling, dominating the room.

"It's still warm enough to have drinks on the terrace," Adelaide said, leading them further into the house. "But we'll have dinner inside. Once the sun sets, it becomes quite cool."

They walked through a large, richly carpeted living room with upholstered chairs and couches, through an open doorway fitted with shuttered doors, and onto a spacious flagstone terrace.

Rebecca and David chose seats on a white wrought-iron love seat with green and white striped cushions. Paul and Adelaide chose the matching couch opposite. Architectural lamps diffused light on glass-topped tables. Music was playing in the background and floral fragrances from surrounding bushes floated about in the light breeze.

A maid came to take drink orders. Another arrived pushing a wheeled cart with plates and several trays of canapés.

"So," Adelaide said, sitting back and rubbing her hands together. "What have you two been up to?"

David and Rebecca shared a conspiratorial look. "You mean in addition to the hours we've spent alone behind closed doors?" David asked.

Adelaide's eyes traveled from David's to Rebecca's, to Paul's. She grinned. "Well, hooray for you. But, yeah, what else?"

"Were we supposed to be doing something else?" David asked.

Rebecca poked him in the ribs. "David!"

"Actually," he continued, winking at her, "we've really had a fine time. The afternoon of my arrival, Rebecca took me on a tour of the Lawler art collection. Then, after a delicious dinner of: sherried consume, veal scallops sautéed with tarragon, broccoli soufflé, and mixed green salad—all of which she'd had prepared in advance—we went to a benefit concert given by your symphony orchestra."

"Following brunch this morning," Rebecca said, "we spent time at the art museum. After coming home, we swam and relaxed around the pool until it was time to come here. And you, Addie? What have you and Paul been doing?"

Their drinks arrived and they paused for a mutual toast.

"What have Addie and I been doing?" Paul repeated, setting his drink down on the coffee table. "On Friday, Addie prepared an exceptional dinner of medallions of venison with port wine gravy in my honor. Afterwards, we sat in front of a fire and talked until two in the morning."

"I take it you're staying here, Paul?" Rebecca asked, avoiding her sister's glare.

A slow flush crept up beyond his collar. "Yes, Addie was generous enough to put me up, but I'll be returning to New York tomorrow."

"Besides, Becca," Adelaide said, eyes narrowed, "we *both* know this place is big enough to sleep ten."

"Which reminds me," Rebecca said, quickly changing the subject. "I've been thinking."

Adelaide rolled her eyes. "That's the first sign of trouble."

"As I was about to say," Rebecca continued, trying to hide a smile, "earlier I was telling David how much fun it would be if I were to throw a party once the paintings have been sold or at least are scheduled to be sold. If I had it here in Las Vegas, between this house and mine, no one would have to stay in a hotel."

"Fair enough," Adelaide said.

"And," David said. "I suggested that instead, everyone should come to New York and I'll host the party." He put a hand over Rebecca's. "Since we'd be celebrating your success, Rebecca, we should be the ones giving the party for you."

"Either arrangement sounds fine," Adelaide said. "As usual, it would depend on when. You'll probably be back from the west coast after a week or so, Becca, but my return will depend on what Carting Plus has in store for me. I guess I'll find out at the annual board meeting. Tallying up the past year's activities will be number one on the agenda." To the subsequent silence, she added, "Before matters erupted at Broker Industries, labor problems, instigated by the Mob, developed at Carting Plus. In the end, the governor had to summon the National Guard."

"I remember reading about that," David said. "At the time, I was in San Francisco on business."

"And if I remember correctly," Paul said, "at the start of it, Bill Height sent Brian out to investigate."

"Small world," Adelaide said. "Getting back to celebrations for a minute, though it might seem premature, has anyone given any thought about Thanksgiving? I know it's traditionally considered a family day, but who says we can't include family? Paul? I'll start with you. Do you have plans?"

"None at the moment. My family lives in San Francisco, and since my moving to New York, we've rarely celebrated that particular holiday together. I do go out for Christmas, however."

"David?"

He shook his head. "No. No plans at the moment."

"Becca?"

"It sounds wonderful, although I doubt any of the paintings will be sold by then."

"I know," Adelaide interrupted. "But let's say you and Georges have at least an auction scheduled for them."

"In that case, combining that with Thanksgiving would be great."

"If you're planning to include Georges, don't you think we should check with him before making any definite decisions?" David asked.

"Absolutely," Rebecca agreed. "In fact, I just remembered that I forgot to call Gabrielle yesterday to see if she's heard from him." She looked at her watch. "I'll try her now." She hesitated, "It's a bit late in Paris."

"Try anyway," Adelaide said. "Do you have her cell number?"

"I do. It's here in my bag." Rebecca dug it out. "I'll use the phone in the library."

She was back in twenty minutes.

"I presume you reached her?" David asked.

Rebecca reclaimed her place next to him on the love seat. "Yes. She said Georges arrived back in Berlin two days ago and met with the director of the Neue Nationalgalerie. Then, due to the recent release of declassified documents belonging to the ERR, he stayed in the hope of examining them. He was supposed to call this afternoon, but so far, hasn't. She said it might be that he's intending to call me instead. What's interesting is that he took his driver Jacques Duprée with him."

David threw her a look. "You mean he drove Georges all the way to Berlin?"

Rebecca shook her head. "No. Georges reserved a car, and he and Jacques flew to Berlin. Georges told her that the reason was that it would save him time moving from place to place. The Neue Nationalgalerie is not on Museum Island with the other museums, but on Potsdamer Platz. However, Gabrielle feels the real reason is that someone has begun following him. On the day before he left, he received a threat telling him to drop his current investigation. Since then, when he's in Paris, he posts Hulot at the gallery, a guard near his apartment, another guard near Sally's, and takes Jacques with him when he's out and about. Since he was traveling outside the country, he took Jacques who, according to Gabrielle, was a body guard for various government officials before moving to France from the U.K. six years ago."

Adelaide looked up. "You mean like 007 he was part of MI6?"

"And people say I have an imagination!" Rebecca said with a laugh. "I really have no idea, Addie. I would guess so. What I find disturbing, though, is that now, like me, Georges is being followed. To top it off, he's also received a threat!"

David spun a look at her. "What's this about 'like me'? You're being followed? Since when?"

"Since just before Addie and I went to Paris for Brian's wedding. Someone in a large, black car has been following me, similar to the way it did after Jeffrey's death. Unknown to me at the time, the CIA got involved and it stopped. Then recently, it started again."

David took her hand. "Rebecca, I think there are some things you need to tell me."

She glanced at Addie who avoided her gaze and looked at Paul.

"I haven't brought it up, David, because there hasn't been time to explain, and I didn't want to spoil our visit together." She paused. "After Jeffrey was killed . . ." she went on to tell him about how the CIA had helped put an end to her harassment. "Then when Addie, Sally and I returned from Portugal . . ." and she told him about Bruce Ross, Jack Deevers, and her suspicions about Jeffrey's death.

David stared at her. "All this is *in addition* to the calls?"

She looked at him and nodded.

Fortunately, at that point, dinner was announced.

CHAPTER TWENTY-EIGHT

The meal was served in the dining room adjacent to the library where the fire had caused considerable damage and Brian had been burned. No one alluded to it, but Rebecca saw that David took notice. Fortunately, everything had been restored and the odor of smoke had completely dissipated. After dinner, they adjourned to the living room for dessert and coffee.

Within the hour, Georges telephoned.

"It's been confirmed," he told Rebecca over their transatlantic connection. "Both the Kirchner *and* the Kandinsky were hanging in a gallery of the Kronprinzenpalais at the time the Nazis closed it in 1936 and fired the director, Ludwig Justi. Amazingly, those two paintings, along with a group of others from that particular gallery, were subsequently overlooked by the Nazis during the *Entartete Kunst* purge in early 1937."

"And you know for a fact that before the war they were owned by the museum?"

"Only one, the Kirchner. The Kandinsky was on loan from a local dealer who was a friend of Justi's. At some point, this same group of paintings was taken to the Reichsbank on Werderscher Markt and remained there for an undetermined period of time. Unlike the rest that had been evacuated to one of the salt mines for storage, they accompanied a group of Modern and Contemporary paintings to the Jeu de Paume, presumably to be used by Goering and Bruno Lohse for bartering or exchange."

I can't believe it. "How on earth did you uncover all this?"

"It started with a hunch involving the Kirchner. As it was a very early work, it seemed too unusual for it not to have belonged to a museum. Next, Jacques helped me review what lists we could find of the art the ERR removed from museums. From there, we hit gold. Thanks to the

Claims Conference, in collaboration with the U.S Holocaust Museum in Washington, we were able to examine not only the records of Rose Valland, but also the recently released database of art objects processed through the Jeu de Paume between late 1940 to the summer of 1944. That's where we found the Kirchner. Later, we also discovered the Kandinsky. After that, the trail ran cold. From that point on, we have nothing until your husband's grandfather purchased them."

"Illegally, of course."

"Oui.

"How do you think they got to Madrid?"

"Smuggled, one presumes. Probably through one of the Vatican Ratlines along with gold and other valuable loot taken from victims of the War. As you know, the Ratlines were initially established for humanitarian reasons to help refugees shuttle safely from place to place. As time went on, however, it also benefited some of the most notorious Nazi war criminals. Nazis left Europe for destinations throughout the globe. Thousands went to America. But a number, known for the most heinous crimes, went to South America. The Vatican hoped that, should the Soviet Union decide to initiate World War III, the Nazis would help fight against them. Adolf Eichman, Joseph Mengale and Klaus Barbi were three who benefited from the Ratlines. Barbi went to Bolivia, Mengale and Eichman went to Argentina. Your paintings, however, went to Madrid, probably packed in a crate with others. One of the main Ratlines ran through Madrid. Turns out, it was the hub of smuggling activity, especially for art and refugees.

"Unfortunately, the cessation of hostilities did not herald the end to trafficking in stolen art. In many cases, it increased. Those involved were taking advantage of the post-war chaos to get as much business completed as possible. Only recently have I been able to obtain lists of once reputable international dealers who took advantage of the situation. Interestingly, one is Gustav Mendes, the person in Madrid from whom your husband's grandfather bought these two pieces. Unfortunately, time has not allowed me to investigate the Mendes Galleria. It's my guess that Mendes sold him even more works."

Rebecca's thoughts were in a whirl. *Since Deitrich Radtke not only worked there but also signed the sales slips, he had to have been party to this kind of activity from the beginning. Once Jeffrey called and mentioned there was a problem with a provenance, Radtke had to have recognized that Jeffrey's knowledge could pose a problem. So he lured Jeffrey . . .* She gasped, "Oh, God!"

David glanced at her. The color was gone from her face, and she was holding the phone, trembling. He gave her hand a tug. "Rebecca? What's up? Are you okay?" When she didn't reply, he reached over and gently took the receiver from her.

"Georges? Yeah, she's still here, but it appears your news has come as a shock."

"*Merde*. Probably because what I told her all but confirms that her husband was murdered. Tell her I'll call again tomorrow, but earlier, say around noon your time. I'll be staying in Berlin another day to make sure I have everything I need. Tell her that as soon as she can, she *must* notify Bruce Ross at Interpol and her CIA contact in Las Vegas and tell them about the Mendes Galleria. If she's up to it, tell her to do so as soon as we hang up. And now, *mon ami, adieu, bon nuit,* and good night!"

David hung up and gave Rebecca's hand a squeeze. "Rebecca?"

"Becca, what on earth did Georges tell you?" Adelaide asked, concern evident on her face.

Rebecca closed her eyes for a minute then, covering her face with her hands, she started to cry. "I knew it! I just knew it!"

With a helpless look at Adelaide, David dug out his handkerchief and handed it to Rebecca.

Mumbling a "thank you," Rebecca took it and dabbed at her eyes.

At last, after a drink of water, she haltingly told them the rest of her conversation. "I can't believe he's discovered where those two paintings came from. Their lack of a complete provenance was beginning to create a big problem, and I wondered if I'd ever be able to sell them. Talk about luck."

"And lucky to find someone who's persistent and has a very perceptive mind," Adelaide added.

"Indeed," Rebecca sniffed. "Thank heaven for Georges Lartigue. I guess if all goes well, he and I will be going back to Paris sometime after Thanksgiving. From there, I imagine we'll go to Berlin and return the Kirschner and the Kandinsky to the Neue Nationalgalerie."

"In that case, Rebecca, "David said, trying to sound positive, "there's your reason to celebrate." He looked at Adelaide. "If we're serious about getting together, why don't you and Rebecca come to New York for Thanksgiving? Hopefully, Georges can arrange to go to Berlin afterward and it would mean that you, Rebecca, could fly to Europe from Kennedy. Of course, it will also mean that one or two might have to stay in a New York hotel." He and Rebecca shared a look, but she quickly looked away. "And, if it makes everyone feel better," he continued, "you can all help me shop and do the cooking. But we don't need to settle all the logistics now. We still have a couple of weeks.

"In the meantime," David said, placing his hand over Rebecca's, "Georges insisted that either tonight or first thing tomorrow, you call your contacts at Interpol and the CIA and tell them what he's discovered about the Mendes Galleria."

"Yes. In fact, why don't I do that right now? Just thinking about Dietrich Radtke is enough to send me into orbit."

* * *

"What a great evening," David said, on finishing his meringue glacé. "I'm so relaxed, I can't bear the thought of returning to the real world tomorrow."

Adelaide laughed. "Well, if all goes well, you can return the favor in November."

"Right. Let's hope it works out." He looked at Rebecca. "How are you doing?"

"I'm fine now, thanks."

"I presume you reached your two contacts as Georges requested?"

"Yes." She blinked back tears and sniffed.

He glanced at the clock on the mantle. "I really hate to break this up, but we should get going."

"What time is your flight tomorrow?" Paul asked.

"Continental at eleven. And you?"

"The same. I'll look for you in the lounge before boarding."

Addie and Paul accompanied them onto the porch.

"Goodnight and many thanks," David said, giving Adelaide a kiss on the cheek.

"G'night, Addie," Rebecca said, hugging her sister. "Speak to you tomorrow."

"Are you feeling better now that you've spoken with Bruce Ross and Deevers?"

"I don't know because I'm seething with frustration and anger over the fact that Jeffrey was set up to be murdered."

Adelaide studied her. "Becca, I hope you're not thinking of doing something crazy like taking some form of revenge."

"Certainly not without help."

David gave Paul a two-finger salute. "See you in the a.m. In the meantime, don't do anything I wouldn't do," he added with a wink.

"Speak for yourself, pal," Paul said.

David hooted a laugh. "Touché."

As she and David walked to the car, Rebecca held up her keys. "Would you mind driving?"

"Not at all. You're sure you're okay?"

"Yes, thanks. Only a little weary." She looked at him and smiled. "Think you know the way?"

"If not, I know where I can find a good navigator," he said, opening the passenger side door for her.

Top down, David and Rebecca rode in silence. Other than the steady hum of the motor and music playing softly on the radio, there was no other sound.

With a black cashmere shawl loosely draped across her shoulders and her head resting against the back of the seat, Rebecca luxuriated in the cool evening temperature.

Learning some of the history behind the Kirchner and Kandinsky, while a relief, also made her realize that the easy part was over. It was no longer important whether she or Georges ever discovered how they got to Madrid, because it was clear they'd been confiscated once they'd left the Kronprinzenpalais. It was also clear the Mendes Galleria sold them to Ernst Lawler. *All I need now is to find where Jeffrey might have kept a list of dealers involved in the illegal sale of art and turn it over to Interpol.* As requested, she'd already searched his desk and fastidiously gone through his drawers, briefcases, shoes, coats, and other clothes in both their houses to no avail. Discouraged, she had grown more concerned as the calls had become more persistent, always insisting she knew where "it" was.

David swung the car off the main road and edged up the driveway, pulling to a stop in front of the house and switching off the engine.

Placing his arm across the back of the seat, he turned and caressed Rebecca's cheek with his fingers. "You've been very quiet since your talk with Georges. Is what he told you the only thing that's bothering you?"

The absence of a smile reflected her mood. "I now have several emotions warring inside of me: shock and sorrow over Jeffrey's death and a need for revenge." She looked at him and reached for his hand. "I'm sorry, David. I didn't mean to put a damper on your last evening."

He brought their joined hands to his lips and kissed her fingertips. "Impossible, Rebecca. Impossible."

They looked at each other and Rebecca realized she was holding her breath. Then slowly but steadily, he brought his mouth down to hers.

The kiss was gentle, his lips cool from the evening air. Rebecca's emotions, already stirred by the night's events, now came alive. She leaned into him, instinctively parting her lips as he slipped his tongue between them and deepened the kiss.

She stroked the side of his face then gasped as she sunk her fingers into his hair when he tongued the inner chambers of an ear. Reaching for her hand, he moved it across his lower torso and slid toward her on the passenger seat.

Her pulse rate surged. Angling toward him, she rose onto her knees and slipped off her shawl and shoes. Then, one hand on his shoulder, she eased up her skirt with the other and, moving one leg across his, settled onto his lap.

The pressure of her against him produced a moan. Reaching up, he loosened her hair and ran his fingers through it as it fell away onto her shoulders. He then skimmed his hands down her back, and caressed her buttocks and thighs.

She let her head fall back, moaning as his hands stroked her. Moving to her chest, he fondled her breasts, teasing the tips through her clothing until they were upright against his palms.

She leaned forward, kissing him deeply, and then trailed her lips over his face while her body began a slow, uncontrollable rhythm against his legs.

"You're driving me crazy," he groaned a moment later. Unbuttoning her blouse, he separated the fabric and unhooked the sheer, lace brassiere.

Her skin was luminous in the darkened light. Taking both breasts in his hands, he caressed them while his mouth licked and nipped their dusky tips.

"Oh, David . . . mmm," Rebecca sighed as chills of pleasure spiraled through her.

Minutes later, she removed his tie. Unbuttoning his shirt, she ran kisses across his chest, enjoying the male scent of him.

He slid his hands onto her hips, compressing and releasing them in time with her rhythmic motion. Running them under her skirt, he explored her thighs above the tops of her stockings. He stroked higher and she gasped. He moved higher yet, and she gripped his shoulders and said his name.

Arching away from him, she leaned back and depressed a button on the side of the steering wheel, prompting the seats to tilt and slide backward and affording them additional room. Loosening his belt, she unzipped his trousers and let his arousal fill her hands. The look and feel of him left her breathless.

"Easy, Rebecca, easy," he panted.

She stretched out on the seat next to him, and continued her gentle massage until he pulled off her bikini panties and rolled between her legs. Rising onto his elbows, he inched into her and began to move. Moaning softly, Rebecca clung to his shoulders and moved with him.

"God," he gasped, a few minutes later when she cried out and they climaxed.

Neither spoke as minutes passed and their breathing returned to normal.

Rolled on one side, David brushed the hair away from her face. "You're so beautiful," he said, his voice thick.

Gazing up at him, Rebecca realized she'd probably fallen in love with him in Greece twelve years before. Those few days, however, had been pure fantasy. She'd known and accepted that, and until recently, had never looked back. The difference was that what had just happened between them was anything but a fantasy, and along with the chaos now in her life, its implications terrified her.

Returning his smile with effort, she said, "And you, David, are *very* handsome."

He shook his head in protest, but before he could reply, she pressed two fingers against his lips and said, "Did I ever tell you that when I saw you come down the stairs and step into Victor's that night in Greece, I was convinced the atmosphere had played tricks on me and you were actually the human counterpart of a Classical Greek sculpture of Apollo?"

His deep chuckle resonated through him. "You were either mad or it was the drink." He lifted his head and looked at her. "Are you sure it was only Campari and soda you had in that glass?"

She giggled and kissed his neck. "Stay. I'll fix us breakfast, follow you to your hotel and drive you to the airport. But tonight, I'd like you to stay."

He smiled and fingered her hair. "I thought you'd never ask."

She pulled his head down and kissed him. "Thanks."

"Besides," he added, "the thought of going back to the hotel alone tonight is at best a bleak one."

After another few minutes, they rearranged themselves and got out of the car. With arms locked together, they walked into the house.

As soon as they were inside, someone with binoculars stepped out from the trees at the edge of the property and retreated toward the road.

CHAPTER TWENTY-NINE

Rebecca had been home from California for two days when Tom Hutchins called. "How was your trip?"

"It was wonderful, Tom. Thank you. To what do I owe your nice call?"

"You may not think it so nice when you hear what I have to say."

Her breath caught. "And that is?"

"Because of the ongoing scandal surrounding Broker Industries, the insurance companies involved decided that there was enough evidence of wrongdoing to warrant further inquiry as to how construction contract bidding was done and to whom contracts were awarded. Since you worked for the company and Jeffrey was one of Broker Industries' major project managers, the reinvestigation committee wishes to interview you to ask if you ever discovered, or Jeffrey ever mentioned, anything about the company that could help with the investigation."

"Surely they can't be serious?"

Tom sighed audibly. "I'm afraid they are."

"First, it's a terrible thing for them to expect me to comment on anything Jeffrey might have said because it would be hearsay. Second, Jeffrey never brought work home or discussed his job. In fact, it was a miracle I even knew he worked there." *Similar to my not knowing he was working for Interpol!* "As far as interviewing me, however, though I'm not pleased, I realize I have do it."

"Thanks, Rebecca. Again, I'm sorry about this."

"Addie and I are going to New York on Sunday the twenty-second for Thanksgiving. From there, I may have to go to Paris and possibly to Berlin. If I must meet with anyone, can it be arranged for early next week?"

"That doesn't give us much time, but I'll see what I can do. And Rebecca?"

"Yes?"

"I know you said Jeffrey never brought his job home, but do you ever remember him making any sort of casual remark or acting in a way that might have made you think he was uncomfortable working at B.I?"

"Someone else asked me that the other day."

"Oh?"

"No one you'd know, just a friend who was curious. I told him what I just told you, that Jeffrey never discussed his job. Nor do I remember his acting oddly at any time while he worked there. But I'll give it some additional thought."

"Thanks. What about the phone calls? Do they continue?"

"Yes, they do. Only now, they're more frequent and, according to Clarissa, more intimidating. She's nervous about being here alone during the day. Fortunately, her husband recently retired and can be here with her."

Rebecca realized that while Tom had known about the telephone calls, he knew nothing about her being followed or her involvement with Interpol and the CIA. *And as for Jeffrey, he knows nothing about him being murdered. Nor does he know about Georges Lartigue . . . or David for that matter.* "Tom?"

"Yes?"

"There're some vital things I need to discuss with you. Addie's due home tomorrow and I'd like to arrange a time when the three of us can meet, hopefully this week?"

"Vital, you say? Hold on." A minute later, he was back on the line. "How's my office, Thursday at ten?"

Rebecca checked her calendar. "That's the day after tomorrow. It's fine with me. To be sure, I'll check with Addie. If you don't hear from me, we'll see you Thursday at ten."

That evening, Rebecca attended a dinner party at her neighbor's. Under normal circumstances, she would have walked, but the news of Georges' being threatened and followed, coupled with the increased phone calls and news about Jeffrey's death, had her nerves on edge. Instead, she put the top up on the convertible and drove the quarter of a mile.

When she arrived home around ten-thirty, she was about to put the car in the garage, but changed her mind. The exterior house and garage lights were on and leaving it out front was easier and more convenient. *Besides, I have the panic button in my purse.* Decision made, she locked it and left it out front.

She was halfway to the house, when someone grabbed her from behind. In one continuous movement, a thick, calloused hand yanked her head back and covered her mouth, while a large arm pinned her against a rock-hard, muscular chest. In the struggle, she dropped her purse.

"You don't get it do you, Mrs. Lawler," a deep male voice said against her ear. His sour breath was making her stomach churn. "If you value your life and don't want to end up like your dear husband, sweetheart, you're going to find that list he was making and follow the directions you'll get after that. Understood?" To emphasize what he said, he tightened the arm around her waist and yanked her head backward, wrenching her neck and causing bits of light to float around in her eyes. She tried to nod, but he was holding her so tightly, she couldn't move her head.

The next moment, bright light flooded the area. *Who turned on the property lights*?

With that, Jack, Clarissa's husband, came around from the back of the house carrying a shotgun, aimed it in the air and fired above their heads.

Rebecca's assailant released her so suddenly, she fell to her knees on the driveway, ripping her stockings as she did. Jack fired in the air above the fleeing man. "For good measure," he told Rebecca after retrieving her purse and helping her into the house. "Wasn't aiming to kill him, though I had good reason."

"How did you know I was here?" Rebecca asked.

"Heard the car drive up."

Rebecca was sure the gun's blast had rendered her deaf, but once they got into the house, she was relieved to find it had not. "Thank God you came out when you did, Jack," Rebecca croaked once they were safely inside.

"The skin on your chin and around your mouth is all red," Clarissa said, inspecting her.

Rebecca touched it and recoiled. "It's tender, too. That brute's fat hand had rough calluses. He was covering my mouth so tightly he bruised me."

She winced as she rolled her head from side to side, "My neck's stiff too. And just look at my knees!"

"Go upstairs, take a shower and doctor those scrapes on your knees. I'll make you an ice bag to hold on your chin and neck."

"Thanks, Clarissa. I can't help thinking how fortunate it was that you and Jack were here."

The next day, Rebecca notified Deevers, who insisted she tell him when she expected to go out in the evening. Within the hour he'd reported it to Bruce Ross.

That afternoon, Deevers appeared and presented her with a Glock G19, nine-millimeter, compact handgun. Despite her stiff neck and skinned knees, or no, he escorted her to the firing range used by the local police department and instructed her for two hours. Afterward, Rebecca decided that whenever she was in Las Vegas, she'd make a point of practicing thirty minutes twice a week.

"What's the point of having a gun unless you know how to use it?" she told the captain.

After returning from the firing range, she again went through all of Jeffrey's things with Clarissa's help. But as before, she found nothing. Resigned, Rebecca dropped onto the bed and looked at her housekeeper. "Clarissa, whatever am I going to do?"

Addie returned the following afternoon, and Rebecca told her about being attacked. Fortunately, she'd been able to cover the discolored skin around her mouth and chin with makeup so that Addie wasn't as upset as she might have been. The next day, they met with Tom Hutchins and brought him up to date on everything.

* * *

As promised, Rebecca met with members of the reinvestigation committee the following week. Adelaide met her afterward.

"I see you survived. Are you all right?"

Rebecca nodded. "Yes, surprisingly enough."

"Tell you what," Adelaide said, hooking her arm through Rebecca's, "let's drive into town and I'll treat you to lunch."

"Aren't you supposed to be at a meeting or something?"

"I excused myself," Adelaide said with a grin, "you know, an executive privilege kind of thing?"

"Then if you don't mind, let's go out to the art museum where the atmosphere's less frantic."

"Suits me. Would you like me to drive?"

Rebecca looked at her. "No, why?"

"I just thought that after this morning's ordeal you'd like to put your head back and relax."

Adelaide's offer reminded her of the last night she and David were together. Heat rose to her cheeks.

"On second thought," Rebecca said, handing over her keys, "that doesn't sound like such a bad idea."

Adelaide laughed. "I'll say this much, the suggestion certainly has improved your color."

Rebecca smiled. "Yes, I seem to be feeling better already."

While she was in California, David had surprised her with his frequent phone calls. Interestingly enough, she also heard twice from Stan O'Neill.

Besides being extremely nice, Stan's attractive, interesting, considerate, and if it wasn't for David . . . It troubled her to know that he'd headed the investigation into her brother-in-law's murder and John Norman's suicide. *Therefore, he has to know about John and me.*

"And so," Adelaide said, bringing her back to the moment, "do you want to talk about what went on in your meeting?"

"First they went over everything in minute detail as if to verify what they already had. Next, they proceeded to ask questions about Jeffrey's attitudes and actions such as whether he ever indicated that he was suspicious or dissatisfied with what he saw or suspected was going on within the company or while he was on site. You know, that type of thing.

"Jeffrey was there ten years yet, during the seven we were married, he never brought the job home. He believed in leaving it where it belonged—in his business life, not in his personal one. But Tom and I now believe there had to have been something else going on. Otherwise, why reopen the investigation? Thankfully, it wasn't as bad as I anticipated. Now, if I could only find the list Jeffrey was supposed to have been making."

"What about his study? Could something be in there?"

"In addition to searching the house in Portugal, Clarissa helped me go through everything, including Jeffrey's study, again this past Sunday."

With a sigh, Rebecca rested her head back and glanced at the side mirror. "Addie?"

"Yes?"

"Notice that big black sedan two cars back, the one with the out-of-state plates?"

Addie looked. "Yes."

"How long has it been behind us?"

"It drove out of the parking lot right after we did. Why?"

"Because it's the same one that was following me before we went to Paris and it's the one that's been following me since."

"Really?"

Rebecca studied the image in the mirror. "Positive."

Adelaide looked again. "Could be a coincidence."

"Except it was waiting for me this morning when I pulled out of the driveway."

Adelaide shivered. "All this is beginning to give *me* the creeps. Why not ask Clarissa's husband, Jack, to go out with you when you go?"

"I have my Glock right here," Rebecca said, patting her purse.

"Then at least let Jack chauffer you around so you have a free hand in case you need to use it. Seems to me you can't very well manage both."

"That's not a bad idea. I keep hoping that if we can hold on until we go to New York for Thanksgiving, we can forget about it for a couple of days. Trouble is, now that Georges is coming, whoever is behind this will be sure to have us followed in New York."

They were halfway through lunch when Adelaide said, "By the way, I made hotel reservations in New York."

Rebecca looked up, fork poised in the air. "Oh?" She knew David was hoping she'd stay with him but she was ambivalent. "I mean, fine. Where?"

"The St. Regis. And Becca?"

"Hmm?" Rebecca said, glancing up from her salad.

"While the room's a double, I only booked it for one."

Rebecca straightened. *Oh! That means I now have to . . .* She stared at her sister.

"Oops," Adelaide said, and lowered her fork. "I just thought you and David . . . well, that you and he might have made other plans. Sorry if I overstepped by assuming too much. The room's big enough, a small suite actually, and you're more than welcome to join me."

Rebecca cleared her throat. "You're right, David's hoping I'll stay with him, but I haven't given him an answer. To be honest, Addie, I'd rather begin by staying with you. David and I . . . I mean it's been twelve years."

"You do like him though?"

"Yes!"

"And the two of you seem to get along like gangbusters."

"True."

"Are you in love with him? Sorry, you don't have to answer that."

Rebecca let out a sigh. "It's all right. I don't mind answering."

"Well, now you don't need to. Has he any idea?"

"I haven't said anything."

"Has he?"

Rebecca shook her head. "No, but it's still a bit early for us, don't you think?"

Adelaide laid a hand on Rebecca's arm and smiled. "Not really. Even though it's been twelve years, it's not as though you've just met."

Rebecca thought back to their night on the beach in Greece and felt her color rising. "I guess I have to agree with you there. But we've each lived a wholly different life in the meantime. We might find we have nothing in common. Then what? The entire situation is terrifying, if you want to know the truth."

"Why not just relax, enjoy your time together, and see where it leads? Seems to me you have enough troubling you at the moment. Why add to your woes by trying to outguess the future? You'd probably be wrong anyway."

Rebecca suppressed a laugh. "Thanks, Addie. It's reassuring to know I can always rely on you to lift my spirits." The conversation made her uneasy. *When David and I are together, it's almost too good to be true. When we're apart, I'm restless. And not knowing how he feels unsettles me even more. I need to change the subject.*

"To get back to New York/Thanksgiving, if you don't mind, I'd prefer to stay with you at the hotel. I'm just not comfortable starting out at

David's. It makes everything just a bit *too* convenient, as if I'm a sure thing. We've only just begun seeing each other."

"Smart gal. I have to hand it to you, Becca. I think I'd find that decision difficult. He's a pretty neat guy, but you're right to let it play out naturally. If it's destined to happen, it will. When we get back, I'll call the hotel and tell them that the one will be two."

"Thanks, Addie. Stalling my decision was making me more and more anxious. Discussing it has helped, and I appreciate your understanding and support."

"Funny enough, I feel better, too. Guess I picked up on your anxiety."

"And now, I'm even beginning to get excited," Rebecca said, laughing.

"Me too. Let's pay the check and get out of here. And this time, you can drive me."

As they rode along, Rebecca noticed the same black sedan following them.

CHAPTER THIRTY

By the middle of November, Miranda's search for an attorney had led to nothing but dead ends.

At Legal Aid, she learned that, even though pressed for funds, she was neither indigent nor a current resident of any of the New York areas they serviced.

But at the New York Legal Assistant Group, her hopes soared. They said her current non-resident status would not pose a problem. Since the declaration of death had been filed in New York, the inquiry would only involve reviewing the records of the New York State Court of Appeals. Should they agree to take the case, a fee could certainly be negotiated.

Miranda's momentary bliss was shattered, however, when they added that the only obstacle they could see was that since her husband had been the one to file for the declaration, reversing it might necessitate involving him. That would take time, and it might be several months before she'd have an answer.

It was the last straw.

"Trapped!" she screamed at the startled individual across from her. "That's what I am, *fucking trapped!*"

Shouting a stream of obscenities, she swept whatever was on the desk in front of her onto the floor. Standing, she grabbed anything else she could lay her hands on and sent it flying across the room. Then, removing the glass water pitcher from the desk, she held it at eye level and dropped it on the floor. After that, she fled.

Head throbbing, she ran blindly through the streets, giving little thought to her whereabouts or her destination and unaware that Odile Allard was following, ready to call Payne Whitney.

At last, out of breath and near exhaustion, Miranda hailed a taxi. Although still agitated, she was able to give the driver the name and address of her hotel.

Once in her room, she called the airline and booked her return flight. As she started throwing things into her suitcase, she again thought of her predicament.

"God *damn* you, Georges Lartigue, leaving me no choice!"

Divorce him? And give that son-of-a-bitch husband of mine the satisfaction of ridding himself of me? Never. He'll have to kill me first.

* * *

On Thursday the week before Thanksgiving, Georges arrived at New York's Kennedy Airport into the welcoming arms of Sally. The weeks alone in Paris, haunted by thoughts of Miranda, were at last behind him, and he hugged her tightly as he came into the terminal from customs.

"This time I have a car for you, and Mr. O'Reilly over there," Sally said, indicating a man in a long black coat and chauffer's cap waiting by an exit beyond the crowd in the lobby, "will be our chauffeur."

"I don't care if he's the devil himself, *cherie.* It only matters that I'm away from Paris, away from the worry over Miranda, away from . . ." He decided not to mention being followed or the threats—the second one coming just before he and Jacques left Paris for New York.

Traffic into Manhattan was heavy, but soon they were pulling up in front of the St. Regis Hotel on East Fifty-fifth Street. Sally waited in the car with O'Reilly while Georges checked in. Two hours later, Georges was preparing dinner in Sally's apartment while they both enjoyed a glass of Meursault.

"I never knew you were a gourmet cook," Sally said, watching him sauté the truffles for the Bordelaise sauce to accompany the filet mignons.

"Ah, but if one is a gourmand, necessity dictates that one be a gourmet cook, *n'est-ce pas?"*

"I'm very glad you're here," Sally said, sliding her arms around him and giving him a squeeze. "I've missed you."

Georges extinguished the flame under the pan and added its contents to the sauce. Then, he turned and enveloped Sally in his arms. "And I have missed you more than I thought possible."

Georges had business appointments on Friday, but Saturday was free. It turned out to be a clear, cloudless, fall day, and he and Sally spent it out and about in New York, stopping by the Carlyle Hotel on Madison Avenue for a cocktail in the late afternoon.

Rebecca and Adelaide arrived Sunday and checked in at the Saint Regis as planned. When Rebecca told David her plans, the news initially dashed all his hopes of sharing his apartment with her for the few days. Fortunately, his better judgment told him to be patient.

On Monday, with Jacques hovering nearby, Georges met Rebecca at the Oak Room in the Plaza Hotel for lunch. He brought good news. "Our bid representative, Marie Hélène, has managed to sell the two pieces we left with Drouot: the Ludwig Meidner drawing of Potsdamer Platz and the Kandinsky watercolor-and-ink drawing. You'd like Marie Hélène, Rebecca." He smiled, eyes sparkling. "Not only is she beautiful, she handled the auction process like the professional she is, resulting in her netting you top price."

"Wonderful! I wish I could have been there. How was the trip to London?"

"Short. By prior arrangement with Christie's, I dropped off the Max Beckman street scene and the Degas sketch of the nude. They're scheduled for auction this Friday. Marie Hélène will again be our rep. So, Rebecca, it looks like you'll soon be a very rich woman."

She laughed. "Don't forget, part of it is your commission."

Georges looked as if he was about to protest, but she reached across the table and laid her hand on his. "Don't you even think of saying no. I'll never be able to tell you how thankful I am to have found you, Georges. Despite the terrible odds I left you with on those two confiscated pieces, you forged ahead. It's a wonder you didn't walk away and leave me to fend for myself. Oh,that reminds me. I must send Senhor Carlos something. Would you help me chose an appropriate gift? After all, he's the one who introduced you to me. I only wish Jeffrey had lived long enough to appreciate what you've done."

Georges turned his hand over and grasped hers. "*Je regrette*, Rebecca. I haven't had the chance to say how devastated I was when I realized the evidence on Radtke and the Mendes Galleria all but proved your husband was murdered. *Mon Dieu!*"

Tears filled her eyes and she squeezed his hand. "Thank you. I greatly appreciate the sympathy." She reached into her handbag for a tissue and blew her nose. "Despite the news confirming my worst fears, the knowledge of it brought closure and ended the suspended sense of dread. As you advised, I notified Ross and Deevers as soon as we hung up. Ross told me that, at one time, the Mendes Galleria had been on Interpol's watch list. Thanks to you, now Interpol has even more to go on." She waited a beat. "Jack Deevers gave me a gun."

"Non!"

"Yes! A Glock, nine millimeter handgun."

He stared at her a minute then broke out laughing. "Pardon, Rebecca," he said a moment later. "It's just that I'm having a *trés difficile* time imagining you holding a gun."

"I'll have you know I'm a damn good shot!" But her attempt to appear insulted failed and she was soon laughing.

"Speaking of regret," she said at last, "I feel responsible for your being followed and receiving those threats. If it hadn't been for the two paintings I took to Lisbon, you'd never be in this mess."

"Ah, *non*, Rebecca. *Non.* You should not feel that way. It's not the first time I've been threatened. Receiving the occasional threat is part of this business. After all, provenance research, especially involving stolen art, comes with a certain amount of risk built in."

"Makes me feel as if we're involved in some kind of espionage."

"But think about it a moment. We *are*, Rebecca. Indeed we are." He started to chuckle. "Pardon. I'm still having difficulty imagining you with a handgun."

Rebecca held up her purse. "I have it right in here." She opened her purse. "Shall I take it out and show you?"

Looking about, he held up both hands in protest. "*Non,* Rebecca*! S' il vous plait, non*!" But he was still chuckling as he paid the bill.

That evening Rebecca and David got together for dinner with Georges, Sally, Addie, and Paul. They met at the main restaurant in the Carlyle Hotel. The combination of an excellent menu, the refined elegance of plush chintz-covered banquettes, Aubusson rugs, and mirrored alcoves set off by a dramatic six-foot floral arrangement, did much to soothe Rebecca's overall anxiety as well as Georges' concern over Miranda.

The following day was Tuesday, and Rebecca and Adelaide helped David do the food shopping. Later, joined by the others, everyone pitched in to help him cook dinner. Georges took charge of the fireplace and soon had a decent fire going. Afterward, they sat around an antique oak trestle table in the living room to enjoy the meal.

"So this is the famous silver bedroom?" Adelaide asked, entering.

She inspected every detail. She opened the bathroom door, and peered in. Centered in the middle of the room was a partially sunken, Jacuzzi-style, double-sized, gray bathtub with chrome fixtures. Installed along one wall was a pair of matching sinks. A toilet and bidet were placed along another, and a glass-enclosed, walk-in shower with multiple jets was on an angle in the far left corner opposite the entrance. Mirrors lined the walls over the sinks and indirect lighting, controlled by rheostats, bordered the vaulted ceiling. Radiant-heated, gray flagstone tiles lined the floor.

"Do much entertaining?" she asked David, who'd come to stand beside her with the others.

"Addie!" Rebecca scolded, but David interrupted.

"I do, but only by advance reservation. Select patrons refer to the suite as 'David's Seraglio.'"

Adelaide threw her head back and laughed. A moment later she said, "Once you get to know me better, David, you'll realize my comments are often masked by my admiration. Your place is spectacular, very 'guy-like' and, well, spectacular. A real winner. In fact, I'm drooling."

"After seeing your fabulous home, Addie, I take that as a true compliment. Thanks."

Unable to resist the urge to tease, he added, "But later, should either you or Paul like to use any of the facilities, the management would be only too happy to oblige. A dip in the tub enjoys a wide reputation."

"I can't believe you!" Rebecca said, giving him a poke as she and the others watched Paul struggle with a blush.

"Don't worry, Rebecca," Paul said. "I have ways of getting even with your friend."

CHAPTER THIRTY-ONE

By Wednesday, most of the preparation for Thanksgiving was done. Paul and Adelaide were spending the day and evening together, and Sally and Georges were teaming up with Brian and Carrie.

Overjoyed at the prospect of at last spending an evening alone with Rebecca, David made reservations for a night of dining and dancing at the Rainbow Room on the top floor of Rockefeller Plaza. His frustration had been building all week and was now at an all time peak. To have her near, to laugh with her, drink with her, prepare food with her, and share knowing glances with her yet not be able to get his hands on her, had taken its toll.

The evening finally arrived and the weather was made to order—clean and crisp with a festive feeling in the air. He picked Rebecca up at her hotel, and when he saw her coming toward him dressed in a rich brown velvet suit and wearing his earrings, his heart leapt into his throat.

"David," she said, beaming.

"Hi," he said, taking her hands in his and giving her a kiss. "As usual, you take my breath away."

She smiled. "You always say the most wonderful things."

"Because you make it so easy."

Tucking her hand in the crook of his arm, they left the hotel and got into a cab.

David had requested a table near a window. Once the waiter seated them, David ordered them drinks and helped Rebecca remove her jacket. Then, overwhelmed with the need to have her in his arms, he pulled her to her feet and onto the dance floor.

She looked great, smelled great and—with the soft, supple texture of her satin blouse under his hand—felt great. During their recent time apart, he began to realize he no longer wished to spend so much time away from her. But she was here now, and that's what mattered.

The band took a break so they returned to their table.

"See anything that looks good?" David asked, glancing up at her as they perused the menu.

To Rebecca's dismay, her stomach was doing cartwheels. She avoided looking at him afraid that if he knew, he'd think her foolish. She'd looked forward to being with him all week, and now that she was, her nerves were giving her grief. *Whatever's the matter with me? Anyone would think I was on my first date. Plus I'm terrified of being followed, forever looking around corners and down streets.*

In the end, she settled for two appetizers—a pear and walnut salad with goat cheese, and shrimp scampi. David ordered potato and leek soup and a main course of venison.

He reached across the table and took her hand. "I've really missed you."

His touch left her short of breath, but she managed to smile and squeeze his hand. "I've missed you, too, David."

"I can't tell you how happy I am knowing Clarissa's husband moved in and Deevers gave you a gun. As far as your being attacked . . ."

Rebecca stared at him. "Word travels fast. How did you know? Oh, let me guess. Addie told Paul and he—need I say more? I hadn't mentioned it because I didn't want you to worry. What could you have done? At least now Jack's there and has a shotgun, and Deevers is in the wings, so to speak. Added to that, Tom Hutchins is about to have the most up-to-date wiretap installed on the telephone."

"Okay, okay. I'll back off. I'll be damn glad when all those paintings have found a home and no one's after your hide." He smiled, relieving the tension.

"Nor Georges'," Rebecca added.

"Right. Nor Georges'," David repeated. He'd been so preoccupied with thoughts of Rebecca that he'd forgotten about the threats to Georges.

They took time to enjoy their meal, interspersing each course with sessions on the dance floor. During the last number, David eased back and looked at her. "Want to stop and have a nightcap after we leave here?" *Like my apartment?*

"Mmm, good idea. We can stop at the King Cole bar in the St. Regis."

Damn. Oh well. "Why not?" David replied. "Seems as good a place as any."

They were sitting at a table in the King Cole bar, each nursing a brandy, when David put his hand over hers and said, "Come back with me tonight."

There it was. The moment she'd been anticipating.

"Oh, David, I'd really like to but I'm sharing a room with Addie."

"All the more reason."

"I . . . I know, but I don't know how to . . ."

"What? Let her know we want to sleep together?"

"I think she already knows that."

He gave her hand a tug. "Then what's the problem?" When she remained silent, and averted his gaze, he added, "Rebecca, I'm dying for you, to undress you, to touch you, caress you, and to have you do the same to me."

She looked down at their joined hands. "How about if I come prepared to stay tomorrow?"

"Because I'm selfish enough to want you tonight."

She looked up at him, and he saw it in her eyes. *My God, she's upset.*

He kissed the back of her hand. "I'm sorry, Rebecca, I don't mean to press you." *Yes, I do, damn it.* "It's just that I . . . that I . . ." She looked so beautiful . . . and so sad. He'd never seen her sad. His heart melted. "The fact is, I'm in love with you, Rebecca, and I'm concerned about what's troubling you."

Her whole face brightened. She looked at him, and he saw her eyes were filled with tears.

Now what? Shit, I've gone and made it worse.

Leaning against him, she pulled his head down and kissed him.

His mind spun out of control and he plunged his tongue into her mouth. With his heart rate surging, he slipped a hand under the table and slowly ran it up between her legs, then came to his senses.

"Rebecca," he gasped, interrupting the kiss. "We have to stop. I'm already bursting with want for you. Let's get out of here." He signaled the waiter.

"I can't believe you actually said you were in love with me."

He thought back and chortled. "Well, what do you know? So I did." He needed the comic relief.

"And I'm in love with you."

Her statement both surprised and thrilled him. "You are?"

She nodded. "Yes, I am."

The waiter brought the check and David put down a credit card.

He looked back at Rebecca and grinned. "Well, I'll be damned."

"I promise to come and stay with you tomorrow."

"Deal!"

David accompanied her up to her room, but before either spoke, they were in each other's arms. Then with great effort, David released her. Tilting her chin up, he kissed her again. "Until tomorrow then."

Smiling through her tears, Rebecca nodded.

He trailed his fingers down one side of her face and, with one last smile, left.

Because of the late hour, Rebecca opened the door of the suite as quietly as possible. Tip-toeing in, she saw a piece of hotel writing paper on the floor and bent to pick it up. Seeing it contained Adelaide's handwriting, she scanned it. Adelaide was spending the night at Paul's. *David. Oh, David!* With a squeal, she tore out of the room and down the hall toward the elevators, rounding the corner just as one of the doors slid shut. "David! Oh, David!" she mumbled, pounding on the call button.

For a minute, she thought of using the adjacent "Million Dollar Stair," when the elevator came.

She started to get in but hesitated, waiting to see if the man inside was going to come out. He didn't. Before she could react, he grabbed her upper arm and pulled her against him as he stepped out.

Her instinct was to scream. Then she felt something hard press against the side of her velvet jacket. *My God! He has a gun!*

"All right, Mrs. Lawler, let's the two of us take a little stroll back to your room. I know your sister isn't there and your boyfriend just left. It'll just be the two of us. Cozy like. We'll have a nice little chat and you *will* tell me where your husband kept that list." Terrified, her mind reeling, Rebecca let him pull her back toward the room. *Think! Think!*

When they got there, she saw the door was shut and remembered hearing it lock when it closed earlier. *We can't get in without the key.* They stopped in front. She was still holding the note from Adelaide.

"The key is in my handbag."

"Then, reach in, and *slowly* take it out. And don't think of trying anything either. Remember, I'm the one with the gun." For emphasis, he shoved it against her side.

Her heart was beating so rapidly. She was amazed she wasn't trembling. Her velvet handbag's narrow strap was over her left shoulder which meant her hands were free. She folded Adelaide's note, and, holding the handbag in her left hand, she opened the clasp with her right. After sliding the note inside, she felt about for the key and encountered the gun. She held her breath. *Do I dare? Will the bullet hit him? If it doesn't, will he then shoot me? Don't think, damn it. Do it!!*

Her captor was standing on her left, holding her left arm. Noting the nozzle of her gun was pointing to the left, she didn't give it a second thought and grasped the hilt.

Another jab with the gun. "You're taking too damn long. Hurry the hell up!"

Angling the nozzle of the Glock upward, she pushed it against the side of her bag, and . . . fired.

Despite the thick carpeting, the sound of the shot produced a deafening echo, and for a minute, during which her assailant continued to hold her by the arm, nothing happened. Then his weight shifted, and he sagged against her.

Suddenly a door opened. Then two. Then another. Seeing her chance and using all her strength, Rebecca shoved her attacker away from her. As he toppled sideways onto the floor, still holding the gun, she saw a hole in the side of his jacket begin to ooze a dark, wet substance.

The sound of screams brought her up short, rescuing her from her momentary shock and making her realize she'd not only wounded or killed someone, but her hand was in her purse still holding the gun! She also realized no one knew who she was or what she was doing there standing next to a wounded man lying on the floor holding a gun. She let go of the Glock and frantically groped for the key.

In the meantime, someone yelled, "Call the police!"

"Yes," someone else yelled. "Call the police."

She ignored them and continued searching for the key. *At last.* Pulling it from her bag, she inserted it into the door and pushed it open. Hastening to the phone, she dialed the front desk. "Help! Please! Someone call the police! A man attacked me on the seventh floor and I shot him." She replaced the receiver and collapsed on the bed. That's when the trembling started.

Several minutes later, the telephone rang, startling her. She reached for it. "Yes?"

"Mrs. Lawler?"

"Yes?"

"This is the front desk checking to see if you're in the room. The police have just arrived and want to come up. There's also a gentleman here who insists on coming with them."

Who the devil? She trusted no one. Then she had a thought, "By any chance, would the gentleman's name be David?" She was shaking so violently it was difficult hanging on to the receiver. *If I could only stop trembling!*

She heard the desk clerk ask. "He says it is."

"Oh, please, please. Tell the police to let him come up."

"I'll see what I can do, Ma'am."

"Thank you." A sob caught her off guard, and for a minute, she buried her face in her hands and let the tears come.

A few minutes later there was a knock on the door. "Mrs. Lawler? It's the police. Please open up."

Still wary, she put the chain on before opening it. Several officers stood outside. The one in front introduced himself as Captain Murray. David, looking stricken, was hovering behind them. She slipped off the chain.

She noticed the crowd had diminished but she couldn't make out if there was a body on the floor.

David walked past the officers and pulled her into his arms. "Rebecca? What? What in God's name happened? You're shaking all over! Where's Adelaide?"

"Sir?" one of the officers said, "I'm afraid we need to speak to Mrs. Lawler first."

"It's all right, David," Rebecca said, holding on to him and trying not to dissolve in tears. She looked at the officer. "May he at least sit with me while we talk?"

"As long as he doesn't interrupt."

"May I ask him one question first?"

"If it's a quick one."

She pulled back and looked at him. "David, how is it that you're here?"

"On my way out, a former associate of mine came into the lobby. I hadn't seen him in a while so he and I went into the bar for a drink. I was in there when I heard about the commotion up here. When the police came in and I heard your name and floor mentioned, my heart stopped." He pulled her close. "I never want to go through anything like that again."

"All right, Mr. Neville. It's late, and we do need to start. Otherwise everyone will be here until dawn." He smiled, "And I don't need to tell you what that would do to your taxes."

David nodded, "I understand." He gave Rebecca one last hug before they walked across the room and sat on a settee.

By three in the morning, The police were finally finished with their interrogation and the body on the floor outside the door had been removed. Rebecca had told them everything from the time she and David left the King Cole bar. She also told them about Jeffrey's death, her attempts to sell the art, her association with Interpol—giving them the names of Bruce Ross and Jack Deevers and the reason she was given a gun at all.

"Damn good shot," the coroner had said, "especially for a beginner. When the lady fired, it appears the angle of the gun was such that the bullet went upward into the right side of the chest, clear through the heart, and exited between the third and fourth ribs on the left side. He was probably dead by the time he hit the floor."

In the end, Rebecca had to surrender both the license and the weapon.

"Don't worry," Captain Murray assured her. "Once everything checks out, they'll be returned to you, probably within the week. Your Mr. Deevers chose well. The Glock has the reputation of being the safest gun. There's no chance of it going off without pulling the trigger. Once it's fired, it immediately resets the safety. It's lightweight, too. Our detectives like it because it's so easily concealed."

After requesting that Rebecca notify him if she planned to leave town any time within the next few days, Captain Murray and the others left.

Once they'd gone, David wrapped his arms around her. "I'll help pack your things. No matter what, you're coming home with me. You'd have been coming in a matter of hours as it is. And you never told me what happened to Addie."

It was then that Rebecca remembered the note. She reached in her handbag and handed it to David. "I think this'll answer your question. As soon as I read it, I ran after you. I was trying to get the elevator when that god-awful man grabbed me. And, yes, I'm coming home with you. I'm too exhausted to argue even if I wanted to."

CHAPTER THIRTY-TWO

Thanksgiving Day arrived at last. Rebecca had sufficiently recovered from her narrow escape from death, and David was hosting the event as planned. Thankfully, everyone was in a festive mood.

Each had contributed in some way to the meal. Paul and Adelaide brought an appetizer of fresh oysters; Carrie and Brian, an apricot glazed, apple-cranberry tart; and Georges and Sally, three types of wine: for those who preferred red, a St. Émilion, white, an Alsatian Traminer, and for desert, *Dom Perignon* champagne.

But the main course was the host's, and David outdid himself. The turkey was browned to perfection. Filled with delectable wild rice, walnut, and raisin stuffing, it was served with a lightly sweetened, thick, brown, truffle gravy with cranberry chutney on the side. The vegetables consisted of a whipped potato-yellow turnip combination and buttered string beans, *aux amandes.*

"It's great to know you cook too," Adelaide said as David arranged the delicious-looking bird on a serving platter.

"*Adelaide,*" Rebecca groaned, looking at her sister in exasperation.

With a handful of parsley poised midair, David said, "Hey, Addie, cooking just happens to be the *least* of my prowess."

"Touché, David," Rebecca said, wrapping her arms around him and giving him a hug.

"Gee. Lucky Becca," Adelaide muttered, which brought an "I can't believe she said that," from Rebecca and raucous laughter from the others.

"I'm so glad you decided to come on this trip with Georges and me, Sally," Rebecca said, during the meal.

"When Georges suggested it, I realized I had no fashion projects pending. The idea was too tempting to refuse."

"Then you're also going to Berlin?" Brian asked.

"I'm planning to."

Brian gave Rebecca one of his trademark smiles. "You have to be excited."

"You're right, I am and even more so because of the provenance issues we started out with. Truth be told, I can hardly believe it."

"Georges said the reason you're going is to return several pieces of confiscated art to the Neue Nationalgalerie."

"Yes, the two paintings that were stolen by the Nazis before being smuggled to Madrid. Sometime in the late 1940s they were sold to my late husband's grandfather, Ernst Lawler."

Brian fingered his glass. "Returning them is most generous."

"It's kind of you to say, Brian, but knowing they were stolen and later sold illegally left me no choice."

"Speaking of generosity, Rebecca," Carrie said, smiling at Brian when he took her hand, "my organization is indebted to you for your substantial donation to our grants program."

"I was more than happy to give it. Feeling about art the way Jeffrey and I did, it gives me great pleasure to know the money from the auction at Drouot will go toward helping artists get grants for studio space. Otherwise they may never get the chance to work in such an environment."

"Perhaps you'd like to come to one of our events."

"I'd love it."

"Terrific. I'll add your name to the mailing list."

Dessert was served along with the champagne; Georges insisted on pouring. Before resuming his seat, he said, "I have some interesting news, especially for those of us involved with Holocaust art and it's provenance.

"Perhaps you remember hearing about the Washington Conference of Holocaust Era Assets that took place in 1998. It had been formed in order to approve principles that would encourage and enable victims or heirs of collections confiscated by the Nazis to come forth and establish claims. Despite the improved access to archives and records made available to researchers, progress has remained slow.

"Recently, the Czech Republic held a follow-up conference to assess the progress, review the practices currently in use for provenance research and restitution, and establish new methods aimed to improve those practices. Needless to say, this is especially encouraging news for me and my family. It gives us hope that one day, one or more of the paintings confiscated from my parents' home in 1940 will be found."

"Hear, hear," David said. He and the others raised their glasses in a toast.

Since Adelaide had scheduled a meeting for Saturday morning at Broker Industries, she left for Las Vegas Friday afternoon. Apprehensive about returning to the St. Regis alone after Rebecca's frightful experience, Paul had helped move her things from the room at the hotel to his apartment Thanksgiving morning.

Still suffering the effects of her narrow escape from death, Rebecca was only too glad to spend Friday inside. Besides it was raining. David had an appointment to meet a client at his gallery at ten so, at Rebecca's insistence, he left her curled up on the couch watching TV. When he returned at five o'clock, she was up, showered and dressed. She had fixed him a vodka martini—with a twist of lemon peel the way he liked—and she was in the kitchen preparing something that smelled marvelous.

"Creamed turkey in a crepe, compliments of Julia Child," Rebecca answered when David asked what she was cooking.

"Accompanied by *haricots verts* and a mixed green salad," she added.

David walked over and encircled her in his arms. "Despite what you've been through, you look as wonderful as ever."

Rebecca kissed his cheek. "Tell me, did your client buy anything today?"

"As a matter of fact, she did."

"So the client was a she, hmm?"

David chuckled at her attempt to appear jealous. "Yes. She purchased a Georges Braque woodcut and a blue and white, ten-inch round ceramic plate by Picasso."

"My, not a bad haul for a rainy day."

David pulled her against him and closed her mouth with his.

Saturday was cool, but the bright sunny atmosphere lifted everyone's spirits. How could they not? On a day like this, New York was in its glory. David was close to talking Rebecca into going to Central Park and letting him show her how to skateboard when the police called.

The officer on the phone told Rebecca that if she came to the Seventeenth Precinct in the Citicorp building at 167 East 51st Street, she could pick up her gun. Suspecting that Rebecca had no desire to negotiate the subway, David called his car service. As he punched in the telephone numbers on his iPhone, he was reminded of the last time he'd used the service—the night he and Elise Crawford ended their relationship. He briefly wondered how she was.

David and Rebecca arrived at the Seventeenth Precinct and were asked to wait, but it wasn't long before Captain Murray appeared and took them into his office. Rebecca's Glock lay on his desk. Murray got right down to business.

"As soon as we returned to the precinct the other night," Murray began, "I telephoned Jack Deevers. Despite the hour, he already knew what had happened. Were you aware that you were being followed that evening, Mrs. Lawler?"

"I'm not surprised. Someone's been following me for the past several months. Why?"

"Because Jack Deevers had a detective tailing you that night. The man followed you and Mr. Neville into the King Cole and sat in the corner after ordering a club soda with lime. Once he saw the two of you leave and get on the elevator, however, he figured you were spending the night together and returned to the bar. He saw Mr. Neville come back with his friend and was still there when I arrived with the other officers. The detective managed to eavesdrop on our conversation then followed us up to your floor on another elevator. Once he saw what happened, he telephoned Deevers.

"I've put two detectives from the crime division in charge of running a background check on the individual who attacked you, Mrs. Lawler. As luck would have it, the man's fingertips had been roughed up so that we couldn't get a clean fingerprint. He was also carrying bogus ID. Immediate identification, therefore, has been impossible. Obviously, he was a rouge operative, in other words, someone for hire. Once we have the dental records, it shouldn't take long to identify him. You and your late husband are known for being sizeable art collectors, Mrs. Lawler, and Deevers is certain that whoever hired the man has ties to or is actively involved in black market art . . ."

"In other words," Rebecca interrupted, "he buys and sells stolen art."

"Exactly. Deevers has notified Bruce Ross."

Rebecca waited a beat. "I'm still a bit hazy about everything that happened the other night, Captain Murray, but I believe I told you that Monsieur Lartigues and I are leaving for Paris on Monday?"

"You did, and you're free to go. Your gun has been registered with the NYPD. Nevertheless, should you have to use it again, please try to do so in some other borough besides Manhattan."

Unsure of his tone, Rebecca studied him. When she saw the hint of a smile begin to crinkle the corners of his mouth, she laughed. "I have to admit you had me there for a moment, Captain Murray."

The three of them stood, and Rebecca extended her hand. "I can't thank you enough for everything, Captain. I was in a pretty bad state when you saw me the other night."

"That's understandable, and you're welcome. Under the circumstances, you were lucky everything turned out as well as it did. Have a good trip to Paris." He looked at David. "You going too?"

"Unfortunately, not this time," David answered.

Murray looked back at Rebecca. "Then at least try to stay safe. Come back to New York soon."

"I will," Rebecca said, "but doubt I'll stay at the St. Regis."

Murray grinned as he shook David's hand. "If I'm reading things right, I suspect you won't have to."

When Rebecca at last let David convince her to go rollerblading in Central Park, he invited Georges and Sally to go with them. David knew that wherever Georges went Jacques went with him. David also knew that Jacques' presence would lessen Rebecca's feeling of vulnerability. As it turned out, rollerblading was just what Rebecca needed to help her forget her recent nightmare. She quickly learned the skill of balancing and maneuvering on the blades and by the end of the afternoon, she was in high spirits. With Jacques in tow, the five of them taxied back to David's apartment. While Georges built a fire, David called a local Chinese restaurant and ordered in a selection of dishes for dinner.

David and Rebecca spent Sunday alone. Rebecca packed her clothes and made sure she had all the necessary information needed to return the two paintings to the Neue Nationalgalerie in Berlin. As she packed, she felt the first stirrings of excitement she'd had in weeks. Though her positive outlook had returned, she was still haunted by the memory of being hunted down and manhandled.

After a light supper, she and David retired to the couch and sipped after dinner drinks while watching "Analyze This," starring Robert De Niro and Billy Crystal.

Once the film was over, David slid his arm across Rebecca's shoulders. Pulling her against him, he planted a kiss on the top of her head. "I just want you to know how happy you've made me by agreeing to come and stay."

"The same holds true for me," she said lifting her face for his kiss.

Two hours later, they were no longer on the couch but wrapped together in a blanket on the floor in front of the fireplace after making love. Embers from the dying fire glowed sending constant low-level warmth into the room.

Rebecca laughed softly.

"What's so funny?" David asked.

"Does lying here like this remind you of anything?"

"It sure does. Our first time together in Santorini."

She raised her head and looked at him. "You really *do* remember, don't you?"

David propped himself up on an elbow. "How could I forget?"

She ran a finger across his lips. "I really do love you, you know."

He kissed her. "I love you too, Rebecca. I'm going to miss you like crazy."

"Wish you were coming."

"So do I. Unfortunately, I have a meeting with a very influential client. If it weren't for the fact that he and I made the date two months ago, you couldn't keep me away."

Several more minutes passed. "Rebecca?"

"Mmm?" she said against his chest.

He swallowed. "Would you consider it premature if I suggested we take a crack at living together?"

Cold water could not have sobered her more. She was momentarily at a loss for words. *Live together, at this stage of my life, feeling the way I do about you? Not likely.* But she knew he was expecting an answer.

Tucking the blanket around her, she sat up and looked at him. "You mean as a trial run to see if we continue to get along?"

He reached up and pulled her down to him. "Gee, Rebecca, hearing you say it like that makes it sound so cold and so contractual."

Well, that's what it is, isn't it? She said nothing until she was able to get a handle on her emotions. She wasn't about to compromise the way she felt just to live with him.

Instead, she said, "It's very tempting, David. It really is. But as you know, my life at the moment is very unsettled. Before I consider making that big a decision, I first need to sort several things out. The phone calls continue to harass Clarissa, and no matter how much I've searched, I can't find anything resembling the list Jeffrey was supposedly making."

David tilted her chin and kissed her. "You don't doubt my feelings for you, do you?"

She looked at him. *Why can't things ever be simple?* "No. I don't doubt them."

"I thought that living together would serve to strengthen our feelings toward each other."

How could anything possibly strengthen the way I feel toward you now? She was crushed and deflated. She ran her hand across the soft golden hairs on his chest, and said, "I'm sorry if I've disappointed you, David. It's just that right now I, I can't."

He gathered her to him. "Rebecca . . . Rebecca, please . . . don't shut me out." He kissed her forehead, looked down and her caught her gaze. "Won't you at least promise to think about it?"

His plea softened her resolve, but she dropped her eyes before saying, "Yes, David. I promise."

He tightened his embrace and nuzzled her ear. "Thank heaven."

But despite the promise, he sensed her distance.

It was the anticlimax to a perfect five days with David, Rebecca thought as she gazed out the window of the Air France jet taking her to Paris. But after the initial shock, she again recognized that nothing worthwhile is ever simple.

The bittersweet ending was that Stan O'Neill just happened to be on the same flight, in the same section as she, Sally and Georges.

No, nothing in life is ever really simple.

CHAPTER THIRTY-THREE

They arrived in Paris the next morning, Tuesday, December first. After Rebecca checked into the Manoir St.-Germain-de-Pres, she went to the gallery and worked with Sally and Georges for several hours before leaving to have lunch.

Returning to the hotel that afternoon, she telephoned David as promised, then spent a quiet evening soaking in a hot tub, ordering from room service, and retiring early.

On Wednesday, she again went to the gallery where she and Georges spent the better part of the day preparing paper work releasing her ownership of the Kandinsky and the Kirchner to the Neue Nationalgalerie.

David telephoned her at six that evening Paris time, but Rebecca was out having dinner with Stan O'Neill and came in too late to return the call. As always, she'd enjoyed the evening with Stan, but was distracted by a message she'd received from Clarissa saying that the phone calls had become more threatening and, unless she and her husband were assured of having additional protection, they might have to leave. On top of that, someone continued to follow her. As a result, Georges had Jacques drive her to and from the gallery each day. To complicate matters further, thoughts of David were constantly on her mind.

By Thursday afternoon, the paintings were packed and ready to go to Berlin. Rebecca and Gabrielle had just taken them to the rear of the gallery when they heard a commotion out front.

"Fiend! Bastard! How dare you sue for divorce!"

Gabrielle looked at Rebecca. "Miranda!"

The two of them rushed out in time to see Miranda fly at Sally, knocking her off her feet and into a wall. She went limp and collapsed on the floor. Instantly, Georges started toward her.

But Miranda was quicker. Eyes wild, her hair in disarray, she seized a matting knife from a counter and charged Georges.

"You filthy bastard!" she screamed. Knife in hand, she swung her arm up and brought it down, cleanly slicing through Georges' shirt and striking his left arm near the shoulder.

Then, everything happened at once.

Gabrielle grabbed a large cardboard portfolio of unframed prints and hurled it at Miranda, unbalancing her as it struck its target dead on. In the meantime, Rebecca grabbed a roll of paper towels, tore off a dozen or more sheets, wadded them up and helped Georges apply pressure to his wound.

At that point, Hulot and Jacques ran through the door into the gallery. Seeing their opportunity, they began to close in.

Yet again, Miranda was faster. Finding her balance, she pirouetted around and brandished the knife in front of her. "Don't even think of it," she yelled and, with a nod toward Georges, added, "or I'll cut you just as I did that son of a bitch over there!"

Hulot and Jacques charged, but Miranda, now ever wilder, dodged past them laughing hysterically and ran toward the door. The two men followed with Jacques on his cell phone barking instructions. Seconds before they reached the door, Miranda dashed through it and ran toward the street. A moment later there was a screech of brakes and a loud *thunk.* Then silence. No one inside the gallery moved.

A groan from Sally broke the spell.

Rebecca ran over to her while Gabrielle went to Georges who'd managed to drag himself onto a chair and was pressing the wad of paper towels against his wound in an unsuccessful attempt to stem the flow of blood running down his arm. Seeing his pallor, Gabrielle grabbed more towels and convinced him to get down on the floor again. After, quickly retrieving his jacket from the office, she folded it and used it for a pillow.

Kneeling, Rebecca carefully pushed the hair away from Sally's forehead. "How are you doing?"

Sally touched the left side of her head and grimaced. "Hurts."

Rebecca put her hand near Sally's and felt a large lump. "Do you hurt anywhere else?"

"Ankle. My right ankle. It's numb. I can't feel it."

Rebecca looked down and saw there was a moderate amount of swelling around Sally's right foot and ankle.

"I'll get some ice." Getting up, she sprinted toward the office.

Seeing the blood continuing to flow down Georges' arm, Gabrielle tore off more paper towels. Removing those soaked with blood, she pressed the thicker wad firmly against his shoulder.

"Sally. Oh, Sally," he repeated over and over.

"She's just coming around. Rebecca's with her."

George twisted his head from side to side. "Sorry. So sorry to have caused all this."

"Tsk, tsk," Gabrielle shamed. "Don't be foolish. Miranda was supposed to be dead, remember?"

The sound of sirens pierced the air.

Supplies in hand, Rebecca was on her way back to Sally when the police and ambulance crew walked in. The police questioned Hulot while Jacques and the medics helped with the wounded.

Taking Rebecca by the hand, Gabrielle pulled her into Georges' office. "Sit," she commanded. Withdrawing two small tumblers and a bottle of Spanish brandy from a cabinet, she poured them each a glass. "Drink," she instructed, handing one to Rebecca.

Rebecca drank a portion of the liquid, closed her eyes and leaned back against the chair. But she immediately thought of David and opened them again. Gabrielle was sitting behind Georges' desk, drink in hand, staring at the ceiling. "*Finis*. Perhaps at last it's finished."

They downed the last of their brandies and walked back into the gallery. A police officer and Hulot approached. "They're taking Monsieur Lartigue and Mademoiselle Livingston to the American Hospital for treatment," Hulot said.

"What about the other . . ." Rebecca asked gesturing toward the street where a second ambulance had pulled up.

The officer shook his head. "We're sorry, mademoiselle. The lady expired a few moments ago."

Rebecca shivered and was glad she'd had the brandy. The appalling tragedy left everyone in state of shock.

"Rebecca, if you'd be good enough to go with my brother and Sally," Gabrielle said, "I'll stay here and clean up."

"Of course. I'd be happy to. I'll get my things from the office."

"Call me when you know something," Gabrielle said when Rebecca returned.

"How long will you be here?"

"I'll wait for your call. There's food in the refrigerator and wine in the cooler. I shouldn't want for anything."

"Gabrielle, why not give me your cell phone number in case you find you're tired and want to go home."

Gabrielle wrote it down, and the two of them followed Sally and Georges as the medics wheeled their stretchers out to the waiting ambulances.

* * *

At five p.m., New York time, that same Thursday, David again telephoned Rebecca's hotel and left a message. But when he hadn't heard from her by Friday evening, he was overcome with sense of dread. Heart sinking, he realized she'd probably already left for Berlin with Georges and Sally, and he'd 'blown it.'

Miserable after a dinner of snack foods and three glasses of wine, he telephoned Adelaide. It was eight in the evening, Las Vegas time, but fortunately Adelaide was home and answered on the third ring.

After starting off with general cordialities, David got down to basics and detailed the reasons for his misgivings.

Adelaide remained silent.

"Addie?"

"Yes, David. I'm here. Just trying to think of what to say. I guess what immediately comes to mind is that the two of you obviously have different views about your relationship. Funny thing is, once I saw you two together, there was no doubt as to how you felt about each other."

Getting no response, she continued, "I'll try and explain. Okay?"

The wine had made his mouth dry. "Sure. I mean, fine. Okay."

"You love her?"

David rested his head against the back of the couch and closed his eyes. "Yes."

"And she loves you."

Raising his head, he came to full attention. "Is that a question or a statement of fact?"

"A statement."

"Then why has she rejected the idea of us living together?"

"Because she's beyond that."

"Beyond that?" He sat forward, elbows on knees. "I don't understand."

Adelaide sighed. "When Rebecca returned from Greece that first time after college, there was a noticeable difference in her. It was as though she'd found peace with herself and with the world. Everyone noticed the change, but none of us knew the reason.

"I figured something extraordinary had to have happened, but she was right out of college and I just assumed she'd had a glorious vacation in a wonderful place. Only later did I realize her behavior was somehow connected with whatever had happened in Santorini.

"Then you came to Portugal, walked back into her life, and I knew what else had happened in Santorini. She'd fallen in love with you, David, and the experience had been fantastic enough for her to label it 'a fantasy.'"

Silence.

"Believe me," Adelaide continued. "Rebecca was devoted to Jeffrey and loved him very much. Their relationship was possible, don't you see, because in her mind she'd already shared the fantasy with you. That freed her so she could move on."

Running his fingers through his hair, David laughed self-consciously. "I, I don't know what to say."

"Rebecca's what I'd call a consummate dreamer, David, a true romantic. If she hadn't spent that time with you, I doubt anyone would have measured up to her ideals. But now you've reappeared and are anything but a fantasy, and she can't compromise the depth of her feelings simply to move in with you. There has to be more.

"Therefore, my advice is this: If living together is all you want or can manage, let her go. To put it bluntly, get out of her life."

David choked on a laugh. "Well, gee, Adelaide, why didn't you say so?"

She laughed too. "Okay, then."

"Then what?"

"What's the verdict?"

"I know this much, I can't, won't, let her disappear from my life."

"So?"

He ran his fingers through his hair again. "Wow."

"Wow, is not going to do it, David. But, take your time. I don't mind waiting. It's the rest of your life you're deciding, after all."

To relieve the tension, he got up and started to pace. "Okay. Now you're sure, sure how Rebecca feels about all this?"

"Is my name Adelaide Thomas Broker?"

"The last I knew."

She laughed again. "Then, yes, David, as sure as if it was I."

"What should I do?"

"What do you want to do?"

"Fly to Paris, grab her and . . . marry her." He suddenly felt as if the weight of the world had been lifted from him.

My hero. "Wonderful! But there are a couple more things."

He sat down again. "Yes, and they are?"

"One, you should know that earlier today, Georges had a close call when his ex-wife rushed into the gallery, knocked Sally down and went after Georges with a matting knife, cutting him and almost severing a ligament in his shoulder. Rebecca . . ."

David's heart stopped. "Yes. Rebecca?"

"Rebecca and Gabrielle were in the back of the gallery and fortunately weren't involved."

His relief was palpable. "So they're all right?"

"Yes. They're fine."

"You're sure?"

"Yes! In fact, Rebecca accompanied Sally and Georges to the hospital. Sally suffered a mild concussion and sprained her ankle. Unfortunately, Georges needed surgery and has to spend three days in the hospital."

"*God!* And the ex-wife?"

"When Georges' security guards tried to apprehend her, she ran screaming from the gallery into the path of a car. She was pronounced dead at the scene. According to Rebecca, she had a long history of mental illness. On learning that Georges had started divorce proceedings, she went over the top."

"Geez, Addie. Is this for real?"

"Incredible, isn't it?"

"I guess that means no one will be going to Berlin. What a disappointment that has to be."

"Yes. A big one. But plans are already in the works to reschedule the visit. The museum wants to hold a reception in Rebecca's honor."

Hopefully, I'll be with her. "Where's Sally now?"

"Rebecca took her to Georges' apartment and spent the night with her."

No wonder she never called me back.

"But David?"

"Yes?

"There's even more. Rebecca is coming back to Las Vegas on Monday."

"Why so soon?"

"Someone broke into the house and ransacked the place. Deevers, Tom Hutchins and I have been over there most of the day."

I can't believe this. "Sounds like whoever has been harassing Rebecca is getting desperate. How'd they get in?"

"Someone familiar with the security system gained access and put aluminum foil across the contacts. While the contacts weren't physically connected, they behaved as if they were. The system registered "on," when, in effect, it wasn't. When the house was breached, no alarms went off. Clarissa suspects that whoever was involved worked on the system a few weeks ago when there was a power failure. Setting it up to fail was a piece of cake."

"But what was important enough to interest two security technicians? The art collection?"

"Deevers said he thinks the men looking for Jeffrey's list are responsible. He also said that whoever decided to use these particular goons—his word, not mine—was stupid. Professionals would have saved time and done a more efficient job. Added to that, professionals are very neat. A useful piece of information, wouldn't you say? I hope you're taking notes."

David chuckled.

Pause.

"Adelaide?"

"Yes?"

"I'm on my way there as soon as I stop at my parents' in Weston, Connecticut."

"Your parents? You need permission?"

This time, he laughed out loud. "No! I want to stop and get a ring my grandmother gave me."

"What a guy. Call me and let me know when you plan to arrive."

"I will. And Addie?"

"Yes?"

"Thanks. You're the best."

"Yeah, well . . ."

CHAPTER THIRTY-FOUR

"Am I ever glad to see you," Adelaide said, embracing Rebecca at the main terminal of Las Vegas' McCarran International Airport Monday afternoon. She held Rebecca at arms' length noting the strained expression and dusky shadows under Rebecca's eyes. "How was the trip?"

Rebecca managed a smile. "Not bad. Just long. Hello Tom."

He gave her a hug. "Even though Adelaide said you were unscathed from that disaster in the gallery, it's a relief to see it's true."

Rebecca nodded. "And when the memory fades, I'll be even better."

"Are you up to speaking with the police?" Adelaide asked. "Deevers and Bruce Ross are here too."

"They are? Do you think I can freshen up and have a cup of tea first?"

"Why not?" Adelaide said, threading her arm through Rebecca's. "Just let me ask our chauffer if that will that be a problem. Tom?"

Tom relieved Rebecca of her luggage. "No. My afternoon's yours."

"I was thinking, Becca," Adelaide said once they were in the car. "Since the repair to your security system has only just begun, you might feel more comfortable if you came to stay with me. Once you've spoken to the police, Tom can drive me home and you can follow in your car. That way, it'll be there in case you need it."

"Good idea. All I can say is that this so-called 'list' these criminals claim Jeffrey was making, must be crucial to their very existence. For them to physically abuse and threaten me, invade a New York hotel to come gunning for me, and ransacking my house . . . The only reason Clarissa's husband, Jack, has been staying there with her for the last two weeks is that, whoever calls, leaves threats. Seems now someone is carrying out those threats. The unnerving part is that I *still* can't find anything that even resembles any kind of a list!"

Adelaide looked at Tom. "I thought the calls were being traced."

"The police are working on it. The problem is, whoever makes them either uses a one-time throw-away phone card or a pay-as-you-go mobile. The police can trace where the phone card was purchased but not who purchased them, unless the buyer uses a credit card. The pay-as-you-go mobile doesn't require a registered address. It's also untraceable."

While Rebecca unpacked and took a quick shower, Adelaide telephoned the local police and learned that Jack Deevers and Bruce Ross were also on their way over.

"The police said they'd be here within the hour," Adelaide told Rebecca over a cup of tea in Jeffrey's study.

Clarissa was ringing her hands while her husband stood by looking glum. "You should have seen this mess," she said, "drawers upturned on the floor, books and papers strewn everywhere. And that was just in here. Wherever there was a drawer, it was pulled out and the contents were dumped on the floor. As for the bedrooms . . ." She shook her head. "Jack and I straightened things up as best we could once the police said it was all right. We both feel so guilty, Mrs. Lawler. If we only hadn't gone out to do the food shopping."

"Clarissa," Rebecca reassured, "put that idea right out of your head. There's not a reason in the world why either you or Jack should feel guilty. Who could have imagined that the system had been tampered with during the power failure?" She looked at Jack and smiled. "Besides, if it hadn't been for you when that horrid man grabbed me out front, I don't know what would have happened."

Rebecca began to look through the folders Clarissa had stacked on the desk. She leafed through letters, old contracts, meeting notes, and paid invoices. After twenty minutes, she stopped and sagged back against the chair. "This is a waste of time. Clarissa and I already went through these weeks ago."

The doorbell rang.

Tom looked at Rebecca. "That'll be the police."

"I'll go down," Clarissa offered.

A few minutes later, they heard heavy footsteps on the stairs and four men appeared at the door.

Rebecca stood and extended her hand. "Hello again, Detective Bradley, Detective Moore. How are you, Deevers? Hello again, Mr. Ross."

"How are you, Mrs. Lawler?"

"Welcome to my disastrous-looking home. All of you remember my sister, Adelaide Broker, and her attorney, Tom Hutchins?"

"Indeed we do," Bradley said.

"Sorry Mrs. Lawler," Bradley said. "I know you just arrived home so we won't keep you longer than necessary."

"These days, it seems the end of a trip is the best time to get me," Rebecca said, trying to appear lighthearted.

An hour later, the detectives, Deevers and Ross finished inspecting every room in the house and were on the verge of leaving.

"I wish we could have found *something*," Rebecca said. "I've tried to think of every place Jeffrey would have kept such a list. I even asked Adelaide to have his former office and files searched again at Broker Industries. I'm at the end of my rope. Even a shopping list would look good at this point!" She glanced around at the serious faces. "Sorry. Just trying to lift my spirits." She looked at Deevers. "I can't thank you enough for giving me that gun. It saved my life, you know."

"So I heard. Self protection is the reason I gave it to you."

"Has Interpol come up with anything as to who's chasing me?" Rebecca asked Bruce Ross.

"Too early to say for sure. We're getting there. The Mendes Galleria is again under surveillance, and we did take Radtke back to Headquarters for interrogation. Don't know if he can be charged with conspiring to murder, however. We'll have to wait and see. I think we shook him up, though. I'll be working with Deevers for the next few days if anything comes up."

"Hopefully, nothing will," Rebecca said, wishing she felt as confident as she'd like to.

"Anyone as hungry as I am?" Rebecca asked once the detectives had gone. "It's half past six."

"Yes, as a matter of fact," Adelaide said. "Are you about ready to go?"

"Give me ten minutes to throw some things in a suitcase and I will be."

Tom smiled as he watched Rebecca climb the stairs. "Despite everything, she still seems to have plenty of energy."

"Tell me about it," Adelaide said.

"Perhaps now's a good time to speak to Clarissa and Jack about the phone calls."

"Mind if I tag along?"

Tom laughed. "No, of course not."

Fifteen minutes later, Rebecca came looking for them.

"I'm going to stay with my sister for a few days, Clarissa. If either you or Jack need me, call me there."

"All right, Mrs. Lawler. I felt badly about the message I left you in Paris but now that two officers are patrolling the property, Jack and I will stay. Don't go worrying about us either. You concentrate on taking care of yourself and getting some rest. You look tired, more than you should from jet lag."

"Don't worry. Getting some rest is just what I plan on doing."

Once outside, Rebecca put her suitcase in the convertible's trunk. Though it was a clear evening it was cool, and she decided against lowering the top on the Mercedes.

Since Tom and Adelaide were already in Tom's car, Rebecca tossed her handbag on the passenger's seat, and slid behind the wheel. Switching on the ignition, she buckled herself in and drove off.

As she turned from the service road onto the main highway, she glanced in the rear view mirror fully expecting to see Tom's car. Instead, a large black limousine, this time with foreign plates, drew up behind her. *It must have been waiting for me at the foot of the driveway.*

Her mouth went dry. *Who the devil is this? Where are Tom and Addie?* She pulled the panic button from her purse and pressed it three times. *This time, I'm taking no chances!* It was the signal for 'Help! I'm in trouble.' The read out would appear on Deevers' receiver and show exactly where she was.

Glancing in the mirror again, Rebecca saw that Tom's car was now directly behind the limousine.

She gunned the motor, accelerating to 75 mph. So did the limo, but the maneuver left Tom and Adelaide further behind.

She slowed. So did the limousine.

Her knuckles were white from gripping the wheel, but she concentrated on staying calm, hoping that Deevers and Ross would respond.

Several moments passed. When they were only minutes away from the turnoff to Adelaide's, the limo sped up and nudged Rebecca's car from behind.

The impact caused the Mercedes to swerve and Rebecca's head to snap back against the headrest. But luck was with her, and she managed to maintain control.

What followed was a different story.

The limousine increased its speed and, drawing alongside, struck Rebecca's car broadside.

This time, the convertible swerved violently, and it took all of Rebecca's strength to keep it from going off the road.

She glanced out the window and saw her attacker pull away in preparation to strike again when something inside her snapped.

Within seconds, the last few years of her life flashed through her mind. She realized that after Jeffrey's death, she'd allowed herself to become a victim, sheltering herself in some sort of never-never land to nurse her grief. Rather than taking charge of her life and moving ahead, she'd allowed her life to take charge of her. *No wonder these thugs are after me! Well, you can all go to hell!*

Infused with outrage and fury, without thinking of the possible consequences, she floored the accelerator. The car shot forward, streaking in front of the oncoming limousine, cutting it off and forcibly clipping its right front fender with the rear bumper.

The Mercedes swerved slightly, but due to the level of acceleration, was basically unaffected by the hit. Not so with the limousine. Careening from side to side, it again became a threat.

One glance told Rebecca she was quickly approaching the turnoff for Adelaide's. Tightening her grip on the wheel, she directed her speeding vehicle toward it while pumping the brakes. Then, slamming her foot down on the clutch, she downshifted.

The engine made a terrible grinding noise and she braced herself for the fast, difficult right-hand turn. At that instant, a rifle appeared in the passenger-side window of the limousine and fired at the Mercedes' rear tires, one after the other. The rear section of the convertible sagged. For several seconds the undercarriage dragged on the pavement, throwing off sparks like sparklers on the Fourth of July.

The brakes were now ineffective, and, due to her momentum, it was all but impossible for Rebecca to alter the direction of the car. As she completed the turn, the Mercedes skidded onto the narrow shoulder, flipping over once as it plunged down the ten-foot embankment where, after teetering precariously on one side, it at last settled back on all fours amidst a cloud of dust and dirt.

CHAPTER THIRTY-FIVE

Over the weekend David made reservations at the Las Vegas Hilton. On Thursday he was on a two p.m. flight. Since Rebecca was returning on Monday, he felt having Tuesday and Wednesday would allow her some time alone before he appeared on the scene Thursday afternoon.

His mother had been happy to see him, and after her initial surprise, was delighted to learn the purpose of his visit. She was especially pleased to discover who the young woman was who was lucky enough to have snared her son. She'd formed a positive opinion of Rebecca at Brian and Carrie's wedding.

David waited while his mother opened the safe and removed two black velvet boxes. She handed him one.

Nestled inside was a magnificent perfectly round, two-carat, pale yellow diamond that lay flush within its old-fashioned platinum filigree setting.

David stared at its simple beauty and tried to imagine how it would look on Rebecca's finger. His grandmother's two dinner rings had gone to his brothers, Larry and Brian. This had been her actual engagement ring.

"Do you also want the wedding ring?" his mother asked, opening the second box holding a narrow platinum band with matching small, yellow, diamonds.

David swallowed hard. "No, Mother. Keep it for now. First things first."

What he didn't want her to know was what he most feared—that Rebecca might refuse to see him altogether.

On arriving in Las Vegas, he rented a car. But before starting out, he pulled out his cell phone and called Adelaide.

"Broker residence," a female voice answered.

Then a man took over. "I'll take that, Louise. Hello? This is Tom Hutchins. How may I help you?"

"Tom, this is David Neville."

Through the windows of the foyer, Tom watched Adelaide help Rebecca out of his car.

"Yes, David. Hello. Where are you?"

"At McCarran Airport. I promised Adelaide I'd call as soon as I got in." Then his heart skipped a beat when he heard Rebecca's voice.

"David? It's David? Why is he calling here?" Next, he heard Adelaide's voice.

"Becca, wait until Tom finishes. In the meantime, come sit down."

"David," Tom repeated, "Do you need a ride?"

Rebecca looked over her shoulder. "Need a ride? Where *is* he? Tom?"

David could hear her voice but not what she was saying. "Thanks anyway, Tom. I've rented a car. Is there anything I should know before I come out?"

"Nothing that won't keep until you get here. Adelaide can fill you in."

"Get here?" Rebecca said. "Wait. Tom, please, let me talk to him."

David braced himself. His heart stopped when he heard her voice.

"David?"

He swallowed. "Yes?"

"Where are you? Are you coming to Las Vegas?"

"I'm in Las Vegas, Rebecca."

"*In* Las Vegas?"

"Yes, at the airport about to drive out."

"What a wonderful surprise." She sounded happy enough, but her voice was weak and he could have sworn he'd heard a choked sob.

"Rebecca, is everything all right?"

She drew a deep breath. "Yes. At least, it is now. I'm sorry for the way things ended between us at Thanksgiving, David. Perhaps we should think about having another talk."

"No."

"No?"

Shit. "I mean there's no need to because I don't *want* to talk about it again."

Silence.

"Damn it, Rebecca, I'm so nervous and tongue tied I'm mixing everything up and saying all the wrong things." *Hell.* "Marry me."

"What?"

Courage. "I said, marry me. I don't want to talk about us again unless you agree to marry me."

"David!"

"Well?" He held his breath. *Dare I hope*?

Now she was laughing. "I can't believe . . ."

"Yes?"

"I-I don't know. I can't think!"

"Then don't." He held his breath.

"Yes."

"What?"

"Yes! "

"Say it again."

"I said my answer's, yes!"

He closed his eyes and put his head back against the seat. "Halleluiah."

"How soon can you get here?"

Alert once more he answered, "Know anyone with a helicopter?"

"You're funny."

"No. Delirious! You're sure you're okay?"

He heard her sigh. "Yes, David. I'm okay."

He started the engine. "I'm on my way."

"Don't speed. I'd like you here in one piece."

"Ditto." Chuckling to himself, he added, "Oh, and please give my best to Adelaide."

CHAPTER THIRTY-SIX

David eyed the cane, cervical collar, facial abrasions, and the swelling and large bruise on Rebecca's forehead that had begun to spread into the orbit of her left eye. "I *knew* something had happened. I just knew it." He and Rebecca were holding hands sitting across from Adelaide on the enclosed terrace of the Broker home. "I can't imagine you doing what you did in the first place. But then to have someone *fire* at you . . . Your actions alone could have killed you. Did you even consider that?"

"There wasn't time. I was so furious. All I could think about was foiling their attempts to kill *me*."

David looked over at Adelaide.

She shrugged. "What can I say? Tom and I were paralyzed watching 'stunt woman' do her thing. I almost passed out when that rifle appeared and . . ." She shook her head and looked off into space. "It was like watching a horror movie in slow motion. The worst was being unable to do anything about it. As soon as we could, we pulled over and scrambled down the embankment while I frantically tried to dial 911!"

"And scream my name," Rebecca added. "I did hear that."

"Right," Adelaide agreed. "I was screaming Rebecca's name while Tom called Detective Bradley's hotline." She looked back at Rebecca. "Neither of us could believe you survived. Thank God for the roll bar."

David gave Rebecca's hand a tug. "It's a damn good thing you were driving a Mercedes."

"Yes," Adelaide agreed. "Believe me, I've been thanking every saint from Agnes to Zoticus."

"It's understandable how you got the whiplash," David said. "But where did you get the abrasions and the bruise?"

Rebecca gently fingered the area. "I struck my head against the side window just as the airbag activated and the car flipped over. The sudden inflation of the air bag caused the abrasions. The collar's a precaution."

"What about the cane?"

"It's difficult to walk because I'm so stiff. I need the cane for support."

"The auto mechanic told her it was a good thing the car did roll," Adelaide said. "Had it struck the bottom nose first, both she and the car would be in critical condition."

"He also said that despite losing the two rear tires, the car's momentum contributed to the roll and its ultimately landing right side up." Rebecca grimaced as she tried to shift position. "I'm chafed and sore from the seat belts holding me in. Thank heaven for seat belts. Otherwise . . ."

"*Otherwise?*" David stared at her. He leaned back and ran his fingers through his hair. "So, where's the car now?"

"In a shop somewhere," Adelaide answered. "The police arrived with an ambulance and a tow truck. Once they got Rebecca out, they hauled the car away. She was taken to the emergency room where they gave her a thorough examination. She wanted to go home, but they wanted to admit her for observation. In the end, I overruled and made her stay. Tom and I brought her home just before you arrived."

"Have the police found either the men or the limousine?" David asked.

"Thanks to Rebecca's panic button, Deevers and Bruce Ross immediately got in touch with the local police and arranged for a road block. They encircled the limo on the highway and arrested the two men."

David squeezed Rebecca's hand. "That's one down. What about the phone calls? Are you still getting them?"

"Yes. Neither Jack nor Clarissa answer so whoever it is leaves a message."

"What kind of message?"

"After threatening us, the person asks where the list is. Ha! If I knew where it was, we'd no longer be in this situation. I'm beginning to think Jeffrey was bluffing when he said he was making one. Actually, I don't really believe that. It just felt good to say it."

"The whole bloody thing is a nightmare," David said. "Trouble is, it's no dream." He looked at Rebecca and their eyes held.

"Tell you what," Adelaide said, "I'm going to see Louise about some lunch."

When she'd gone, David carefully took Rebecca in his arms and kissed her. "After you left for Paris," he whispered against her ear, his chin resting against the cervical collar. "I had the awful feeling I might never have the chance to do that again." He shifted. Digging into a pocket, he produced the velvet box and opened it with one hand.

Rebecca gasped. "David! It's so beautiful! It takes my breath away."

"It was my grandmother's engagement ring. She gave it to me the year I graduated from college with the hope that one day I'd use it in the same way. Rebecca, will you marry me?"

She looked at him and smiled. "Yes, David. I will marry you."

Tears in her eyes, she watched him lift the ring from the box and slip it on the ring finger of her left hand. "It's a little loose," he observed, "but we can have it resized or have a band put in across the back."

Rebecca stared at the magnificent gem.

After a minute of silence, David said, "Hey?"

Two tears escaped and ran down her cheeks. Then she laughed. "Sorry, I'm a bit overwhelmed." She extended her hand and wiggled her fingers as she watched the diamond's fire catch the light. "It really is gorgeous."

"There's also a matching wedding ring."

"There is?"

"Yes, but I wasn't sure we'd get this far so I didn't bring it."

Rebecca laughed. This time the musical lilt was back in her voice, "We probably have a little time before that."

"What would you say to our getting married now?"

She looked up. "*Now?*"

He laughed at her expression. "What I mean is while we're here in Las Vegas, some time in the next few days." He lifted her hand to his lips. "I lost you once twelve years ago. Then because I behaved like an ass, I almost lost you again. But now, after your accident and with guys gunning for you, I won't let you out of my sight again until we're married. So, if you're up to it, what about getting married," he hesitated, trying to visualize a calendar, "the day after the day after tomorrow?"

Rebecca looked at him as if he'd just arrived from Mars. She counted on her fingers. "You mean *Sunday?*"

"Yes. Sunday. I think they have weddings on Sundays."

"You're crazy!"

"Shall I come back later?" Adelaide asked, coming into the room.

David leapt up. "Addie, don't leave! You should be the first to know that, if Rebecca feels she can manage it, she and I are thinking of getting married Sunday."

Adelaide stared at him. *This* Sunday?" Just then she spotted the diamond on Rebecca's hand.

He nodded. "Yes. At the Little White Wedding Chapel. It has drive-through service and supplies free witnesses. We'll only need one witness, because we have you.

"Of course, if you prefer," he said, looking at Rebecca, "we can hover over The Strip in a flowered hot air balloon at the Little Chapel in the Sky." *I'm behaving like an ass again.* He tried harnessing his excitement.

"Wherever did you hear about all this?" Rebecca asked.

"I read about it on the plane."

"Isn't the Little White Wedding Chapel where Frank Sinatra was once married?

"The very same."

Adelaide sat down.

"We can pick up wedding rings on our way to the Marriage License Bureau," David suggested.

Silence.

"Are you always this decisive?" Rebecca asked.

David looked at her, remembering when and where he'd heard that question before. "When it concerns my best interests."

She smiled. "Oh? And this does?"

David leaned over and kissed the tip of her nose. "I think this time all three of us know the answer to that."

"I always knew that under that gorgeous head of blonde hair of yours lay a caveman mentality," Adelaide said, laughing.

In the next two hours, David called The Little White Wedding Chapel, lucked out and booked the chapel for six p.m. Sunday. He phoned the Hilton and cancelled his reservation for that night, then called the Bellagio and reserved a suite for Sunday in the name of Mr. and Mrs. David Neville.

In the meantime, Adelaide arranged to have a limousine on hand for the next few days and made reservations for a champagne dinner at Le Cirque in the Bellagio for Sunday evening.

They were about to have lunch when Tom Hutchins and Jack Deevers walked in.

"I tried calling you, Adelaide," Tom said, "but both your lines have been busy so I decided to stop by and tell you . . ."

"Tom! Oh, this is perfect. You can be the other witness."

He came to an abrupt halt. "*Witness*? Witness for what? Don't tell me something else has happened."

Adelaide laughed loudly and came forward. "Hello again, Deevers."

"How are you, Adelaide?"

"All right, what's up?" Tom asked

"David and I have decided to get married Sunday," Rebecca said, "and we need two witnesses. Addie's one, and we're hoping you'll agree to be the other."

When he remained silent, Adelaide chided, "Don't tell me you have something already planned for Sunday evening, Tom? What could be more important than being a witness to something as wonderful as this?"

"You're right," Tom agreed, grinning. "I'd be honored." He turned to Rebecca and David and shook their hands. "Great news, you two. Congratulations."

"Yes. Congratulations," Deevers said. "Best of luck."

"What time is this big event taking place?" Tom asked.

"The wedding's at six," David answered.

"Followed by a dinner Adelaide is giving for us at Le Cirque at eight," Rebecca added. She looked at Jack Deevers. "Would you accept an invitation if I asked you to come? It would be one way of thanking you for helping save my life."

"Thanks, Rebecca. That's very kind of you. Unfortunately, I'm needed elsewhere that day." To Adelaide's look of concern, he added, "But Rebecca can still reach me with the panic button if you need me."

"That's at least some consolation. We'll save you some wedding cake and a bottle of champagne."

"Great!"

"Sounds like the reception means formal, Tom said."

"Yes. And when you talk to your wife, Tom," Adelaide said, "please extend both the wedding and reception invitations to her. We'd be delighted if she can join us."

"Thank you. Knowing my wife, she'll be looking forward to it. Now, if you'll excuse us, Deevers and I'll get out of your hair."

Lunch had just been served when Rebecca exclaimed, "Oh!"

Adelaide looked at her plate, "Something wrong with the food?"

"No, No. I was just thinking. If we get married Sunday, none of our friends will be there. And what about your parents, David? Or mine? Don't you think we should wait until everyone can be with us?"

"You can always call and shock the hell out of them, on Monday," Adelaide suggested.

Everyone laughed. "Leave it to you, Addie," David said. He reached for Rebecca's hand. "What about considering Sunday's ceremony as preliminary and have a more formal wedding later—perhaps in the spring—in California, or Connecticut . . . or Santorini?"

"Santorini!" Rebecca repeated. "Wouldn't it be incredible to have it in Santorini?"

Their eyes met and David kissed her fingertips. "Speaking of friends, how are Georges and Sally? Have you spoken to them?"

"Georges is out of the hospital but will be laid up for several weeks. He'll need therapy on his arm and shoulder. Sally got a medical leave from her job so she could stay with him and continue the physiotherapy on her ankle."

Just then, Tom and Deevers walked into the dining room.

"Oh, Tom," Adelaide said. "You're back."

"We didn't go anywhere, yet."

"In that case, pull up a seat and join us. I also need to apologize. With all the excitement, I forgot to ask what you and Deevers came to tell us before I ambushed you."

Tom grabbed a chair from against the wall and sat. Deevers remained standing. "Deevers and I stopped by to tell you that the authorities caught the individuals responsible for making the phone calls. They also happen to be the same ones who've been following you in the black sedans."

"Individuals? Sedans? How many are there?" Rebecca asked.

"At the moment, we know of four."

"Is one of them the person who attacked me in my front yard?"

"Yes," Deevers said. "And the same one who shot out your tires."

"Nice fellow. Any relation to the person who kidnapped me in the St. Regis?" Rebecca asked.

"I'm surprised you have any sense of humor left," Deevers said. "The night of your car accident, both the driver and the man who shot out your tires—who is the same one who grabbed you in your front yard—are linked to the same international network as the man who attacked you in Manhattan. The others following you in the sedans are local ready-to-hire thugs who get paid in cash for each job. Their assignment was to follow you in hopes of unnerving you so that you'd give in to the network's demands. Since you wouldn't cooperate, their plan that night was to take out your tires if hitting you broadside didn't send you off the road. If you happened to get killed in the process, so be it. I have to commend you on the way you handled the situation, Rebecca. That was some pretty serious driving you did."

"In addition," Tom added, "you and Adelaide are to be congratulated for remembering the details on the sedan's various license plates."

Deevers looked at David. "With Rebecca and Jeffrey out of the way, the network would have most assuredly turned their attention to you figuring that you'd be the one with the list."

Silence

"Okay," Tom said slapping his thighs and standing. "Thanks for the lunch invitation, Adelaide. Unfortunately, Deevers and I have things we need to do. Oh, my wife says 'thank you.' She's touched you asked her to join us Sunday evening. She told me to say she accepts enthusiastically. So," he said, starting toward the door, "until we see you at The Little White Wedding Chapel, please try to stay out of trouble."

CHAPTER THIRTY-SEVEN

"I still can't believe we're actually doing this," Rebecca said as she and David walked into The Little White Wedding Chapel on the famous Las Vegas Strip, Saturday afternoon.

Smiling, David held the door for her. "By *this* do you mean getting married or getting married here?" Upon noticing an advertisement on display, he pointed to it and said, "Perhaps you'd prefer to have the ceremony like that in a helicopter."

Steadying herself with the cane, she grabbed his sleeve and tried to pull him away. "*No* thank you." She was still quite stiff and had taken a Tylenol to help alleviate a dull headache, but given the chance, she would never have postponed what they were doing.

She had to admit The Little White Wedding Chapel did have a certain charm. The staff couldn't have been nicer or more helpful, expertly fitting David with formal shoes, a dress shirt and tuxedo.

David insisted she carry some kind of flowers. She chose a spray of pale green phalaenopsis, with another to wear in her hair.

After they finished at the chapel, David told their driver to stop at the Tower of Jewels on Sahara Avenue so they could pick out wedding rings. On the way, he again mentioned his grandmother's ring. Rebecca made no comment but, when they were in the store, she said, "I'm sure your grandmother's wedding ring is beautiful, David. But if you don't mind, I'd really like to have one of my own. Perhaps we can use your grandmother's as a guard ring instead."

David put his arm around her. "Anything, Rebecca, anything at all."

Rebecca looked at the woman behind the counter. "Is it any wonder why I love this man?"

The woman laughed. "Seems to me you've both been very lucky."

While David was looking in another jewelry display case, Rebecca remembered how the saleswoman's eyes had widened when she saw her walk in with a cane, black eye, facial abrasions and neck collar. Rebecca winked at her. "You can put your mind at rest. I got even with him. I hit him back."

Fifteen minutes later, they walked out the door with their rings—Rebecca had David's plain gold band in a box in her purse, and David had Rebecca's simple filigreed platinum band, boxed, in his pocket.

With a hand on her elbow, he cast her a sidelong glance as they left. "So you got even with me by hitting me back, did you?"

"That poor woman was trying so hard not to stare, I just thought I'd help her out."

Gently putting his arm around her, David leaned in and kissed her cheek. "Know something, woman?"

"What?"

"I love you."

Rebecca looked at him. "Know what else?

"What?"

"I love you too."

Following brunch on Sunday, David left to pick up Rebecca's flowers and his dress clothes. On his return, he carried the clothes to the same guestroom he'd used on his previous visit. *Could it have been only six weeks ago?*

Chuckling, he opened the door and walked in. *Boy, when I make up my mind, I sure make up my mind!*

At five, dressed and ready, he knocked on Rebecca's door. "Need any help in there?"

"I'm just about ready," Rebecca answered. "Come in."

"Isn't this supposed to be bad luck or something?" he asked, opening the door and stepping into the room. "I mean seeing the bride before . . ." He stopped. She was radiant, her skin a golden blush against the ivory-colored, silk-pongee fabric of the dress. Full sleeves, gathered into a wide band skimming the wrist, accentuated the slimness of her knee-length, horizontally tucked skirt.

"Bad luck or not," Rebecca said, smiling, "I'm never going to get anywhere until someone helps me button the back of this dress."

David went to help but as he reached for a button, he caught a glimpse of the lace-trimmed satin chemise underneath. Parting the opening of the dress, he slipped his hands inside. His actions exposed the bruised, chafed areas the seat belts had left on Rebecca's neck and shoulders, and he was again reminded of her close call with death.

Relief pulsed through him as he tenderly caressed the abraded areas before replacing his fingers with his lips.

He nuzzled her ear. "God, Rebecca. When I think of what could have happened . . ."

He caught her scent and instinctively slid his hands over the chemise's sensuous fabric to the front and over her breasts.

"Oh, David," she moaned. "I'm not sure we have time."

He straightened, slowly withdrawing his hands. "You're right. Sorry. Kind of lost it there." He cleared his throat. "Now what is it you need me to do? Button these buttons back here?"

"Mmm. Yes," she said, backing into him.

The arousal in his groin was still growing, and as their bodies touched, David yelped and jumped backward. "Stop! Otherwise I'll have to leave you with the whole thing hanging open."

"All right," she laughed. "All right. But you started it. It was too tempting not to tease."

"Guilty as charged," he said with his hands on the buttons.

A few minutes later he finished buttoning and stepped back to admire her, marveling at the way the dropped waist bodice molded itself to her slim form. He also liked her green shoes. "Need any help with your bag?"

She snapped it closed. "Yes, thanks. Even though it's light, I don't think I can manage it and the cane. I'll ditch the collar and the cane when we get to the chapel. When you get downstairs, have yourself a prenuptial drink."

"I think I'll pass on the drink and have a Coke instead. Can I get you anything?"

"No thanks."

"And you're sure you can manage?"

She sent him a big smile. "Thanks, David. I'll be fine."

Rebecca came down the stairs twenty minutes later and David got another look at her. The cane and cervical collar were gone but she was holding on to the banister and carrying a small green fabric purse. As usual, her hair was up and she'd fastened the single phalaenopsis above one ear. Single pearl earrings and the yellow diamond engagement ring were her only jewelry.

Beaming, David approached her. "Always beautiful, but today as my bride, you look exceptional."

She ran her gaze over him. "And what you do for that cutaway, my-about-to-be husband, defies description."

He laughed. "Why, thank you, Mrs. Lawler." At her quizzical look, he added, "And that's the last time anyone will be saying that."

"Hearing you say it was a shock, but only because I haven't had time to think about it. But look what I just found." She extended her hand.

"They look like keys to me."

"They are, but they're Jeffrey's. I think they were the keys to his office at Broker Industries. I can't think of how they got in this silk clutch. Obviously, I must have put them in there."

"When was the last time you used the purse?"

"I don't remember. It had to have been for another dressy affair. Perhaps Jeffrey asked me to carry them. But why? Take a look at this long one. Doesn't it resemble the kind used on a safe deposit box?"

David took the keys and examined them. "You're right. It does."

"Jeffrey never kept a safe deposit box that I know of." She thought of Bruce Ross. "But then again, I didn't know he'd been working for Interpol either. There was certainly no mention of a safe deposit box in his will or the trust. Perhaps it was for a lock box he kept at work."

"Why not bring them along and show Tom?"

"Good idea. For the time being, I'll keep them in the purse."

"We should probably be going."

"Right. Come with me while I say goodnight to Jack and Clarissa."

They'd just started toward the kitchen when Rebecca stopped suddenly and grabbed his arm. "David!"

Alarmed, he reached out for her. "What's wrong?"

"That key, you know, the one that looks like it belongs to a safe deposit box? You don't suppose it *is* to a safe deposit box, one in which Jeffrey kept the list I've almost been killed for?"

"Regardless, Give it to Tom. He and Deevers can work it out."

"I'm surprised whoever ransacked the house didn't find them. The bag was way back in a corner on the top shelf. I guess they didn't see it."

And so, on Sunday, December twelfth, David and Rebecca were married at The Little White Wedding Chapel in Las Vegas. Afterwards, Adelaide, and Tom and Jane Hutchins helped them celebrate with a champagne dinner at Le Cirque. It may not have been the wedding Rebecca had envisioned, but she was marrying David and that's what really mattered.

CHAPTER THIRTY-EIGHT

David took the rest of the week off. He wanted to make sure the work on Rebecca's security system was completed before he and she left for New York. He'd managed, by telephone and computer, to keep up with his business and was confident he was on top of things. On Wednesday, Adelaide called and came over with Jack Deevers and Tom Hutchins.

Rebecca had given Clarissa and her husband some time off. David was making coffee for them while they sat around the table in the breakfast nook of the kitchen. Rebecca was no longer wearing the collar or using the cane, but her black eye had become more obvious.

"On the phone, Tom, you said you had information about the keys I gave you."

"That's right, Rebecca, I do. You were correct. That long key did belong to a safe deposit box, one that was rented in the name of Emil Jeffreys."

"Emil is Jeffrey's father's name. No wonder it was never mentioned in either the trust or the will."

"But," Tom continued, "the owner's address was listed as a post office box in Faro, Portugal."

Rebecca shook her head. "None of this makes any sense."

"Unless you consider that it may have been one way Jeffrey was hoping to conceal what he was doing," Deevers said. "It took Tom and me several days to locate the bank that had the safe deposit box. Turns out it was the Brigadier branch of the Nevada State Bank on Las Vegas Boulevard South. We learned that after the rental fee had not been paid for six months, the bank had the box drilled open, impounded the contents, and sent it to the state capital as unclaimed property. We got the necessary court order and claimed it."

"And?" Rebecca asked, the suspense all but killing her.

"As you suspected, the contents consisted of several copies of a list of galleries and agents who continue to profit from the sale of counterfeit and stolen art," Deevers continued, "predominately art the Nazis confiscated during the War. It's quite a list. On it, of course, is the Mendes Galleria. I'm sure that comes as no surprise."

"What happens now? Will you prosecute? What will happen to Deitrich Radtke?" Rebecca asked, finishing the last of her coffee.

Tom looked at Deevers. "It's pretty much out of my jurisdiction at this point," Deevers said. "Bruce Ross will be taking over from here. It's my guess that Interpol will bring charges against the Señora Galina and the Mendes Galleria, possibly closing it. As for Radtke, as guilty as he must seem to you, unless there's definite proof he lured your husband to his death, there's little that can be done about charging him with conspiring to murder. But, he is guilty of buying and selling stolen art and will be charged and have to answer for that. You can at last relax and begin to enjoy your new life with David. You've done a great job cooperating with us . . . Mrs. Neville."

Rebecca looked at David. "Doesn't *that* sound nice? But, Deevers, please call me Rebecca."

"All right, Rebecca. I was about to say that I'm sure I include Interpol when I say thank you for all you've done."

"That's it, then?" David asked. "Rebecca's free from her responsibility to you?"

"She is."

"What about the gun and panic button you gave me?"

"The gun's yours to keep if you want it. Just be sure to keep the license up to date and practice regularly. As for the call button, you can keep that too. I'll just have its signal deleted."

Rebecca thought a minute. "Perhaps I should apply to be an undercover agent with the CIA or Interpol like Jeffrey was."

"I'm sure they'd be happy to see you any time," Deevers said.

David slid to Rebecca's side and put an arm around her. "Over my dead body you will."

"But just think of how exciting it would be," Rebecca chided.

David cast her a look of disbelief. "Haven't you had enough excitement in the past few weeks to last a lifetime?"

Rebecca laughed. "Of course. I really wasn't serious."

"I'd love to stay longer," Deevers said, tightening his neck scarf and pushing himself out of his chair. "Unfortunately, I really have to get going." He turned to shake Rebecca's hand, but as he did, she slid off her chair, stood on her tiptoes, and kissed his cheek. "Merry Christmas, Deevers."

"Thanks," he sputtered. "How nice. I don't often get *that* kind of a farewell. Well, it's been grand. Merry Christmas everyone." And with a final wave, Deevers walked out.

Adelaide poured more coffee.

"I guess now I'll have to tell Jeffrey's parents and sister about everything," Rebecca said, resuming her seat with a sigh.

Tom finished his coffee. "I probably should be going, too."

"Wait," Rebecca said. "I'll walk you out. I need to stretch my legs. They stiffen up if I don't move about."

"I'll come along, with you," Adelaide said.

"Thanks for everything, Tom," Rebecca said kissing his cheek when they got to the front door. "I can't tell you how much we appreciate your help."

"Yes. Thanks, Tom," Adelaide said, also giving him a kiss on the cheek.

David got in line. "Thanks, Tom." When he moved as if he was going to kiss him, however, Tom balked, "Wait a minute!"

"How nice it is to relax," Rebecca said, when they were having coffee and desert after dinner at Adelaide's. "The trouble is, the excitement I felt once Deevers confirmed my suspicions about that key is fast giving way to fatigue."

Adelaide rolled her eyes. "Of course, it has nothing to do with jet lag, narrowly escaping the jaws of death and getting married."

Rebecca laughed "Right. But the longer I sit here, the more difficult it'll be to get out of this chair at all."

"My feelings won't be hurt if the two of you want to leave."

"I know," David said, getting up from the couch. "So I think we'll do just that." He held out a hand out for Rebecca. "Thanks for dinner, Addie."

"Any time, you two, any time."

Rebecca was so drowsy when they got home, David told her that if it weren't for her injuries, he'd throw her over his shoulder and carry her to bed.

"Caveman style, right?"

"No," David said, "They dragged their women around by the hair."

* * *

The call from Rebecca's former mother-in-law, Inès Lawler, came through the next day announcing the death of Abuelita—Jeffrey's father, Emil's, ninety-nine year old mother, Jeffrey's grandmother.

"Rebecca," Mrs. Lawler said, "Abuelita left you several paintings. Therefore, my dear, would it be possible for you to come to Madrid for the reading of the will on Monday, the twentieth? That way, you can claim them right away."

"I'm so sorry to hear about this, Mana," Rebecca said.

"We'll certainly miss her, but we are grateful she was with us for so long—remaining feisty as ever, I might add."

"I'm also deeply touched by her generous gift," Rebecca added.

"She was very fond of you, Rebecca, and knew the paintings would be well cared for. I was told you'd tried to reach us in Greece and apologize for the tardiness in getting back to you. Unfortunately, this is the first opportunity I've had."

"I wanted to tell you I'd remarried."

"Oh, my dear, that is marvelous news! I've always said you're much too lovely to remain single. I hope when you come you'll bring the lucky man."

Just then David came into the room, walked over and gave Rebecca a nip on her neck, at last minus the collar. "Of course I'll come, Mana, and you can be sure David will be with me."

"His name is David?"

"Yes. David Neville." She looked at him and he bit her neck again. She poked him in an attempt to get him to move away.

"This is all very exciting. How nice to have such good news to follow the sad."

Her comment reminded Rebecca of the news she'd soon be telling the Lawlers about Jeffrey. "All right, Mana. I'll call the airlines as soon as we hang up. Where can I reach you?"

Inès Lawler gave her the telephone number. "And plan on staying here with us," she said. "That way we can spend a little more time together."

Rebecca thought of Abuelita's beautiful home with its lush furnishings, antique oriental carpets, collection of paintings and other pieces of art. "We'd love to. Thank you."

"Good."

"I'll call you as soon as we know our plans."

"I look forward to it. Goodbye for now, my dear."

"Goodbye, Mana. See you soon."

"I take it *mana* is the familiar term for mother-in-law?" David asked Friday morning when they were about to leave for their flight to Spain.

"It's Greek and doesn't mean mother-in-law as such," Rebecca said. "*Mitera* is actually the Greek word for mother. But in time, Mother Lawler, as I used to call her, suggested I call her Mana because of our close relationship."

"Come to think of it, I've never been to Madrid," David said when they were at last on their way to the airport in the Broker Industries' car that Adelaide insisted they take

"It's a wonderful city," Rebecca said. "It's a shame we'll only be there for three days."

She slipped her hand into David's. "It was very generous of Abuelita to leave me those paintings." She started to laugh. "What are we going to do with more paintings?"

"Who knows? But I wouldn't worry about them now. Wait until you've seen them before making a judgment. For the moment just consider them a wedding gift from someone you've always been fond." He looked at her and grinned. "Besides, for all we know, they might be prize pieces worth a small fortune."

Rebecca gave his arm a playful push, "Oh, you!"

He studied their joined hands. "Those rings look especially nice on you, Mrs. Neville."

Rebecca held her hand up and studied them. "They do, don't they? And I wouldn't change them for anything in the world." She looked at David. "It's no wonder I chose you out of the thousands."

He threw his head back and laughed. "I had no idea you were up against such a formidable decision." He leaned over and kissed the tip of her nose. "My sympathies, dearest wife."

CHAPTER THIRTY-NINE

Madrid,
Tuesday, December 21

"Thank you so much for everything Mana," Rebecca said, giving her mother-in-law a big hug as she and David prepared to leave for Madrid's Barajas Airport in Abuelita's chauffeur-driven car.

"No, thank *you*, my dear, for coming on such short notice and for bringing this wonderful man," she said, turning to David and giving him a hug. "It's reassuring to know that Rebecca's in such good hands."

David kissed her cheek. "You flatter me, Inès."

"No, she doesn't," Emil Lawler said, shaking David's hand.

"That's most kind. Thank you."

"Goodbye, Papa," Rebecca said, hugging him and giving him a kiss.

She was about to release him when he held onto her and said, "And thank you, Rebecca, for telling us about Jeffrey. Inès and I know how difficult it must have been for you."

Throat tight, Rebecca could only nod.

"Don't forget to let us know when you want to come to Greece," Inès Lawler said.

"Rebecca and I thought we might like to do that in the spring."

"Then we'll count on it. Spring is the loveliest time, as you know. Flowers and their perfume are everywhere."

The Lawlers walked them to the car where the butler was helping their driver, Luis, slip the well-packed paintings into the trunk before adding the luggage.

Inès Lawler threaded her arm through Rebecca's. "It's so good of you and David to detour your trip through Paris before returning to New York so you can deliver those paintings to your friend, Monsieur Lartigue."

"I'm afraid to let them out of my sight. I'd never forgive myself if anything happened to them. It was an enormous relief to learn Georges chartered a plane for us. It makes traveling with them so much easier and saves David and me a great deal of worry. They're insured, of course. But how do you insure irreplaceable works of art? The fact is, you can't. We'll be two very happy people once they're back in Georges' hands."

"Rebecca's right," David said. "Both of us are looking forward to celebrating with him and his family."

"To think that lovely Klimt portrait of *Emma* that my father-in-law bought so many years ago had once hung in the Lartigue home in Brussels," Inès Lawler said.

"Along with the other Klimt painting, the small Picasso, and the Emil Nolde Abuelita left me. I remember seeing those once before when I was here visiting, but I never saw or knew anything about *Emma.* What a shock it was to find it here! And that was before I realized what it was. For Abuelita to have given it to me . . . well, I still can't believe it."

"It should be interesting tracing where they went after the Nazis stole them," Inès said.

"David and I are amazed the small Emil Nolde watercolor wasn't destroyed. So many of his works were towards the end of the War."

"Monsieur Lartigue had to have been overjoyed when you telephoned."

"Speechless is more like it," Rebecca said, smiling at David when he snaked his arm around her waist. "I don't know who was more excited, he or I. He told me he'd always hoped but never dreamed he'd recover *Emma,* let alone anything else. *Emma* was always the one painting foremost in his mind. His mother will be ecstatic. He called me his angel and then broke down and cried. At which point so did I. I just may start again," she said, searching her handbag for a handkerchief.

David handed her the one from his breast pocket.

Inès looked at her former daughter-in-law. "What will you do with the other two?"

David and Rebecca exchanged glances. "After we check their provenance . . ." David started to say, but was interrupted by the arrival of a dark blue Mercedes coming up the driveway. It stopped behind the car Luis was packing with their things. To Rebecca and David's surprise, Bruce Ross stepped out from the passenger's side.

"Thought I'd come by and see how Rebecca is doing."

"Thoughtful of you stop," David said.

Rebecca nodded. "It is indeed. I'm doing fine, thanks. I still have the black eye, as you can see. At least now, I can walk without the aid of a cane. Bruce, you surprise me. Normally you catch me just as I *arrive* home from a trip." Realizing the Lawlers might not know who he was, she introduced him.

"So," Ross continued, glancing into the trunk, "you're headed for Paris?"

"Word travels fast."

"You have the correct documents for those?" he asked, pointing to the packaged paintings.

"Of course."

"Want me to check them to be sure?"

"Now I'm even more suspicious." Reaching into her purse, Rebecca produced two envelopes and handed them to him. "Did you really just stop to see how I was and say goodbye or is there another reason?"

"The police are doing random baggage checks on the highways approaching the airport." He opened the envelopes and looked through the slips inside. "You're right," he said, returning them to her. "These are fine. I understand you're taking a charter."

"As I said, news travels fast. Yes. Georges arranged it."

Ross smiled. "Sure beats commercial travel these days."

"By the way, how is everyone at the Mendes Galleria?"

"Another time," Ross said, looking at his watch, "when you're not on your way to catch a plane. Don't worry. I'll be in touch once we complete the final details of the investigation."

"I plan on annoying you until you do," Rebecca threatened, still suspicious of his visit.

"In the meantime," Ross said, grasping David's hand, "take good care of this girl."

"That should be easy, if she behaves."

Rebecca shot him a look. "*Behaves*?"

"Yes," David said, obviously enjoying the tease. "No more stunt driving for a start."

But before she could say anything more, Ross took hold of her hands. "I want to thank you again for your bravery, dedication, and steely constitution, Rebecca. We'll miss you."

Rebecca answered by leaning forward and kissing his cheek. "Goodbye, Ross. And please say goodbye again to Deevers."

Once he said farewell to the Lawlers, Ross got back in his car.

"I don't believe that story of why they stopped here for one minute," Rebecca said, watching the car disappear down the driveway. "I suppose recent experience has taught me to be suspicious of everything."

David slid his arm around her. "Even me?"

"No, silly."

"Was that the same Mr. Ross who Jeffrey was working with?" Emil Lawler asked.

"Yes. He's really quite nice. He thought very highly of Jeffrey and was greatly saddened by his death."

"Before Mr. Ross arrived, David," Ines Lawler said, "you were telling us what you and Rebecca might do with the other paintings."

"Oh. Right. I think I was saying we'll pool them with those we already have and try to decide which ones to weed out and where to hang them."

"David's a dealer," Rebecca explained, "so it shouldn't be difficult to find customers for any of ours we might want to sell."

"One of these days, however," David said, putting his arm around her shoulders and pulling her against him, "we have to give some thought about where we want to spend the majority of our time: Las Vegas, New York, or Portugal. After we go to Paris, we just want to go back to New York, enjoy the fact that we're married, and celebrate Christmas with our friends and families." He looked at Rebecca. "As Christmases go, we couldn't have asked for a better one."

"And what a wonderful Christmas it will be for you," Emil Lawler said, bending to give Rebecca's cheek another goodbye kiss.

"You and Mana have a wonderful Christmas, too, Papa. "

"Thank you, my dear. We will." He looked at David. "We' ll be sharing it with Jeffrey's sister, her husband, and their two children."

"Goodbye again," Inès said once Rebecca and David were in the car. "Good journey and take care of those bruises and that head injury."

"Don't worry. I'll make sure she behaves," David promised.

"There's that word again," Rebecca said, laughing.

Luis closed the door, said something in Spanish to the Lawlers, and slid behind the wheel. With David and Rebecca waving, he slowly pulled away.

Rebecca nestled into the depth of the leather seat. "Don't you think it's incredible, David?"

"You mean the paintings belonging to Georges' family?"

"Yes. I'm still in shock. Talk about serendipity."

"And to think it all began when you took those two paintings to Lisbon."

Rebecca reached for his hand. "Actually, my darling husband, I like thinking it all began when you and I met in Greece."

He gave her hand a squeeze. "Wasn't that our lucky day?"

She snuggled against him. "Mmm. You can say that again."

"Tell me again when your parents arrive?"

"The afternoon of the twenty-third. The same day as Addie, and if all goes as planned, the same day as Georges and we do."

"And they're booked at the St. Regis?"

"My parents are, yes. I don't know about Adelaide. My guess is that she'll stay with Paul, especially since he chose to spend Christmas in New York instead of going home to be with his family."

David feigned surprise. "All because he didn't want to miss celebrating with us?"

Rebecca laughed. "While that might have had *some* bearing on his decision . . ."

"It probably has more to do with someone whose name begins with 'A.' Paul's a special guy. He was the one who hauled Brian out of the fire in Adelaide's library. After that, he never left the hospital for three days and nights. He finally booked a room in a hotel, but he continued visiting Brian daily until he escorted him back to New York *six weeks later.* If he and Addie do have something going, she certainly could do worse."

"I remember Brian mentioning Paul's taking care of him at the wedding reception. What's his field of expertise?"

"He's a computer specialist, one so sharp that Brian insisted he be with him on the Broker Industries' insurance reinvestigation. Because of his ability to obtain and analyze information in half the time it takes anyone else, his clients line up."

"Really? Well, I've no idea if Addie's ready for something serious, but she seems to enjoy having him around." Rebecca sighed and lowered her head to David's shoulder. "I'm excited about spending Christmas in New York, David, but the best part is I'll be celebrating it married to you."

David slid his arm around her shoulders and placed a kiss on top of her head. "In fact, if we weren't spending it there, I think my family would disown me. Mother, of course, knew I was hoping to become engaged to you, but neither of us had any idea we'd be getting married so quickly.

When she asked if I wanted to take grandmother's wedding ring, I told her no."

Rebecca looked up.

"Remember, at the time, I wasn't sure you were even speaking to me."

"You're right. I was pretty upset when I left for Paris. The trouble was, I started to miss you and was so distracted that when I went out with Stan that Wednesday evening, he must have wondered what in the world was the matter with me. Then Sally and Georges were attacked, and all I could think of was how much I wished you were there."

So that's why she didn't call me back that Wednesday. "Well," David said, drawing her closer, "happily that's all behind us."

"Speaking of Georges, we must have a special celebration for him in New York."

"We will."

"And then I'd like to hibernate for a time . . . you know, just hole up and go nowhere. I'm so tired right now, I think I could sleep for a week."

He rested his cheek against her hair. "Then you should do just that. Given everything you've been through—not to mention commuting between continents—it's a wonder you have any energy left at all."

"Fortunately, I'm able to sleep on planes."

David chuckled. "I've noticed. Like a log."

CHAPTER FORTY

Rebecca hadn't been paying much attention to where they were. She knew it was near the airport. Planes could be seen taking off and landing in the distance. Feeling the car slow, she picked her head up from David's shoulder. "What's going on?"

"Seems the police are pulling the odd car over to speak with the drivers."

"That's right. Remember? Ross said he wanted to check the documents for the paintings because the police were randomly inspecting cars."

"Luis, do you know anything about this?" David asked.

"It happens sometimes, señor. Probably a security check." He stopped in front of the two officers who were flagging them down and rolled down his window.

What followed was a series of questions from the *policia* and answers, from Luis. There was an exchange of documents.

Rebecca looked at David. "I hope this won't affect our flight."

"I doubt it. Let's wait and see what happens."

"Damn!" Rebecca muttered.

David glanced at her. "I don't think I've ever heard you swear."

"I've learned a lot these past few months."

The officers returned the papers and said something to Luis. He made no reply but pulled over to the right shoulder of the road and stopped, switching off the ignition and getting out of the car. When the officers came over, Luis took them around to the back and opened the trunk. A few minutes later he came along to Rebecca's side of the car and gestured for her to roll down the window.

"Señora, your passport, airline tickets and the papers you have on the packages in the back. The *policia* want to see them."

"They want . . ." Rebecca started to say, but stopped when David put a hand on her arm. "Do what they ask. Otherwise, we'll be here for hours and it will precipitate some kind of international Armageddon."

She had to agree and surrendered the documents to the *policia* as requested.

Luis got back in the driver's seat.

After several minutes, the *policia* returned everything to her and said something in Spanish to Luis. "The *policia* say we go to Terminal Four S."

"Isn't that the cargo terminal?" David asked.

"There are two Terminal Fours, señor. Both carry passengers and cargo. According to the *policia,* Terminal Four S is where you get your charter."

Rebecca looked at David. He smiled and shook his head. "At least *that* part seems clear."

They continued on toward the airport, following directions for Terminal Four and Four S. The area was congested with traffic, but as they drove along, it seemed to ease. Rebecca soon discovered why. An automated shuttle transported passengers and their luggage between the two buildings so there was little need for cars.

At last they came to Terminal Four S. When Luis stopped in front of the check-in area, David leaned forward and handed him their plane and luggage tickets. Luis left to open the trunk but was back in a matter of minutes.

"We must go around to the rear. They say that is where the plane will meet you. You give them your passports and tickets there and they will check you in."

He continued along the front of Terminal Four S until he got to the corner where he turned left and headed toward the back. As they rounded the far corner, to their relief hey saw a small, sleek-looking jet parked forty to fifty feet away.

"Could that be it?" David asked, looking around.

"There seems to be lots of activity over at Terminal Four," Rebecca noted. "Luis," she continued, "would you mind going over to one of those doors at the back of this building to see if there's anyone we can speak with?"

"*Si, señora.*" He got out of the car and walked toward the building. Just before he reached it, a man came out. Noticing Luis, he went over and the two conversed. In another minute, Luis was bringing him over to the car. He introduced him as Ramon, the pilot of the small jet.

David showed him their tickets. "I think that may be our charter over there," he said, pointing.

"You are correct, señor Neville. That plane has been reserved for you. Unfortunately, there's a delay and we have to wait for the okay."

"But everything checked out two days ago," David said. "What seems to be the problem?"

"Something about taking artwork out of the country."

Rebecca could hardly believe her ears.

David laughed out loud. "You know, that's really funny. We're taking this artwork out of Spain because the Nazis stole it from a friend's house in the first place. All we're doing is returning it to its rightful owner." He waved an envelope in the air. "And we have the proper certificates for their export right here."

Ramon shrugged. "I don't doubt what you're saying for a minute, señor. Unfortunately, I'm just the pilot and don't have any influence over the rules. I'm as anxious to get on with this trip as you are."

Resigned, David stuffed the documents back to his inside jacket pocket, and he and Rebecca sat back to wait.

At a loss for words, Rebecca slouched down in the seat and closed her eyes. *So the nightmare continues.*

They waited for what seemed like hours when a police car accompanying a medium-sized gray van with three men inside drove up. *D' Art, Ancient et Nouveau* in elaborate gold lettering was written on the sides. Rebecca and David got out of their car.

One of the men, dressed as if he'd just walked out of Charles Tyrwhitt, the high-end British clothier, left the van and came toward them. A chill ran down Rebecca's spine as a sense of foreboding descended on her. "Oh my God!"

David threw her a look. "What?"

"Radtke. Deitrich Radtke! Jeffrey's killer. I recognize him from my research."

"What's he doing here?"

"Whatever the reason, it can't be good."

As Radtke approached, David reached for her hand and gave it squeeze. "Steady."

"Mrs. Lawler?" Radtke said, walking over, his right hand outstretched. "I don't think I've had the pleasure."

"You're correct, Mr. Radtke. Nor shall you." Then she changed her mind. "On second thought," she said, extending her hand, "I don't think I've ever met a murderer before."

David tightened his grip on her hand. "*Easy.*"

Radtke's expression blackened, his eyes turned the color of dark thunderclouds and looked just as threatening. Rebecca went on, unable to stop herself. "What I'd really like to know, Herr Radtke, is the reason you stood my husband up the day you arranged for his death."

Radtke withdrew his hand. "I suggest you double check your facts, young lady, before you go throwing accusations about so carelessly. After all, *I* was the one waiting for *him*. It was he who stood *me* up. I was still waiting for him when I received word of his tragic accident. I was most distressed."

I just bet you were, given you orchestrated it. "I see. Then since you seem to insist on accuracy, my name is no longer Mrs. Lawler. It's Mrs. *Neville.*"

In a voice dripping with sarcasm, Radtke said, "My apologies. It must have slipped my mind. Congratulations."

For the next few moments no one said a word until David took over and stepped forward. "Mr. Radtke. There's been some kind of discrepancy about our taking Rebecca's artwork out of the country." He produced the envelope with all the papers. "We have all the correct paperwork, including the original bills of sale from the Mendes Galleria and the certificates needed for export. Perhaps you can help by clearing things up so we can all be on our way."

Glaring at Rebecca, Radtke walked over and took the papers David held out to him. A few minutes went by while he reviewed them. Then, he reached inside his jacket and withdrew an envelope. From it he removed several certificates of his own. He passed them to David. "I'm sure you'll see that these certificates pertain to those very same paintings. There's a difference, however." He held out another paper, this one with a red stamp. "Yours are missing this additional government approval needed to remove them from the country."

David and Rebecca examined both sets of certificates. "Frankly, Mr. Radtke," Rebecca said, waving his documents in the air, "both David and

I happen to be experienced collectors and neither of us believe these are authentic. They're very good copies, but they are indeed fakes."

"You and your husband can think whatever you wish, Mrs. *Neville.* But as an official of the government of Spain, I'm here to inform you that the artwork in your car will not be leaving *this* country . . . today or any day."

"Not even when you send them to South America to be copied? Besides, these paintings don't belong to Spain. They were stolen from the Lartigue home in Belgium during the War. It's pretty amazing when you stop to think of how they traveled all the way from small, little Belgium to the Mendes Galleria in Madrid! Because," she continued, annunciating the words and raising her voice, "the Mendes Galleria in Madrid is where Ernst Lawler purchased them! You, Mr. Radtke, even signed the sales slips! Come to think of it, Georges Lartigue, the owner of the paintings, is one of the individuals on your hit list, isn't he?"

Radtke turned to her with a frown. "I'm sorry. Whom did you say is on what list?"

Go to hell. This time she refused to answer. It was her only recourse to the feeling of total helplessness.

"Well then," Radtke said, relieving Rebecca of his papers and pulling on his leather gloves, "the matter is settled. All we need to do is transfer the paintings from your car to ours." He started toward his van but stopped, turning back to David and Rebecca. "Would either of you like to come and make sure we transfer only the paintings? That way you can be certain we don't touch your personal things."

"Just get the hell out of here and be done with it, you bastard!" David exploded, taking a step in Radtke's direction.

Radtke's expression darkened once again. "Temper, temper, Mr. Neville." He motioned to his men. "All right, let's get moving."

As soon as Radtke turned away, David and Rebecca each pulled out their cell phones: David called Georges to tell him they'd been delayed, and Rebecca rang Bruce Ross. Ross was out of the office but his secretary assured her he'd get back to her as soon as she gave him Rebecca's message.

David knew there was nothing he could say or do that would help. Rebecca's frustration and anguish were far too deep. All he could do was be there to offer support. The worst of it was, there was nowhere to go to avoid seeing Radtke and his men make the transfer.

Once back in the car, Rebecca could no longer hold back the tears that slid silently down her cheeks as she watched Radtke and his men steal Georges' family paintings for the second time. Only after the van drove off and disappeared from sight, did David hear her let out a sob.

All this time, Luis remained in the front seat waiting for direction, the scene having taken a toll on him as well.

"Señor Neville," he said at last, "Perhaps if I drive us around to the front, I can go inside and get you and the señora something to drink."

David glanced at Rebecca. "Interested?"

"But shouldn't we wait to talk with the pilot?" Rebecca asked, her voice muddled with tears.

Just then, two police cars and an Interpol van rounded the corner and came toward them.

"Perfect timing," Rebecca mumbled, blotting her eyes with her handkerchief.

Next, two additional police cars flanking Deitrich Radtke' gray van came around the corner of the building.

"Rebecca," David said as he watched Bruce Ross get out of the Interpol van and head in their direction.

She didn't look up. "Hmm?"

"I think you should take a look," David persisted.

With one final sniff, she removed the tissue and opened her eyes. Bruce Ross stood beside the car. David leaned over and lowered the window.

"Mrs. Neville," Ross began, "would you be so good as to come over and identify the individuals in that gray van over there?"

It took a moment for her to realize what he was asking her to do. With a sigh, she left the car and walked over to the van with Ross, all the while trying to resist the urge to lunge at Radtke and claw his face.

"Can you please identify the men who removed the paintings from the trunk of your car?" Ross said. Rebecca pointed them out.

"And where did they take them?"

"Into the back of this van," she said, placing her hand on the door.

"Good. Now which one is the individual who instructed them to do so?"

She pointed to Radtke. "He is." She was looking forward to staring him down, but he continued looking straight ahead and avoided her gaze.

"One last question," Ross said. "Did you actually *see* Herr Radtke and the men you indicated physically remove the paintings from your car and transfer them to this van?"

"Yes. David and I both did. And when I showed them my proof of ownership and export certificates, Herr Radtke insisted the paintings were his and produced similar documents. David and I knew they had to be forgeries."

"Thank you." Ross turned and signaled for the police to have Radtke open the van.

At first, Radtke resisted. But eventually, he and his men got out and opened the doors.

"Have them bring those packages to me, please," Ross ordered.

He beckoned to David and Rebecca. "Are these your paintings?" he asked once they walked over.

They inspected them. None of the packaging had been disturbed. David looked at Ross and nodded but Rebecca said, loud and clear, "They are."

Ross beamed. "Good." He spoke with two of the police officers while the other officers returned the paintings to Rebecca and David's car. Ross then ordered Radtke and his men handcuffed and put into one of the police cars. Once that was done, he walked over to Rebecca and David.

"You have to be very happy."

"Frankly, Bruce," Rebecca said, her eyes swollen and red, "I don't know what I am. Today's episode has all but put me over the top. I'm not even sure I have the strength to fly to Paris." She looked around. "And God only knows what happened to our pilot." She squinted her eyes and peered at him. "Did you ever get my S.O.S?"

"I did. But we were already at the airport when I got the message."

She still didn't smile.

"Rebecca," Ross said, coming over and standing directly in front of her, "do you remember what you told me your goal was when you started out on this venture?"

"Yes. I said it was to sell the art Jeffrey left me."

"But once you realized he'd worked for us and might have been murdered, you changed it. Do you remember what took its place?"

She shook her head. "I-I'm sorry. With everything that's happened today, I can't seem to think." Her mind was refusing to cooperate. "No, not offhand."

Ross continued. "It was after you found that those of us who'd worked with Jeffrey at Interpol also suspected that he might have been murdered . . . off the record, that is."

She nodded. "Now I remember. I said my goal had changed and my primary goal was to avenge Jeffrey's death."

"Think about it minute, Rebecca. Because that's exactly what you've just done. Congratulations."

She made no comment, but stood there frowning and looking confused.

"I think she's in shock, Bruce," David said. "Despite what you've said, I doubt she has any idea what she just accomplished."

Ross smiled and took her hands in his. "By unwittingly allowing us to set you up to work for us again, Rebecca, you've supplied us with the proof we've needed to nab Radtke and close the Mendes Galleria. Both have been on and off our watch list for years, as you know, but we never had concrete proof of their thievery and complicity. Now, thanks to you, we have it and have been able to nab the . . . the . . ."

"Son of a bitch," David interjected.

Ross laughed. "Right, the son of a bitch!"

"But," Rebecca began, "exactly how . . . ?"

"By letting Radtke and his men physically remove the paintings from you car and put them in theirs, then testifying to that fact."

"Oh."

"Do you understand what it is you've done now?"

"Yes. You set me up."

Ross looked at David, who rolled his eyes and held both hands up in protest.

"In a word, yes. But, in doing so, you helped Interpol get its man and you achieved your goal."

Silence.

"To show our gratitude," Ross continued before Rebecca could comment, "Interpol would like to give you and David a proper send off. While I realize the small jet over there is the one Monsieur Lartigue arranged for you, at any moment the Interpol executive jet will arrive and take you to Paris instead. It comes complete with upholstered chairs and couch in the main cabin, and a fully serviced dining area next to it. To further show our gratitude for a job well done, Interpol is also sending along several bottles of Krug Grande Cuvée champagne."

Rebecca looked at her husband. “Did you hear that, David?”

“I did. And I can’t think of anything that could fit the bill better, especially today.”

“What will we do about the charter Georges arranged for us?” Rebecca asked Ross.

“Georges knows about the change in plans.”

“Still, there’s one little detail that’s not quite clear.”

“And that is?”

“Just how did Radtke know David and I were going to the airport with these paintings in the first place?”

“Probably picked up on it when you applied for the export permits.”

Rebecca studied him. “You really expect me to believe that?”

“Can you think of a better explanation?”

“I think you set him up, too. First you came to the Lawlers to see how I was. While you’re there, you just happen to tell us the police were checking random cars on the approaches to the airport.”

“Which indeed they were.”

“Yes. But then you casually look into the trunk of the car and ask if I’d like you to check the documents on the packages in there to make sure all was in order.”

“Guilty.”

“I think you staged all that. What you really wanted was to make sure the paintings were in there because you’d previously arranged it so that Radtke would know about our plans and come on some trumped up charge to take them from me. Then you could nail him. Which is exactly what happened.”

“Is there a reason that bothers you?” Ross asked.

Rebecca thought about it a moment. “I-I don’t know. I think so.”

“If it doesn’t, it should. For me to have done what you just suggested is referred to as entrapment. If proven, I could be arrested. No matter how heinous the crime, entrapment is illegal.”

“Oh.” She stole a glance at him. “Then, you really think Radtke found out about our leaving with the paintings from the export certificates?”

“I repeat. Can you think of a better explanation? Being an importer/exporter, even one dealing in illegal properties, he’d be privy to the arrivals and departures of *des objets d’art*, so to speak. In the end, do you *really* care how he found out? In all probability, the result would have been the same and your participation just as vital. Added to that, you achieved your most important goal, that of avenging your husband's death. And thanks to you, we at Interpol have caught the villain we've been stalking for years."

Rebecca studied him a moment and smiled at last. "You're right, Ross. I'm sorry. I think it's just that so much has happened today I'm having difficulty absorbing it all."

"Believe me, I understand."

At that point, the Interpol jet arrived and taxied in their direction.

Ross looked at his watch. "Good. I was beginning to get worried. So," he said, turning to Rebecca, "as much as I love standing here talking with you, I think you and David should get going."

While saying their goodbyes to Luis, Ross made sure the paintings and all of David and Rebecca's belongings were put aboard.

"Have a great trip, you two," he said, walking them to the plane. "Send me a card from time to time, too, Rebecca. I'd like to know you're staying out of trouble."

"That shouldn't be a problem as long as I stay away from stolen art and Interpol." Then Rebecca surprised everyone by putting her arms around him and giving him a hug. "Thank you so much for all the support you gave Jeffrey and for all you've done to help me." She stepped back and looked at him. "When you think about it, I guess neither one of us could have achieved our goal without the help of the other."

Ross smiled. "Very true. Then you've forgiven me for setting you up so the plan could work?"

Rebecca laughed. "I have."

"Good."

Once Ross and the *policia* left, David and Rebecca boarded the jet, chose seats, and fastened their seat belts in preparation for takeoff.

"I've never flown on a private jet before," Rebecca said, as the doors were being shut. "Have you?"

"Once. Years ago." David laughed. "It was just before I met you in Greece."

"That was a pretty busy summer for you, wasn't it?" Rebecca chided, feeling her tension beginning to ease.

They had just finished dinner and were sitting together on the couch, relaxing over a glass of the delicious champagne, when David said, "I guess the trip to Berlin will be the one that finally brings your project to a close."

"Yes," Rebecca said. "By mid-January, Georges' shoulder should have healed completely. Going to the Neue Nationalgallerie will be the highlight for me. How lucky I was to find someone like Georges. His unique sense of reasoning and dedication to research are responsible for us finding where those two paintings belonged. You can't imagine how I'd agonized over them before he came on the scene. If it hadn't been for Senhor Carlos introducing me to him, I don't know what I would have done."

"Which reminds me," David said. "When I spoke to Georges earlier, he told me to tell you that during his recent research, he came across some photos taken in Munich at the 1937 *Entartete Kunst* exhibit. One photo showed a group of men gathered together in a gallery filled with Expressionist art, modern paintings and sculptures. The names of the men were written on the back of the photograph—Herman Goering, Joseph Goebbles, the exhibition's organizer, Hartmut Pistauer, Bruno Lohse, Ernst Lawler, and . . ." He hesitated.

Rebecca looked at him. "Yes. And?"

David smiled. "Deitrich Radtke."

Rebecca spun a look at him. "You're kidding!"

"Nope. His name was listed on the back with the others."

"How old must he have been?"

"Georges said he was wearing knee socks and lederhosen and looked about sixteen."

"When I first met Ross, he told me Radtke worked part time at the Mendes Galleria and was reported to be in his eighties. So when Ernst came across Radtke at the Mendes Galleria, he had to have remembered seeing him with Lohse at the Entartete Kunst exhibit."

"And connected the dots." David said.

"But what do you think made Ernst write Lohse's name on that sales slip?"

"Does the sales slip have a date?"

"I have to look. I think it does, and I'm willing to bet it's the same date as the one on the sales slip for the Kirschner. If so, then Ernst suspected the painting had been stolen when he bought it."

"Why do you suppose he bought it?"

"I doubt we'll ever know the answer to that," Rebecca said, "but I'm glad he did. Though it caused me many sleepless nights, it will be enormously gratifying when we return it."

"With all your projects wrapped up, you might get bored."

Rebecca leaned over and kissed his cheek. "You forget, dear husband. We still have to sort out what I've inherited and what we're going to do with our two collections."

"First, dear wife," David said, kissing her ear and, taking her hand, entwining his fingers with hers. "We're not going to do anything but sit back and enjoy spending our first Christmas together as husband and wife."

"Agreed. It's pretty great of your family to host Christmas Day, especially since there'll be so many of us."

"It's been a family tradition for years. Fortunately, this year only a small group of relatives will be there. There've been times when there were just too many."

"Are those the times you made a point to be absent?"

David laughed softly, remembering. "Yes, during my vagabond days." He shifted to put an arm around her. "It was also before I met you and you straightened me out."

Surprised, she pulled back to look at him. "*I* straightened you out?"

He nodded. "Oh yes, Rebecca, you did. As I watched you pull away on that last bus for Kamari, I felt more and more dejected, as if bit by bit I was being left with nothing. I knew right then that if I didn't switch direction, that's exactly the way I was going to end up . . . with nothing. So, I changed my flight, went back home and immediately re-registered for college. The rest, to coin a phrase, is history.

"But those few days we spent together in Santorini, were the happiest, most truly carefree days I've ever known." He gave her shoulders a tug, "All because of you."

Tears filled her eyes. "And to think all this time, I never knew."

"Look what fate has done to us, Rebecca," David said, kissing away the few tears that had come to rest on her lips, "because it was there in Greece that I fell in love with you."

Rebecca could only cling to him and kiss him back.

An art collector since the 1970's, Carol Smilgin has worked in an Upper East Side Manhattan art gallery, visited printmakers in their Paris studios, shown artists' work in her Manhattan apartment, and connected artists with galleries in and outside of New York City.

Mother of two married sons, she currently lives with a Turkish Angora cat on Cape Cod where she serves as secretary on the Executive Committee of the Cape Cod Writers' Center.

Provenance is her second novel.

CPSIA information can be obtained at www.ICGtesting.com
265600BV00001B/1/P

9 781462 014699